Always

She had long fair hair and a heart-shaped face. Unwavering blue eyes. She moved with grace. Her tremulous mouth mirrored the complexity of her nature. Gentle as night, yet it promised pleasure.

She was, he thought, the most beautiful woman he had ever seen.

He shifted in his seat and narrowed his eyes for a more intent look at her. Beautiful, yes.

Oh-God-strike-me-with-a-bolt-of-lightning-and-leave-me-for-dead. As beautiful as love.

His breath stopped. She was looking directly at him. Her eyes were clear and guileless.

'I love you,' she said . . .

with love & best wishes to Margaret from Mum.

Christmas 1979.

D1423796

TREVOR MELDAL-JOHNSEN

Always

Collins

FONTANA BOOKS

First published in the United States in 1979 by Avon Books
First published in Great Britain in 1979 by Fontana Books

Copyright © 1978 by Trevor Meldal-Johnsen

Made and printed in Great Britain by
William Collins Sons & Co Ltd, Glasgow

Chapter One

SHE HAD LONG fair hair and a heart-shaped face. Unwavering blue eyes. She moved with grace. Her tremulous mouth mirrored the complexity of her nature. Gentle as night, yet it promised pleasure.

She was, he thought, the most beautiful woman he had ever seen.

He shifted in his seat and narrowed his eyes for a more intent look at her. Beautiful, yes. Oh-God-strike-me-with-a-bolt-of-lightning-and-leave-me-for-dead. As beautiful as love.

His breath stopped. She was looking directly at him. Her eyes were clear and guileless.

"I love you," she said.

His mouth went dry. His pounding heart shook his body.

"I love you," she repeated, her voice calm. "I've loved you since the sun first rose. I've loved you through God-sent catastrophe and man-made disaster. My love has no shame, no pride. It is only what it is, always has been, and always will be. It is yours. All yours. Only yours."

1

He began to cry.

He tried to stop, but the tears fell freely, coursing down his face. He took huge, ragged breaths, but there was no stopping. There was only the weight of grief and regret from some unknown source.

The woman sitting beside him turned to look, her face pale in the dim theater light.

"What's the matter?" she asked. She placed a hand on his arm.

He ignored the woman and stared through his tears at the screen. She was kissing her lover now, silken eyelashes veiling her eyes, her hands cupped softly at the nape of his neck, her honey-mouth melting.

"The End" flashed across the film in that slashing script they had been so fond of in the forties. It faded from view like a lost dream.

They did not talk much on the way home. He drove automatically, allowing his hands to find the way. It was fortunate they could do the job so well, he thought, because he felt strangely lost himself.

Once the woman turned to him and said lightly, "I wouldn't have insisted on seeing that film, Greg, if I'd known the effect it was going to have on you."

"I found it moving," he said with a shrug. But he felt foolish. The inappropriate force of his response in the theater bewildered him. He couldn't remember when he had last cried. Sometime during childhood, when tears had been closer to the surface, he supposed.

"God, I didn't think it was *that* moving," she said.

"No, I guess not," he replied.

But his thoughts had a will of their own. Beneath his now calm exterior, they buzzed and hummed in frantic circles. They demanded an answer he could not provide. And yet, through it all, there was an intangible feeling, like having a word on the tip of the tongue.

They reached his house in the Los Feliz hills and entered the driveway. The crunch of tires on the gravel struck him as a lonely sound, reminding him suddenly of long-forgotten desolate highways and visits to the country as a child. He dropped Sharon off at the door and drove the car to the garage behind the house.

As he walked up the cobbled path through the back garden, he paused for a moment in the darkness and listened, not knowing what he hoped to hear.

The air pulsed with life. The husky smell of daphne tantalized him, and then withdrew with the breeze. Restless cricket tattoos came from a clump of fern on his right; past them, he could hear the soft murmur of water as it fell into the goldfish pond. The sounds and smells of the night came to him with unusual clarity but . . . no, there was nothing here that satisfied his curious sense of expectancy.

A shape came from the shadows, and he saw his cat, Felix, an orange tom with the haughty flat features of a Siamese. The cat rubbed demandingly against his leg and he dropped to a crouch, scratching it behind the ears. The animal slipped away and started for the house. It was hungry and wanted to be fed. Gregory straightened up and followed it. He fumbled for his keys at the back door and the animal miaowed impatiently. When he finally opened the door, it slid in ahead of him and led the way to the kitchen.

Obediently, he opened a tin of cat food and spooned it into a green plastic dish. The animal immediately forgot the presence of its benefactor and began to eat.

Sharon entered the kitchen. She had changed into a loose cotton robe that accentuated the lovely lines of her body when she moved. It was white, enhancing the sheen of her long dark hair.

"Hungry, Greg?" she asked softly, touching the back of his neck. As always, she had adapted herself to his mood. Usually she was almost boisterously communicative.

"Coffee and a snack would be good," he admitted.

They had met several months earlier at a party given by his agent. She had swept him off his feet then. And she continued to do so, for he found it easier to accept her possessive personality than to resist. He thought he loved her, but, like any bachelor facing marriage, he tended to question his feelings whenever he was alone.

She began to wash the percolator. He watched her attack the pot, her movements brisk. She kept the house like a fanatic. They could have eaten off the kitchen floor. He didn't mind, but, on the other hand, he didn't care much either way. His own housekeeping efforts were erratic. It wasn't one of his top priorities.

He thought sometimes that her New York heritage was responsible for her energy level. Even after he'd been East himself, he still hadn't been able to get rid of the preconceived notion that the city consisted of overcharged dynamos running around in diminishing circles. Sharon had come West about a year before, after a modest success on the Broadway stage. She worked fairly steadily in Hollywood, landing guest roles on television dramas, but her greatest asset was a singlemindedness which sustained her through the setbacks and disappointments that an actress in a cutthroat industry inevitably encountered.

He looked dispassionately at her as she took some cheese out of the refrigerator. There was little doubt that she was beautiful; strikingly so, in fact, but it was a sharp, angular beauty of a type to which he had not previously been attracted. After that first night, however, when she had ridden him like a wild storm and drained and replenished him again and again until he had been rescued by daylight, he had grown to feel an attraction to her that helped him through the small irritations she dispensed in her turbulent wake. They were planning to marry in four months.

She detoured with the cheese in one hand and pressed against him. "Why don't you go and relax in the living room. I'll bring the coffee when it's done."

He walked into the living room, took off his jacket, and tossed it onto the velvet couch. Continuing to the bathroom, he peered at the flat, lifeless reflection of his face in the mirror, as if it had a secret to divulge. There were no answers.

Expressive brown eyes, firm but sensitive mouth, stubborn chin. A handsome face, framed by wavy brown hair that curled over the collar. It was a face that women found attractive, but the image in the mirror gave him no clues. He slowly dropped his eyes and turned on the faucet. When he splashed cold water on his skin, he could still taste the salt of the tears he had shed earlier.

He went back to the living room, feeling partly restored, kicked off his shoes, and settled into a comfortable chrome-and-leather chair with a sigh, a stretch, and a cracking of joints in his ankles and knees. Someone had told him it was a sign of vitamin-C deficiency, but he thought it was more likely the effect of a sedentary life in front of the typewriter. He told himself for the hundredth time that he had to get more exercise. Luckily he was tall and naturally slim, and no matter how much he ate and drank, the genetic engineering of his body didn't allow him to put on weight.

Gregory was grateful that Sharon was taking her time in the kitchen. He idly reached over to the telephone answering machine on the table beside him and pressed its buttons. Then he looked up at the ceiling, as if the faces of his callers were projected there.

His agent, Richard Willmer: "Call me at my office first thing in the morning. I've got some news for you."

Clipped, impersonal, the voice gave no hint of the nature of the news. Good? Bad? He would have to call.

The machine beeped.

Michael Horowitz, "one of Hollywood's hottest young directors." His voice had the characteristic stiffness of those who hate speaking to a machine: "Hi, Greg. This is Mike Horowitz. I'm just calling to invite you to a party at my place Saturday night. About eight onwards. Don't bother letting me know if you're coming, man. I'll just see you or not."

Six months earlier he couldn't have gotten Horowitz's telephone number, let alone entered his front door. Then, Greg had sold *the* script, after years of futile attempts. Now the invitations flooded in. His life had fallen into new patterns, for all intents and purposes for the better—but he wasn't sure.

The man's name was Gregory Thomas, and he had been born some twenty-nine years before in Seattle, Washington, where he lived with his parents through childhood and pimply adolescence. His father, Jack, had been a short, stocky man with boundless energy and ambition. Jack had come West from Philadelphia in his early twenties and opened a grocery store in Seattle. There he had met and married Pam, a tall, dark-haired doctor's daughter, who was given to long wistful silences—the content of which, he discovered too late, was not sensitivity or profundity, but simple vacuity. In the absence of anything better to do, Jack's work became his vice, and within a decade he had built his grocery store into a chain covering the entire Seattle–Tacoma area. When his heart had finally stopped beating, crushed under the weight of a crate of Campbell's soup, fifteen-year-old Gregory had displayed the proper amount of grief for the benefit of his mother and all the relatives. However, he was privately quite dismayed at his actual lack of grief.

Gregory and his father had inhabited different planes of reality, planes that merged all too seldom. Obscured by the appropriate social veneer, their apartness had never become an issue. Their relationship had been based on tolerance rather than love, the kind of attitude reserved for someone living in the same house whom one could not help but meet in hallways, outside bathrooms, and around tables.

Once, just after Greg turned fifteen, his father had taken him aside to the study for what he liked to term "a man-to-man," a rare occasion, prompted when it occurred more by paternal guilt than by a desire to communicate.

"Well," his father had begun as always, his bright glance bouncing around the room as if it couldn't contain him, "you're almost a man now, Gregory."

Gregory had nodded at his father's prediction of impending manhood, at a loss for appropriate comment. He felt the man's embarrassment, which only added to his own discomfort.

"Well," his father had repeated, "have you decided what you're going to do with your life? A year or two and you'll be out of school. It's not too early to start thinking about it now, boy."

Jack Thomas had become wealthy, and the study he used as a home office reflected it. The shelves were lined with expensive mail-order, leather-bound volumes of the classics. Some of the gold-edged pages hadn't even been cut. Jack hadn't read a book since school, but he liked books for their air of permanence and distinction, and when he showed visitors around the house and they reached the study, he always waved proudly at the books. Gregory entered the study whenever his father was away and pored through the classics.

Gregory had answered his father's question in a tight, bored teenage voice. "I'm going to be a writer, Dad." He had mentioned it before. Unlike other boys his age, he had never been overwhelmed by life's limitless possibilities. As far back as he could remember, he had wanted to be a writer. Books and films were his spiritual fuel. He survived on them. He had never had any doubt about writing.

"Yes, of course," his father had acknowledged condescendingly, "but what kind of work are you going to do for a living?"

And so it had always been.

His mother, however, encouraged him, making up in ardor what she lacked in understanding of his purpose. Once she had met what she termed "a real writer," and had thereafter been imbued with a faint vision of her son in tweeds, trailing an aroma of rich pipe tobacco and a gentility her husband had never been able to achieve.

After her husband died, she sent Gregory to college. When he dropped out after two years, she insisted he live at home, where she could care for him. Her adoration was bearable to Gregory, but irritating. During an almost daily ritual, she would float into his study, which had once been his father's, on a cloud of maternal pride and watch him peck away at the typewriter until he was finally distracted enough to stop. Then she would invariably ask—always in exactly the same solicitous tone of voice—"Are you writing, Son?" He would nod curtly. "Oh, good," she would say, comforted and sustained. And the ritual would end. It was all she needed to know of her son's hopes and aspirations. She never read anything he wrote. There was no need; her faith was more than sufficient.

When he was twenty-six, Gregory sold his first novel. The twenty-five-hundred-dollar advance, although far from munificent, gave him the confidence to go out on his own. At first, his mother was distraught, not, God forbid, for selfish reasons, but out of concern for him. He finally persuaded her that in order to write for films it was essential that he live in Los Angeles, and she accepted it—but only on the condition that she send him five hundred dollars a month until he could support himself writing.

And so Gregory had joined Hollywood's ranks of waiters, hairdressers, car-wash attendants, department-store clerks, and other imposters who posed as screenwriters. A few options on his work had enabled him to survive, but it had not been easy, even with the money his mother had sent. He was popular with a modest circle of friends and several women whose company he enjoyed. Somehow, he had always managed.

Now, however, in his own estimation, he had legitimized his life. After three years of futile attempts and near-misses, one of his screenplays, a comedy-mystery about two marines on leave, had sold for what he considered an inordinately large sum of money. Since then, he had sold three teleplays. Suddenly he was well-to-do. And now, earlier screenplays that had crossed the desks of almost every studio reader in the city and received comments ranging from "Not for us" to "Not suitable" were being described by exactly the same readers as "super."

Success had brought with it no small measure of cynicism.

Doors previously barricaded now opened without even the persuasion of a knock. Secretaries called him "sir," brought him coffee or tea while he waited (which wasn't often), and hinted at their personal availability. His agent, inviolate behind the walls and prestige of a large international agency, was now always available and spent more time screening him from deals than getting him into them. And to his dismay, his old friends either withdrew out of misdirected respect for his achievement and his privacy, or treated him with obsequious respect. Many of them had been replaced by what he called "instant friends"—sycophants who mistook frankness for sincerity and familiarity for affection.

It was not exactly what he had expected, or, for that matter, wanted. Sharon had been one of the few bright spots on a generally cloudy social horizon.

These were cold thoughts, and he leaned over to switch off the telephone machine, as if the motion would dispel them. He was saved from further introspection by Sharon's entrance with the coffee and crackers.

She handed him his cup and looked closely at the black circles under his eyes and the dejection in the lines of his face. It disturbed her. It didn't fit into her preconception of things. None of his behavior this night had. Normally he was so gay and charming—like a little boy, she often thought. Perhaps that was why she loved him so. It brought out the mother in her. She touched him on the cheek.

"You look terrible, Greg."

For some reason he was afraid of the tenderness in her voice. "I just had a lousy day at the typewriter, I guess."

She allowed herself to be reassured. As an actress, she was familiar with the pitfalls of creative work. The struggle, the doubt, the ultimate loneliness of it. "Well," she said more cheerfully, "have a bath and I'll give you a back rub afterward—guaranteed to cure all ills."

He swallowed some coffee. "God, that woman had an extraordinary face," he said, half to himself.

Sharon picked up the cue. "Who?" She sat on the couch, her legs tucked beneath her.

"That girl in the movie. What was her name? Brooke Ashley?" Her image floated up again, and he rubbed his neck.

"Yes. She died, you know. Not too long after that movie, I think." Sharon's eyes narrowed. "I didn't think she was particularly special. She had that ethereal carry-over from the actresses of the thirties. Since when have you liked nuns, anyway?"

Greg shook his head. "It wasn't that kind of beauty. There was a sensuality there, too."

Sharon's laugh had a hard edge. "Jesus, you sound like a schoolboy with a crush." And then, suddenly, she added, "Tell me, do you cry often?"

Gregory looked up sharply. "What do you mean?"

"Well, we're going to be married. I should know these things." Sharon spoke with a light smile that belied the seriousness of her question.

"I haven't cried since I was a kid."

"Then why tonight?" she said intently.

He spread a palm. "Beats me. Something pushed a button and away I went. There's no way I can explain it."

After a long look, Sharon smiled. "Well, as long as I don't have to put up with it every day, darling. My shoulder couldn't take it." She put her cup on the end table. "I'm going to run your bath. You probably just need to relax."

He watched her walk out and noticed his hand was trembling when he lit a cigarette. She was probably right, he thought. All he needed was a warm bath and a pleasant, relaxing evening.

Later, during the peak of their amorous struggle, their bodies and fates entwined for a moment. Just before beginning their descent, he looked into her emerald eyes, pure and transparent in the vacancy of her ecstasy, and wondered again why the vision of a long-dead actress should have caused him to weep like a child. He had no answer.

Chapter Two

GREGORY AWOKE with a mission. There was something he had to do. What was it?

He lay in bed, inhaling the smell of bacon cooking, watching the early rays of sunlight filter through the lace curtains, listening to the distant clatter of activity in the kitchen.

Footsteps.

"Up! Up!" Sharon said, peering around the bedroom door, her voice as bright as day. "Breakfast in three minutes. The morning's almost over."

His breakfast normally consisted of coffee, a cigarette, and a slow, comfortable emergence from the world of night. But his routine had changed when Sharon moved in two weeks earlier. Now, by the time he awoke, she had already been to the store.

He remembered.

The impulse had hit him just before sleep. Perhaps "impulse" wasn't a strong enough word, he thought. He had been dozing in the moonlight—Sharon supine and sated beside him

—and he had known suddenly that he had to find out more about Brooke Ashley. Just as he knew he had to eat, sleep, make love, work, he knew he had to discover more about her. It was that certain. "First thing in the morning," he had told himself. And then sleep had claimed him.

He scrambled out of bed and splashed cold water on his face. After wrapping himself in a terry-cloth robe, he strode off for breakfast and the responsibilities of the day.

Afterward, when he had eaten too large a breakfast and Sharon had left in a flurry of admonitions and promises, he went to his study. He scrambled through his bookcase, but all he could find was a one-paragraph biography in a ten-year-old almanac.

In 1949, he learned, Brooke Ashley, at the age of twenty-four, had died in a fire. The accident had happened a week after completion of the film he had seen, *The Flight of an Eagle*, a costume drama dealing with a French family in New Orleans. Apparently, her first two films before that had been well received, but this was the one that would have catapulted her to stardom. Instead, she had become a posthumous celebrity.

Frustrated, Gregory slammed the book shut and returned it to the shelf. Compared to the reality of the woman he had seen on the screen, the printed page was lifeless, empty. The information was sparse and one-dimensional. What can dates tell you of an individual? And names? What does that tell you of the person's hopes, goals, dreams? Nothing. How could he relate to that? Gregory felt a shadow of the loss that had encompassed him the night before.

The telephone interrupted his thoughts. It was his agent.

"I thought I told you to call me first thing," Willmer said in his usual blunt manner.

"Sorry, Richard. I got hung up." He felt guiltier than the circumstances warranted. It was probably because he had promised Willmer the treatment for his new film by the end of the week, but the work had so far been torturously painful. He doubted that he'd make it.

"What could be more important than fame and fortune?" Willmer said. "Sometime today you'll hear on the news that your script's been nominated for an Oscar, babe. Best Script."

There was silence. Gregory knew the words he was expected to say, but sometimes success is harder to accept than failure, so he just stood there, thinking of nothing in particular. A spider scuttled from the pile of logs beside the fireplace. He watched its progress.

"Hey, babe, snap out of it," Willmer said, cheerfully misinterpreting the silence. "From now on you've got it made. I'll be able to retire on my commissions from you."

"That's great, Richard," Gregory mustered up. He added more truthfully, "I'm just kind of shocked."

"I understand. Listen, I've got to run. I'll keep you posted. It looks good so far. The studio's going to pump a fortune into promotion. How's the new treatment coming?"

"Fine, I guess." And then the idea struck him. Like most ideas, it came from nowhere. It just appeared and sat there, swelling with potential, waiting to be developed.

"Listen," Gregory continued. "I've got another

story idea. I think it could be dynamite. Can we have lunch?"

There was a slight pause. "Yes," Willmer said. "I can get clear. How about one o'clock at Le Buce? What's the story?"

"It deals with the reincarnation of a famous forties actress," Gregory ad-libbed. "I'll tell you about it over lunch."

"Hmmm. Sounds interesting. Okay. Seeya later, babe."

Gregory replaced the receiver slowly. He lit a cigarette and watched the smoke disperse.

It could be a good story, he thought. It might have something to do with life after death. There were two ways to go: the heroine could be a girl who remembers that she was a famous actress during her last lifetime and sets about retracing her footsteps. Or the hero could be someone who remembers he loved the star during *his* last life and sets about trying to find her. Well, he had till lunch to work it out. Then he'd sell the idea to Richard.

And then there was the Oscar nomination. He didn't know what to think about that. He should have been elated. Instead, there was an uncomfortable sensation in the pit of his stomach. It was fear, he realized. But he had nothing to fear; the fruits of the future were about to fall right into his hands, whether or not he actually won the Oscar.

Incongruously, the vision of Brooke Ashley entered his mind. Tremulous lips parted, blue eyes gentle and understanding, hands outstretched.

He took a deep settling breath and stood up clumsily. His coffee cup teetered on the edge of the end table and slid over. Blankly, he watched the brown blot seep into the white rug.

He knew then—the knowledge filtered through from some subconscious level—that his life had changed in a drastic manner. He had stood at a crossroads and taken an unscheduled turn down a different road. Nothing would ever be the same. And he knew it had nothing to do with the Oscar.

Richard Willmer liked to be thought of as a "young man in his forties." At the age of forty-seven his greatest fault was his vanity, expressed harmlessly in his appearance and in concern about the opinions of others. Although his hair had begun to gray at the temples, he was still trim and athletic, with a healthy tan.

Gregory liked him. He was honest, frank, and had done well for him. All in all, he was a dynamic individual, a super-salesman who could even sell oil to Arabs, his friends claimed. Now, in a reversal of roles, Gregory was selling to him.

They sat outside in comfortable Louis XIV chairs, sheltered from the sun by striped umbrellas. The table was set with a red-and-white checkered cloth and heavy silver utensils. At the tables around them were the rich, and those who wished they were. Across the aisle was a well-known actor, florid-faced and past his prime. He was with a young, wide-eyed blonde with a body as sleek as a jaguar. She didn't speak, except to say "Yes," and her baby-blue eyes never left his face. The modern-day American geisha girl, Gregory thought cynically. At another table two young men, casually well-dressed, alert to all movement around them, gestured at each other with liquid hands. Making deals. Everyone in Hollywood was making deals. Big deals, important deals, fantastic deals, frantic deals, pinning their hopes and their futures on rising clouds of euphoric words. Even the ones who didn't need to were making deals. It became a habit, like going to the bathroom. If you didn't do it, you grew constipated and broke out in pimples. He told himself that he should feel lucky to be one of the chosen few, envied by housewives in grubby little tract houses all around the world. And here he was, making deals with his agent.

They had dispensed with the small talk and were eating perfect omelettes and sipping expensive white burgundy when Willmer was shocked out of his complacency.

"You mean you want to *drop* the Nazi idea?" he asked incredulously. It was the story of a hunt for a Nazi war criminal in the United States. Even though Willmer hadn't yet seen a word of it, he had already created enthusiasm for the project among executives of two studios.

"Only for something better!" Gregory cut in. "And only for the time being. Until I finish this new project."

"But I've almost sold it already."

"It doesn't matter. This thing's so much better, it'll sell itself." And Gregory, flushed with enthusiasm, launched into an impassioned account of his new story.

He'd decided to stay with what he knew. The hero was a writer who saw a film starring a famous forties actress and remembered his past life with her. He had been in love with her, but died in an accident before he could declare his love. She was still alive, but a recluse. The story dealt with his attempts to meet her and persuade her that he was the reincarnation of her long-ago love.

As he listened, Willmer's irritation slowly faded and he became more attentive. It wasn't bad, he decided, not bad at all.

Gregory finished with a flurry of hand signals and looked at him expectantly. "Well?"

Willmer looked down at his wineglass and turned the stem in his fingers. He grinned. "It's good. I've got to admit, it's good."

Gregory laughed, more with relief than pleasure. On the drive to Beverly Hills, doubts had entered his mind. He had found himself questioning his objectivity, wondering whether his emotional involvement, whatever it was, had clouded his judgment.

Willmer continued. "How would you feel about doing it as a book first, Greg? You told me you wanted to get back into books sometime. What better time?"

Gregory rubbed a forefinger behind his right ear. "It would mean a lot more work . . . but I'd really be able to do the story justice that way. Yeah, I think it's a good idea. . . . What if I base the heroine on someone real? I mean, I have someone in mind. She died in the forties, but for the purposes of the book, I'll just pretend she's still alive. It'll be a sort of fictionalized fact. A blend. That way I'll have a tangible figure to research. It'll make it more credible."

Willmer spread his hands admiringly. "Sounds good to me. How the hell did you come up with this idea anyway?"

Gregory grinned at the table. "Beats me. The Muse, I guess. These things just appear out of thin air."

"I don't care whether you saw it in a crystal

ball, man. It's going to make us rich—again."

He drained his wine and looked at his watch. The thought of money always spurred him into action. "Oh-oh. I've got to run, babe. Can't stay for coffee. I've got a meeting at Universal. Keep me posted. And try to do it quickly, will you? When you're hot, you're hot, right?"

He shook Gregory's hand and charged through the tables, already intent on his next deal, his next salespitch.

Gregory ordered a coffee and sat alone, savoring it slowly. He would base the heroine on Brooke Ashley. He would learn everything there was to know about her. Everything.

The Larry Edmunds Cinema and Theatre Book Shop on Hollywood Boulevard has a well-deserved reputation as a reliable source for anything written on the film industry. From the outside, the bookshop looks slightly decrepit, but inside is collected the written history of America's most glamorous business. The shelves are stuffed to the ceilings with books, some long out of print; books running the gamut from glossy photographic paeans to dry, sociological studies. Something for everyone.

Gregory didn't intend to waste any time. He stopped there on his way back from lunch.

He stood in the aisle and scoured the biographical shelf for mention of Brooke Ashley. There was nothing.

A girl with platinum hair and red patent-leather boots looked over at him reflectively. She saw a tall, good-looking guy—maybe even handsome. She appraised him. Those may be blue-denim jeans, but they're imported French and run at least fifty bucks, she figured.

She moved a little closer. "Seen anything on Kris Kristofferson there?" she asked.

Gregory shook his head absently and turned to look for a clerk.

"Brooke Ashley?" the clerk said. "When was she? Thirties or forties?"

"She died in the late forties. I expect that if there's a book, it came out shortly afterward."

The clerk led him to the rear of the store. He pointed to a shelf. "Take a look up there. If we have anything, it'll be there."

Gregory climbed up an ancient foot ladder that creaked below him, and thumbed the titles. Harlow, Cukor, Leslie Howard, Carole Lombard, Swanson . . . the glory that once was Hollywood in a musty corner . . . there! Brooke Ashley.

It was a slim volume, a biography obviously written in a rush, just after she had died, in order to capitalize on the event. The type was large and the center pages were filled with pictures.

He paid for it and went outside, blinking in the bright sunlight. Eager to get home and begin the book, Gregory couldn't refrain from thumbing through the pictures as he walked to his car. Finally, after jostling a woman, he closed the book and concentrated on where he was going.

As he reached the car, a disturbance on the opposite corner drew his attention. It was the Krishna Consciousness devotees. Bald heads glistening in the sun, pigtails waving, saffron robes swaying in worship. "Hare Rama, Hare Krishna," chants and drumbeats.

"Crazy kids," he said to himself, but he smiled tolerantly. Hollywood was still a place that accepted everything and anything with equanimity.

During the drive home, the book sat on the seat beside him like a promise. By the time he arrived, however, some of his enthusiasm had worn off. An accident on Franklin Avenue had backed up traffic for fifteen minutes. Instead of relaxing through it as he normally did, he had tried unsuccessfully to escape by driving up a dead-end street. And, along with that, the combination of wine and heat were beginning to fog him in.

Sharon was home. He pulled up behind her Toyota in the driveway. Normally, her day consisted of an endless round of casting calls and lunches, drinks, appointments with what she called "the people you have to know to get somewhere in this oasis." A day at home was a major event in her life. She was just hanging up the telephone when he walked into the living room.

"Darling!" She kissed his mouth wetly.

"What's going on?"

"I have to leave town tomorrow," she said breathlessly. "Two days shooting in Santa Barbara. It's a Frederick Hill feature. A feature, Greg!" She was pretty in her excitement, emerald eyes flashing, her smile vivacious.

"When did this happen?"

"Today. I tried for the part weeks ago, but I didn't get it. But then the actress who did was in a car accident or something. They needed a replacement fast and called me in."

"That's fantastic," Gregory said. He was genuinely pleased.

She kissed him again. "It's just one scene, but there are a lot of lines. Hell, I wouldn't care if it was just one line. It's a chance to break out of television at last."

It was a good opportunity for her, Gregory knew. Television is usually dreary, piecemeal work for actresses who have been trained for the rigors of the stage. Sharon, with her hyper energy level, found it more monotonous than most. Films were creatively far more demanding. It was, of course, harder work, but the results were correspondingly more rewarding. She had been wanting to make the jump ever since he had known her.

"I'm really pleased for you," he said, giving her a hug.

"What's that?" she said, noticing the book in his hand.

"It's a bio on Brooke Ashley. I've got a new project going."

She disentangled herself and turned to straighten the pillows on the couch. "What's the new project?" She slapped a pillow.

He told her about his idea. "Willmer really liked it. I think it could be something special."

"But so much has been done on reincarnation," she said with a small frown.

"No. That's where you're wrong. Actually, the subject has hardly been touched—except with tainted hands."

She screwed up her mouth. "I think you're just infatuated with that actress."

It was too close to the truth. He dropped the book on the table and walked over to her. He put his arms around her and pulled her hips against his.

"She's been dead a long time," he said into her hair.

"She doesn't seem to be dead to you. Maybe you knew her in a past life."

Gregory laughed. "I don't believe in that stuff. I just write about it."

She looked up at him and smiled. "Well, *I'm* alive." She reached down and found the zipper of his pants.

"Can't argue with that."

"And this is certainly alive," she said, squeezing him. She looked up at him, eyes watchful, tongue peeking from behind her lips.

"Can't argue with that," he repeated, but his voice had grown husky.

She gave him a tug and led him out to the hall and into the bedroom. He fell back on the bed and watched her undress. First, the small exquisite breasts, the flat stomach with its sheen of soft baby hair, and then the long, slim legs. He thought again how beautiful she was.

When she finished undressing she leaped at him, savage in her nakedness. "Lazy bastard," she said, ripping his shirt and demolishing the buttons. Her flesh was warm against his chest.

"Wait. Wait." He twisted away. "I surrender. I'll do it myself. Here, look!" He hopped up, kicked off his shoes, and undressed while she watched.

He surprised himself with his ardor. He simply could not get enough of her. After the initial shock at the transformation of her gentle lover (too gentle, she sometimes thought), she returned as much as she received, and moaned with pleasure.

Afterward, running a finger lightly over his chest, she looked at him with uncharacteristic seriousness. "I really love you, Greg," she said.

She seldom mentioned love, and it caught him

off-guard. Instead of answering in kind, some inexplicable urge made him reply, "I wouldn't hurt you."

She must have sensed his ambivalence, for there was a rare sadness in her smile, and before she kissed him she said softly, "Don't make any rash promises, lover."

It was night. Sharon had gone to bed early. She had to leave for Santa Barbara at six the following morning.

Gregory went into the kitchen and made a sandwich. In a sense, the timing of her departure was ideal, he thought, not without some guilt. A couple of uninterrupted days would enable him to get his teeth into his new project. He opened a beer and took it with him to the study.

He had bought the place, a small Tudor house, about three months before, probably for more than he could afford at the time, but he liked it. The rooms were fairly large, there was a fireplace in the living room, and the kitchen was big and practical with a butcher-block table in its center. But his favorite room was the study. It, too, had a fireplace, and this, more than anything, had clinched the sale for the realtor.

Unlike his father's showcase, however, it was a working room. The windows looked out on the backyard. There was a stuffed couch for thinking and an oak desk for working. One armchair. A hideous green four-drawer filing cabinet in a corner. The walls were covered with shelves. Those that didn't hold books were littered with paper and other typing supplies. Altogether an unpretentious room.

It wasn't really cold enough, but he lit a fire anyway, more for its spiritual warmth than anything else. When the flames took, he sat beside them in the comfortable armchair, the book spotlighted by a tall chrome lamp, and read.

Brooke Ashley was born Marian Harvey in 1925 in Tulsa, Oklahoma. When she was two years old the family had moved to Los Angeles, probably because her father, Robert, was looking for work. According to the biographer, Robert was, for all intents and purposes, a worthless individual, a handyman who attempted a little bit of everything and excelled at nothing. Various reports said he was "charming," "irresponsible," "a dreamer," "a drunkard." Probably, Greg decided, he was a little bit of all of those. One of those unfortunate souls who was always trying to find his sense of balance. Whether or not he found it was unknown. Soon after the child's fourth birthday, he deserted the family for a new life. He was never heard from again.

The mother, Eleanor, had a different kind of star in her eyes. When her daughter was six years old, it was obvious that young Marian would be a beauty. Everyone, from her nursery-school teacher to the corner grocer, thought so. Perhaps her mother had no choice; perhaps the contagion of Hollywood was too great, for even then she had decided that her daughter would be a film star.

"By the time Marian was twelve, she was taking elocution lessons, dancing lessons, acting lessons. Her mother poured every penny she made into that child. She left nothing to chance," an acquaintance of the family was quoted as saying.

And when she turned twelve, her name was legally changed to Brooke Ashley.

Brooke's mother was apparently a strong-willed woman. When the girl was seventeen she began to get bit parts in pictures. At nineteen, she was signed to an exclusive studio contract.

The big break came at twenty-one. The studio boss noticed her. He liked her and he was willing to gamble. The result was a starring role in *The Story of Esmerelda*. The film was by no means a box-office hit, but it didn't lose money. Brooke Ashley's performance was praised by the critics, and it did her career no harm at all. There was another film, and then came *The Flight of an Eagle*, her last and finest work.

Details on her personal life were sketchy. Gregory suspected that the biographer hadn't taken the time to conduct personal interviews and had gleaned most of his information from press and fan-magazine cuttings.

According to the book, there had been the usual Hollywood parties and publicity dates and only one "serious romance."

The dazzling Miss Ashley was seen everywhere the year before her death with RKO executive William Tanner. They were inseparable and attended premieres, parties, and other Hollywood events together. The persistent but unconfirmed rumor around town was that they were planning to marry. Tanner was a good catch for any girl. A Harvard graduate, he was on his way to becoming a name to reckon with in the film industry. Bright, handsome, and wealthy, he was the ideal partner for the rising young star.

But about six months before her death, the romance had ended.

Miss Ashley was seen occasionally at parties with screenwriter Michael Richardson, the man who was to share her fiery death, but there were no rumors of anything serious in their relationship.

Gregory put the book down and went to get another beer in the kitchen. The gossipy prose was beginning to irritate him. Yet his interest in Brooke Ashley had increased. She had been a fascinating woman, mature and gracious beyond her years, according to reports. Maybe, he thought, if she hadn't died, she would have been as great as Garbo or Hepburn. It was a painful thought.

He took his beer back to the study and continued to read.

Films did not dominate Brooke Ashley's life to the exclusion of all else. She had had other interests. Among her friends was the then-famous Hollywood psychic, Olga Nabakov, a Russian aristocrat who gave "psychic readings" to filmdom's elite. Apparently, Brooke's involvement had begun with astrology and with the séances that were prevalent among the dabblers in spiritualism of the time.

She also loved speed. When she died, she owned two fast cars, and three unpaid speeding tickets, among her other possessions. In fact, there was quite a furor when some over-zealous city official tried to get the fines paid out of her estate. Sailing was another love. "The sweep of the water, the spray, the wind on my skin. I feel naked and free." Her quote shocked the matrons of the day.

Her collection of turquoise jewelry became her trademark. The biographer dutifully noted that she owned 132 rings, 75 bracelets and 70 necklaces. All turquoise and all worn by her at one time or another.

And then there was the fire.

It was not without mystery. It happened at the home of Michael Richardson, the screenwriter. Apparently she and her mother were visiting him at the time and all three had been trapped by the flames. The exact cause of the blaze was never discovered, although traces of wax indicated that a candle might have started the fire. All three were burned beyond recognition.

And so ended the short life and career of Brooke Ashley.

Gregory closed the book and put it on the coffee table beside him. He found that his hands were shaking. He told himself that he was tired and ought to go to bed. Instead, he turned off the lamp, lit a cigarette, and sat smoking in the soft light of the fire.

Felix came in and rubbed against his leg. Then the cat sat at his feet and watched the flickering flames with unblinking golden eyes.

Brooke Ashley. He closed his eyes and imagined how she must have died, unable to escape, her body licked by flames, screaming. Her mother and her friend . . . all past the point of panic, beyond the reach of terror . . . experiencing one of the most hideous deaths it was possible to face. If they had been lucky, the smoke got them before the heat. He'd seen a fire victim once, a Vietnam vet who went down in a chopper. The man survived the explosion of fuel, but he told Gregory there were times he wished he hadn't. Every night, without exception, he relived the event in his dreams.

Gregory must have dozed off with his thoughts.

A sound awakened him.

S-s-s-s-s-s-s!

It was the cat. Its back was arched, the fur standing up like wire. It faced the fire. Hissing.

S-s-s-s-s-s-s!

And then he saw the fire flare up. Flames licked at something that had been added to the embers. He leaned forward in the chair for a closer look. It was the book. It was too late to save it. Gray ash was already floating on the hot currents.

He squatted down and dug at the burning book with the poker. The center pages were now burning. He watched as a picture of Brooke Ashley turned black, then gray.

He shuddered as the cat hissed again. Suddenly, he remembered. The book in the fire had been sitting beside him on the coffee table before he had dozed off.

Chapter Three

GREGORY SAT AND WATCHED the embers fade. It was like watching someone die, seeing life drain from the body in stark, relentless stages.

He berated himself for his fancy. Imagination, always his greatest ally, was seeking domination over him.

But . . . what? The cat? No. There was no way Felix could have moved the book from the coffee table to the fire. The coffee table was on his left, the fire to his right. Sharon? He rose quickly and walked down the carpeted passage to the bedroom.

She was asleep, face bloodless in the moonlight, blankets strewn in a disorderly heap around her. She groaned and turned over. Restless.

He walked over to the bedroom window and drew back the light lace curtain. Outside, the green of the garden had taken on a somber gray cast. It was still and quiet.

He went back to the study. The fire had begun to fade as the coals lost their heat. He sat down and lit another cigarette.

Gregory didn't know what to think. What could he think in a situation like this? The only possible solution, the only rational explanation (and for God's sake, he told himself, stay rational) was that he had done it himself. In his sleep. He must have reached over while he was asleep, picked up the book, and tossed it into the fireplace. If he wrote that scene into a script it would be instantly rejected. But truth *is* stranger than fiction. That must have been what happened. There was no other plausible explanation. His emotions had been strange and new during the past two days. Perhaps sleepwalking was just a phase. Maybe he'd start talking in his sleep, too.

The hell with it! This line of reasoning was getting him nowhere, he thought savagely. He *must* have done it in his sleep. It was the only possible explanation.

He stubbed out his cigarette with a still-shaking hand and pulled the wire-mesh screen in front of the fireplace. He bent to pick up Felix, but the cat backed up quickly, fur rising slightly.

"Hey," he said aloud. "I'm not the only one getting weird. Come on, Felix."

He moved his hand toward the cat more slowly, and this time it didn't retreat. He stroked the top of its head gently and the cat rubbed him back.

"Come on, old friend." The animal had been with him for almost five years. They respected each other. It was a serviceable relationship; he'd decided one couldn't expect more from a cat. He picked it up and put it out through the kitchen door. Then he went to the bedroom.

More than anything else, he needed sleep, he

decided. A tired mind plays tricks. He would rest it, nourish it with the balm of sleep.

But sleep holds its own perils. The dream came soon after he fell asleep.

Brooke was wearing something white and silky that clung to her. Her back was bare, the color of alabaster in the dim light of the moon.

They stood on a hill, looking down at the lights of Los Angeles—slashes and pinpricks on a black canvas. He couldn't see his own face, just his clothes: a dinner suit, his shoes.

"I love this city at night," she said. "All those people down there. I wonder who they are and what they dream about."

He put his hands on her shoulders. There was dark hair on his knuckles. He was wearing a gold ring on his right hand, set with a *fleur-de-lis* carved from a black onyx.

"And I love you," he said. "Night or day."

She turned with a radiant smile. "I . . ."

And then she faded. The lights winked out, the hill disappeared from beneath his feet. Blackness. A whistle of wind.

He knew he was back in his bed. Asleep.

But he wasn't alone. A dark figure stood beside him. It was looking down at his sleeping body. He was asleep. His eyes were closed. But he could "see" the figure.

It was a woman. Somehow he knew, even though she was wearing a long hooded cloak that hid her face. He began to sweat. The cowled figure just stood beside the bed, looking down at him. He wished he could see her face. He struggled to open his eyes. *Oh, God! What's happening? Why can't I open my eyes?* He told himself it was a dream. He told himself he could wake up. *This is a dream.*

He could feel the woman's hatred.

And then she spoke. "Stay away," she said. Her voice grated at him. It was coarse, malicious, filled with contempt.

"Stay away from Brooke. Stay away from her."

He struggled. He twisted and turned. He wanted to scream at her, to strike her. *Go away, damn you!* He wanted to wake up. More than anything, he wanted to open his eyes and wake up. He tried, but his eyelids wouldn't move. *Oh, please! Wake up. Please open, please.* He had the terrifying thought that if he didn't wake up now he never would.

He awakened.

His body was drenched in perspiration. His throat was dry. He wanted to retch.

He stumbled into the bathroom and splashed cold water onto his face. He drank thirstily.

He went back to the bed, sat on its edge, and lit a cigarette. Behind him, Sharon stirred.

"Greg? Whatever . . . ?"

He leaned backward and half-turned to kiss her cheek. "Nothing, honey. Go back to sleep."

She mumbled and then was quiet. He envied her escape, and stretched back on the bed, smoking, looking up at the ceiling. Sleep had never been more elusive.

He woke at ten, feeling partially refreshed. So he had finally fallen asleep after all. And in spite of his apprehension, had had no more nightmares. Sharon had left a note on the kitchen table:

You looked so cute, I didn't wake you. I'll call later. Eat some breakfast!

Love,
S.

He disobeyed. He made some coffee and drank three cups with as many cigarettes while he read the paper.

When at last he glanced up and gazed out the window, he realized it was a spectacular day. The kitchen looked out at the garden on the side of the house. Although there was a fence and he couldn't see her, he could hear his neighbor clucking as she went through her daily ritual, feeding the birds. It was an ideal situation: they fed and shat on her side of the fence, then flew over and added life to his yard.

The events of the night seemed to lose their significance in the brightness of the morning. Of course he must have thrown the book in the fire. A strange thing to do, but what the hell? He shouldn't have eaten those sandwiches before going to bed. As a child, his mother had warned him about that. "Indigestion will give you bad dreams, Greg," she used to say. It turned out she was right, for once. There was an explanation for everything. "Ain't it just like the night, to play tricks when you're trying to be so quiet," Bob Dylan had said.

He would start work on the project. He already had an idea for the first scene. He needed to buckle down to his workaday tasks more earnestly and indulge his fancy less. The thought cheered him. He put his coffee cup in the sink and clapped his hands together. "Action," he said aloud.

Felix looked up lazily from his position on the kitchen chair.

Gregory showered briskly, shaved, and dressed, feeling better than he had in days. Work cures all ills, he told himself. It's the universal panacea. Without it, whole populations would go insane.

His enthusiasm faded briefly when he reached his study and faced a blank sheet of paper in his typewriter. It always did. But it was just a stage, and he'd learned to beat it. Just get some words down, any words.

He began to write.

She stood at the top of the stairs, a vision in white.

The motion in the room slowed for him, then stopped. He saw nothing but the vision. Everything else was surrounded by a haze.

She looked directly at him, a smile hovering around her mouth. The depths in her eyes threatened to burst into flame. He walked toward her. The crowd seemed to part for him.

"Hello, there," he said.

"Hello, there," she replied. *(Keep it simple, keep it simple.)*

"You're Brooke Ashley. I saw one of your films."

She inclined her head, accepting his homage. She smiled. It was dazzling. The haze in the room lifted and he became aware again of the hum of conversation around them.

He realized she was holding out her hand. He took it in his, meaning to shake it. Instead he just stood there, a fool, frozen, with a hand burning in his palm.

"Who are you here with?" he asked finally.

She mentioned a name he vaguely recognized.

"Can you leave with me now?" he asked. He realized he was still holding her hand and released it.

"I'll get my coat," she said. Again she smiled with that peculiar radiance, tantalizing him with excitement.

Gregory pushed the typewriter away and read what he had written. It had been fairly effortless and had an easy feeling to it. That was a good sign. But it read like a film script. It was too threadbare for a novel. He needed some background and atmosphere. The party. He should describe it, capture the ambience of Hollywood in the forties.

Research. He needed to do research. Bone up on the period. Inject some detail into the story.

The telephone rang.

It was Steve Sherman, a friend who went back to his first days in Hollywood. They hadn't seen much of each other since he had been going with Sharon. He suspected that Steve and his wife, Liz, didn't care for her much, although they had never said anything.

They chatted. When Steve heard that Sharon was out of town, he could hardly contain his pleasure.

"Come over for dinner tonight," he said. "You've probably forgotten how to cook since you've been living in blissful sin."

Gregory accepted. It would be a pleasant

evening. He enjoyed their company. He agreed to be at their house between six and seven.

He hung up and again skimmed through the pages he had written. He penciled in a couple of changes, but it wasn't what the scene really needed. He decided to concentrate on the research.

The Franklin Potter Film Institute in Beverly Hills squats beside Wilshire Boulevard, an architectural monstrosity, a gauche monument to the pretentious side of Los Angeles' character that the city has never been able to suppress. A hardheaded businessman, Potter had made his fortune in kidney beans, trampling over the bodies of his unfortunate competitors and his even more unfortunate employees, who were for the most part illegal aliens willing to work for a pittance. His only known soft spot was the film industry. He had loved the color and excitement of it. He had been a fan, in the extreme sense of the word, and had been wealthy enough to indulge himself. He had hobnobbed with studio bosses and stars, financed a few films, visited the sets at every opportunity, heady with the excitement of it all. Ah, Hollywood!

Potter's aspirations to immortality were consummated by the construction of the Institute. It was both a research center and a museum, filled with memorabilia, books, scripts, and copies of films long forgotten by a fickle public. It was a gold mine for students and nostalgia freaks, and they came from all over the world to tap its treasures.

Gregory took the elevator up to the library on the third floor. It was a large room, obviously designed with the researcher in mind. There were comfortable, almost luxurious chairs and tables. The tables even had typewriter pads for those who brought their own machines. He walked past several studious figures to the desk at the far side of the room.

A pretty blond woman, tall, with rounded shoulders, asked if she could help.

"I'd like the clipping and still files on Brooke Ashley, please," he said.

The woman hurried back to a row of filing cabinets on the rear wall. After a minute or two she came back carrying two folders. She put them on the desk and copied their file numbers onto a form.

"Please fill in your name and address," she said, pushing the paper over to him.

He completed the paperwork, although he didn't quite understand its purpose. If he wanted to steal anything, he'd need only to put down a false name. He took the folders to a nearby table.

First he looked quickly through the stills. There were about two dozen, mostly publicity poses and shots of her movies, alone and with leading men. There was one picture of her at the age of nineteen. She looked like a schoolgirl, but the signs of character that grew more evident in the later photographs had already begun to emerge.

He pushed the folder aside and opened the clipping file. It was considerably thicker. It began with the usual planted gossip-column plugs: A Face to Watch; Rising Young Star. And so on. Then there was a rash of dating publicity, arranged by the studio. "Seen at the Brown Derby with actor James Stewart was up-and-coming starlet Brooke Ashley." There were interviews, reviews of her films.

During the last year of her life, the press coverage had increased. More interviews, more fan-magazine features.

And then, an item printed about six months before the fire caught his eye:

IN THE LURCH . . . People are wondering why beautiful Brooke Ashley arrived at Dolly Crocket's spectacular Beverly Hills party with studio executive Bill Tanner and left with dashing young screenwriter Michael Richardson? . . .

Shaken, Gregory closed the file.

It was the scene he had just written.

He told himself it was just coincidence. *But, Jesus!* The world was getting to be a strange place, a place where things that didn't happen were happening to him.

He opened the folder and read the item again. It was one of a number in a column filled with titillating questions and implications. It was exactly how he had created the opening scene of his novel. She arrives at the party with someone else, meets the screenwriter. There is instant chemistry between them, and they leave together. An incredible coincidence.

Gregory shook his head. Coincidences *did* happen. It was practical proof of the adage that life mirrors art. He continued reading.

Brooke Ashley's death had kept the newspapers busy for almost a week. She had received far more press attention in death than at any time during her career. One paper suggested that arson had been suspected. The other accounts said merely that the cause of the fire was unknown. A columnist mentioned the rumor that just before her death Brooke Ashley had been considering retirement from acting. Luminaries, who Gregory suspected had probably never even known her, heaped profuse praise on her acting ability, her honesty, her beauty, her attitude to life. Altogether, it was an exhibition of that peculiar plethora of togetherness and admiration that the Hollywood community exhibits when one of its members dies. Never are they loved so much as in death.

Gregory took the folders back to the blond woman at the desk.

"Do you have anything else on Brooke Ashley?" he asked.

"Her films are probably on file. Other than that, you might check the card catalogue to see if there are any books."

As he turned away, she spoke again. "By the way, there's a miniature wax museum on the first floor. If you're interested, there might be a tableau featuring her there."

Gregory thanked her and went to the catalogue file. There was a card for the biography he had read before. The one he had thrown in the fire. Nothing else on Brooke Ashley.

Impulsively, he went back to the desk. The woman smiled patiently.

"Do you have a file on a screenwriter named Michael Richardson?" he asked.

She went back to her cabinets and returned a moment later with a folder. He filled out the paperwork again, but the file was so slim he read it at the desk.

There were only four or five clippings. No pictures. There was also a small biographical entry.

"Michael Richardson, born June 9, 1918, San Francisco, California . . ." followed by a list of the films he had written. His last work had been *The Flight of an Eagle*, which also happened to be Brooke Ashley's last film. Nothing else of note. He handed the file back.

He ignored the elevator and took the stairs down to the first floor, where the guard showed him the passage to the wax museum. It was a large, high-ceilinged room in the rear of the building. He was the only one in the museum.

The figures were all in glass cases. Perfect costumed replicas, three feet high. It struck him as bizarre. Gable and Lombard, Gable and Leigh from *Gone with the Wind*; Cagney, Bogart, Harlow, Tierney—they were all there, presented in scenes from their films with perfectly scaled sets and costumes. There was nothing later than 1950, he noticed. The idea had probably died with its benefactor from lack of interest.

Brooke Ashley's tableau was in a corner. He almost missed it. The scene was from *The Flight of an Eagle*. The model was exquisite. She was looking up, her lips parted. It was almost a plea.

Gregory stared at it searchingly, looking for the human spirit beneath the plaster cast, examining the contours of her face and figure. A turmoil of nameless emotions gripped him. He began to grow warm. Still he stood, unable to tear his glance from the lovely face looking up at him.

He became hotter. Beads of sweat formed on his forehead. He felt them run down his neck.

The small figure of Brooke had her hands outstretched in his direction, imploring. For what? he wondered.

The heat grew unbearable. He began to gasp. His throat tightened, his breathing grew difficult. He tore his eyes away from the tableau and pulled at his collar, as if to loosen it. He ripped at the buttons of his shirt. Then he turned and ran from the room.

Gregory leaned against the hall wall, slowly regaining his breath. He felt nauseous, drained.

He felt as if he had just escaped from a raging fire.

Chapter Four

STEVE AND LIZ SHERMAN lived in a small house off Beachwood Drive. It was by no means luxurious, but it was theirs and they had made it comfortable. Steve was a working actor, one of the many whose names go unheralded but who are recognizable enough for people to stop them on the street and ask where they had met them before. Liz had been a model when they had met. Now she painted and looked after their five-year-old son, Cosmo.

Steve hugged Gregory at the door.

"You shouldn't stay away so long, man," he said warmly. Then he added with a chuckle, "Especially now that you've won an Oscar nomination."

Steve was a big man—not tall—but broad, solid, and permanent, with laugh lines cut deeply into his face. Liz came up, drying her hands on a dishtowel. She was tall and slim, dark hair falling to the middle of her back. She kissed Gregory on the mouth, poking her tongue out just before pulling away. It was an old joke.

"Still a tease, thank God," Gregory said affectionately.

"Hey, all you have to do is call," she retorted. He slapped her on the buttocks. "Cosmo," she shouted. "Look who's here."

A bright-eyed boy, with ink-stains on his face, came tumbling out of the bedroom. "Greg! Hi, Greg!" He grabbed him around the knees and tried to pull him down. "You know what I got? You know what?"

"No, what?"

"A dog! I got my own dog. Come on." He took Gregory by the hand and led him to the back porch. "Isn't it neat?" he said proudly.

A small dog got up off the rug and wagged its tail. Gregory bent down and patted it.

"It's a great dog, Cosmo. What's its name?"

Cosmo looked thoughtful. "Shep and Lassie," he said.

"Good name," Gregory agreed. He went back inside and walked into the living room.

"Want a beer?" Steve asked.

"Save my life." He sat on the couch and put his feet up on the coffee table while Steve went to get his drink.

Liz sat beside him. "You look beat up," she said.

"Yeah, well, it's a tough life." He grinned at her.

Steve returned with his beer, then sat in an armchair. "You look like you've been overworking or something," he said.

"Oh, Jesus! You too," Gregory exclaimed and rolled his eyes. "Spare me from my friends."

"Did I say something?"

Liz explained. "I just told him he looks beat up," she said. "And so he does. Probably Sharon's been wearing him out in the sack. He's not getting any younger, you know." She smiled maliciously.

"Sheathe your claws, woman," Steve ordered. "How are things going with you two? Still getting married?"

"Yeah. Things are fine. How about you? Not divorcing yet?"

Steve held up his hands. "Okay, okay. You made your point. Little touchy, aren't you?"

Gregory grunted into his beer can. "Yeah, I guess. How's things with you, really?"

"Can't complain. Landed a new commercial last week. Dog food. Good loot. They gave me a case of the stuff, but our dog won't touch it. Dog next door won't touch it. Even the stray cat that hangs around the neighborhood won't touch it. Great product."

Gregory laughed.

"I told the account exec about it," Steve continued. "He said his dogs wouldn't touch it either. 'We don't have to eat it, just sell it,' he told me."

Gregory turned to Liz. "How about your paintings? Selling?"

She grimaced. "Oh, sure, like hot tamales. It seems as if everybody wants seascapes. Except mine."

"Maybe you should do those Mexican things," Gregory suggested. "You know, the deer standing at the lake with the moon peeping over a mountain in the background. All in luminous paint, of course."

"Of course," she said.

Dinner was simple: rare steak, salad with vinaigrette dressing, French bread, red wine, good conversation, more wine, and more talk.

Afterward, nursing a mug of strong coffee, Gregory told his friends about his new project.

"You'll be researching reincarnation, then?" Steve said.

"Yeah. And I've got a long way to go. All I know is what I've seen in popular literature and the media. Most of it's probably bullshit. I'd like to do justice to the subject. What's your opinion?"

"I think when you're dead, you're dead, you're dead," Liz said emphatically.

Steve looked uncertain. "I don't know." He frowned. "I used to think it was crap, you know. Delusion, wishful thinking by people who couldn't accept their own mortality. But I'm not so sure now."

Gregory was interested. "What changed your mind?" He hadn't even considered the possibility that reincarnation might be a reality.

"Well, I have this friend. Bob Lion, the actor?"

Gregory nodded. Lion was no superstar, but he was fairly well known. He had met him casually once at a party.

"Well," Steve continued, "he's really into this stuff. And since he's one of the most cooled out and rational people I know, I can't just dismiss what he says as garbage."

"Maybe I can talk with him when I get into my research," Gregory suggested.

"You're wasting your time," Liz said. "You'd probably do just as well if you made it all up instead of researching it."

"Hey, you like Bob Lion, don't you?" Steve said.

"Yeah, I like him. But that doesn't mean I have to believe his particular brand of bullshit."

Gregory listened, amused by the exchange. The incongruity of it affected him. Hell, he thought, here we are practically into the Emancipated Eighties, me and my two intelligent friends, and we're talking about the fact that there is no death. They sit there arguing about it like they'd argue about politics or vacation sites or brands of beer, all with the same lack of involvement. And here I sit with a silly smile on my face, knowing full well that if this were true and could be proven true, it would change the whole human experience and rip apart the foundations of our lives. Things would flip-flop all over the place. Philosophy, religion, even art, would all be sent to the junk heap, turned in for the new model. What would the films he wrote mean then? Something different, he was sure. But what? It was anybody's guess. Too much for him to think through while he sat on this couch with a coffee cup in one hand, a cigarette in the other.

Gregory drained his coffee and got to his feet. "Well, I'm going to split while you two battle it out." He leaned down to kiss Liz. "Thanks for the dinner, love."

She put her arms around his neck playfully and held him there. "If it takes dinner to get you over here, I'll do it again."

"Deal," he said, touching her lips lightly.

Steve and Liz stood in the doorway and watched him drive away.

"He really does looked wiped out," said Liz.

"Yeah," said Steve.

Gregory looked at his watch. It was only a little after 9:00 P.M. For a moment, he regretted leaving. He didn't really want to go home and sit alone in the house. Perhaps he should have stayed and enjoyed the warmth of his friends.

When he reached Franklin Boulevard, instead of turning left to Los Feliz he swung to the right, then turned down Gower to Hollywood. He still had time to make the 10:00 P.M. show at the theater featuring *The Flight of an Eagle*. He decided to see the film again. After all, it had acted as a catalyst before; perhaps it would inspire him still further. Face it, he said to himself, this is really why you left early.

Traffic was thick along the Boulevard of the Stars. He looked at the knots of people scurrying along the sidewalks, drawn there like helpless moths. Poor Hollywood, he thought; it's lost its sheen. The buildings had succumbed to heat and smog and neglect over the years, and they were now caricatures of their former selves. Ever since the pimps and hookers, the hardcore druggies, the runaways and faggots had moved into the area, it had gone downhill at breakneck speed. The only thing preventing Hollywood Boulevard from falling dead on its feet were the movie theaters that still drew crowds from outlying areas. Tourists still came, of course, but now, instead of vying to see stars and glamour, they came to view the freaks and share in the degradation. Poor Hollywood.

He arrived at the theater with five minutes to spare, paid his three dollars, and took a seat in the air-conditioned darkness. The credits rolled, and once again he found himself in a strange, strange world, a world where the barriers of time and space lost their power, a domain created by the immutable illogic of dreams and imagination.

Brooke Ashley's face, magnified many times

by a technology that had taken over the world, subverted his senses. He sank into it, almost felt her breath on his face, tasted the softness of her lips, smelled her perfume, tickled his nose with her hair. He groaned to himself, squirmed in his seat, worshiped, adored.

And then came her final monologue.

"I love you," she said. She paused. "I love you," she repeated. "I've loved you since the sun first rose. I've loved you through God-sent catastrophe and manmade disaster. My love has no shame, no pride. It is only what it is, always has been, and always will be. It is yours. All yours. Only yours."

He did not cry this time, though he had to swallow the lump in his throat. And he had to rub his forehead with both hands. He desperately wished that she were sitting beside him in the dark gloom of the theater so that he could tell her the words engraved in his thoughts. But he did not cry.

Instead, he found himself thinking that something was missing from the dialogue. There was something about time and eternity that should have been there. There had been an incompleteness to the ending, a wrongness he had been unable to ignore. As a screenwriter, he would have added to the dialogue, made it fuller, more complete, rounded it out to perfection.

He drove home quickly, intent on the road. Anger had replaced his earlier emotion. He found himself angry that Brooke Ashley had died, that she had made only three films, that she was not sitting beside him in the passenger seat looking sideways at him as he drove. At one point he leaned impatiently on his horn when the car in front of him didn't move quickly enough at the green light.

What's the matter with me? he asked himself. Am I in love? But if so, I'm in love with someone no longer in the living world. Still, aren't some of our deepest emotions centered on someone who has died, but still lives in memory? *In memory?* How can I remember someone I never knew?

To make matters worse, when he arrived home, he found an annoying message on his answering machine from Sharon: "I've called three times now. Please call me when you get back." She left the number of her motel in Santa Barbara.

"Where have you been?" was her greeting when he called.

"I had dinner at Steve and Liz's."

"Oh?"

"Then I went to a movie."

She softened. "Oh. What did you see?"

"I saw *The Flight of an Eagle* again."

"God, don't you think you're going a bit berserk with that?"

He asked her what she meant.

"I don't know," she relented, catching the warning in his voice. "I guess I'm just disappointed you weren't there when I called."

The conversation took a turn for the better. Sharon told him how the shooting had been going. She told him she loved him, and Gregory said he loved her. She was returning the following afternoon, she said. The shooting had been going better than expected. She missed him. They ended on a warm note.

Gregory yawned. Time for some sleep. He rose and went to look for Felix. The cat was curled up on his bed, asleep. He picked it up and put it outside through the kitchen door.

There was no moon. The garden was still and black, a mass of shadow. Felix yawned once on the step and then took off, disappearing in seconds.

Gregory turned and went back inside. He undressed and got into bed. It had been a long day and he was tired, but sleep eluded him. He lay on his back and went over the events of the day. He thought his reaction at the end of the film had been curious. The insistence in his mind that something had been missing from the script. It was probably nothing—merely a screenwriter's instinct for perfection. Still, perhaps tomorrow he would try to get a copy of the script itself and check it out. Just to satisfy his curiosity.

With that thought, he fell asleep.

There were no dreams.

Chapter Five

GREGORY TOOK THE SCRIPT over to a desk and sat down. The same blond librarian had attended to him. She had called him "Mr. Thomas" and smiled, a surprisingly sudden change of warmth. Either she had remembered his name, or she had taken the trouble to look him up in the records to see who he was. He felt slightly flattered.

The script for *The Flight of an Eagle* had a heavy black cardboard binding. "By Michael Richardson," it said on the cover. He opened it and flicked through the pages, remembering parts of the dialogue. He found the last scene and read it through.

The dialogue was exactly the same as it had appeared in the film.

His disappointment was bitter. He had expected something else, and although he didn't admit it, for some reason it had been important to him. Then he thought of something.

He took the script back to the desk.

"Finished already, Mr. Thomas?" the woman said.

"Yes, thank you," he said. "Tell me, these are the shooting scripts you have on file here, aren't they?"

"Yes. It's either the shooting script, or if that's not available, a transcript made from the film."

"Well, where could I find the original script? The one Richardson did before everybody got their hands on it?"

She frowned at the question. "I don't know. I suppose you'd have to go to the studio that made the film. They'd probably have it in their archives."

He nodded. "Thank you very much for your help. Is there a phone here?"

"In the lobby, beside the elevator," she said.

He found the telephone, searched in his pockets for a coin, and called Richard Willmer.

Willmer came on the line immediately.

"What's happening, babe?"

Gregory told him what he wanted. "I'm going home now. Would you call me as soon as you've arranged it?"

"Sure thing. I'll call in half an hour."

Thirty minutes later, Gregory walked through his front door. The telephone was ringing. He picked it up.

"Richard?"

"Yeah. It's all arranged. Just go to the north gate. The guard will have your name. He'll also give you directions to the archives section. They'll be expecting you and then you can tell them what you want."

"Fantastic! Thanks a lot."

"*Nada*," Willmer said, and hung up.

Gregory quickly made himself a sandwich and then left the house, eating while he drove. He took the Hollywood Freeway to the San Fernando Valley.

The city behind him was already obscured by smog. At the top of the hill he saw that the valley was even worse. He saw the studio in the distance and turned off the freeway. Once the entire valley had been farmland—neat rows of orange trees perfuming the air with their scent. Now, towns covered the floor of the valley in all directions, clustered together, and the air was weighted with lead and carbon monoxide.

When the studio had moved out here, land had been cheap. It had claimed acres of it. But even during its heyday, when it had turned out scores of films every year, it had still looked like a shantytown with its narrow streets and hastily erected buildings sprawling haphazardly wherever there was a spare foot of earth. Since the passing of the age of the big studio, neglect had made it even uglier. The offices now housed dozens of independent producers, and, of course, television had moved in and exercised squatter's rights.

Gregory pulled up at the gate and gave the guard his name. The man consulted his clipboard and waved him politely on.

"Which way is the archives section?" Gregory asked.

The man consulted a map and then gave Gregory a spate of confusing directions. Gregory set off with a prayer. It didn't help much. Halfway there he was forced to stop and ask a gardener for directions.

The archives were located in a red brick building, fronted by a small parking lot. Gregory pulled up in a space marked by a reserved sign and got out of the car.

A short elderly lady with beady sparrow's eyes guarded the desk. Her graying hair was swept up in a bun and she tapped her desk with one finger while she spoke.

"Yes?" she said suspiciously.

"My name is Gregory Thomas. Someone should have called about me."

"Indeed, they did, Mr. Thomas. What is it you wanted?"

"I'd like to find Michael Richardson's original script for *The Flight of an Eagle*."

"I see," she said, shuffling some papers on her desk. She stood up when she had completed the task. "Follow me, please."

Her steps, like her manner, were short, certain, efficient. He followed her down a hall to a small windowless room. It was lined with shelves, each one crammed with neatly bound scripts.

"That film was probably made in 1948. Am I correct?"

He nodded, and she pointed to the second shelf. "It should be on that shelf. The dates are on the spines of the binders. They are in chronological order. Please do not take the script from this room. You may inspect it here. There are no chairs, but there's a stool." She indicated a wooden stool in the corner.

Gregory began to thank her, but before he could get past the first syllable, she turned and walked out.

He ran his fingers along the bindings. They were not dusty. The scripts were filed not only by year, but alphabetically. It didn't take him long to find what he was looking for.

There were two copies of *Eagle*, one marked A, the other B. He pulled them out and flipped to the last pages of one of them. The dialogue was the same as that in the final shooting script. He put it on the floor and examined the script marked A.

"I've loved you since the sun first rose," he read. "I've loved you through God-sent catastrophe and manmade disaster. *I've loved you though my heart stopped beating and my eyes ran dry, through time and in spite of it, for our love has its roots in eternity and cannot fall victim to time or death.* My love has no shame, no pride. It is only what it is, always has been, and always will be. It is yours. All yours. Only yours."

Gregory went cold with fear—and it didn't help matters to realize that he didn't know exactly why. It wasn't an overwhelming fear—that might have been easier to face. This was more a niggling, subversive emotion, one that chipped away slowly but remorselessly at the foundations of his reality. There had been too many things happening that violated his normal realm of experience. He didn't understand them, and wasn't sure he wanted to. Any attempt to do so would be worse than banging his head up against a rock. At least with a rock the outcome would be predictable: lumps on his head. The terror of the unknown is that it is unknown.

Sharon had arrived home a few hours earlier, and she was walking around with a set mouth and creased forehead. She had found Gregory preoccupied and withdrawn. It was not what she had looked forward to. The shooting had exceeded all expectations and she had come back with a sense of personal achievement. The director had liked her work and complimented her on it. She had wanted to share her triumph with Gregory. Instead, he had half-listened to her chatter, his mind obviously on his own work, and it had deflated her cheerful expectations.

She walked into the study to find him immersed in a sheaf of notes, resolved to rescue the situation.

"Greg?"

"Hmmm?" He didn't look up, just crossed something out with his ballpoint pen.

She perched on the arm of his chair and put her hand on his neck. He couldn't ignore her; had no wish to. It was just that the plotting had been difficult and he was at a particularly crucial point. He looked up at her and smiled absently.

"What, honey?"

She smiled brightly, nervously. "Let's go out to dinner tonight, Greg. Afterward we can go to a movie or something."

Gregory shook his head. "I'm not hungry, love. A sandwich will do for me. Besides, I'm at a point here . . . if I just stick with it, I think it'll all be worked out. I just have to find a way for him to remember who he is, and then. . . ."

Sharon removed her hand and rose petulantly to her feet. "Greg, I'm really not interested in hearing about that. I just wish you'd pay me half as much attention as you do to that—that —script!"

"It's not a script, it's a novel," he said patiently. "Just give me a couple of hours, and I'll pay you all the attention you want."

He made a move to touch her, but she pushed his hand away angrily. "For God's sake, Greg.

I've been stuck in Santa Barbara for two days, working my ass off. I need to get out. Can't you think of me?"

Gregory put his papers down slowly and gave her his undivided attention. There was an edge of hysteria in her voice. He had never seen her act like this before.

"Sharon, you know how demanding my work is," he said reasonably. "You've never complained about it before. What's going on?"

Her hands flew up in a gesture of impatience. "Can't you see I'm sick of your work? I'm sick of taking second place. I'm sick of hearing about Brooke-fucking-Ashley! I'm sick of seeing you fall in love with a ghost." Her voice rose to a shout. "You're supposed to love *me*. Can't you give *me* any attention? I'm alive. I'm here. Now!"

Her face was livid. Tight lines pulled her mouth out of shape. Suddenly she seemed ugly to Gregory, and he had to fight the impulse to tell her so, to lose himself in screaming anger. The impulse passed, and for a moment he considered telling her what he had been going through, of the strange things that had happened since he had been working on this story, but an inner voice cautioned him that it would antagonize her all the more.

Instead, he said, "Sharon, I do love you. You know that. But my work is important, too. It's what I live for. It's what I do. And you're going to have to live with that." His voice came out colder than he had intended.

She reached down and grabbed his arm, pushed her face close to his. "Show me that you love me then. Stop working and let's go out. Right now!"

Gregory became angry. "Sharon, that's child-ish. It's emotional blackmail. I'm not going to buy it. You'd better get a little more rational on the subject." But his anger was a weak thing, and that damn inner voice laughed at him and said, Who are you to talk about "rational," you hypocrite? You, with your things that go bump in your dreams and your coincidences and the infatuation that's becoming an obsession. And what about this work that right now is just a continuation of your obsession?

And damned if she didn't shout out, "Ra-tional? Ha! You call having a crush on a dead actress rational? It's not even"— she searched for the scathing word—"adult, for Christsakes!"

She began to cry, and he realized that the scene had gone far enough. He stood up and put his arms around her and pulled her head into his chest. "Sharon, it's all right. Everything is all right."

He could feel the sobs shake her body against him. Slowly, she calmed down and her sobs became sniffles. He gently pushed her away from him and kissed her eyes. He had never been able to face a woman's tears. She stood with her arms hanging limply at her sides, as if she had used up her last ounce of energy.

"I'm sorry, Greg. It wasn't fair." Her voice was mournful. "It's just that I don't want to lose what we have, and I get this horrible feel-ing that it's happening right in front of my eyes and I can't do anything about it."

He held her shoulders and looked at her. "Nothing like that is happening, Sharon. Nothing at all. Everything is going to be fine." He let his hands drop and smiled at her. "Now, how about getting dressed and we'll go out for dinner?"

She shook her head numbly. "No, Greg. You don't have to do that. It wasn't fair of me to lay that on you."

He took her hand and led her out of the study. "No. You were right, Sharon. I'm getting too deep into this project. It'll do us both good to get out and play a bit."

Sharon blinked through her remaining tears. "All right, I'll just be a minute or two." She turned and ran to the bedroom. Gregory watched her go down the passage. He wanted to run after her and tell her he loved her enough to give up everything for her, to reassure her, to wipe away her doubts. But he didn't think he could say it and mean it. He just stood there, feeling despicable.

Dinner went well. Outwardly, at least. Gregory was his charming best. They ate and drank at the Brasserie, and afterward went to a nearby piano bar where they drank some more and held hands as they had when they'd first met. They chatted happily, reminisced, and told each other silly stories. Yet, through it all, Gregory felt as if they were trying to regain something that had been lost, some special intensity of feeling.

Driving back home, he realized that Sharon had been having similar thoughts. She put her hand on his leg and said quietly, "Greg, we had a good time, didn't we? Everything is going to be fine, isn't it?"

Somehow, it touched him more deeply than anything that had happened between them before. Perhaps it was the small, thin voice, or the expression of deep concern he imagined was on her face.

"Yes, love, everything is fine," he said with all

the feeling he could muster, and she relaxed her hold on his leg.

Later, though, as he was washing his face and hands before bed, he happened to glance into the mirror and caught her watching him. The look on her face reminded him of a bar fight he had once witnessed. A big bruiser of a man had picked a fight with a small, nondescript fellow who weighed about 160 with his shoes on, and had pulverized him. Afterward, he had stood looking down at the wreck beside his feet, with its broken nose, the face a bloody pudding. The big man's mouth was slack, sensual, and he licked his lips. But it was his eyes that were revealing. They shone with a curious mixture of hate, derision and love. It had been sickening to watch.

For a moment, before she realized he was looking, Sharon's eyes flickered with similar contradictions. Then she saw him and a veil dropped over her face.

She stepped closer and held his arm. "Come to bed, Greg," she said pleasantly.

He looked at her sharply, shocked by the unguarded expression he had seen on her face. She returned his stare, eyes innocent. He told himself he must be imagining things and allowed her to lead him to their bed.

After he had fallen asleep, the dream came again.

He was standing on the hill with Brooke, looking down at the peppered city lights, exactly as before. They each spoke the same words, and then the scene faded again.

Gregory waited for what he knew would come.

A current of cold air crossed his face. And then he "saw" the dark, hooded figure standing beside him.

She emanated cold, naked hatred. It seeped through his flesh, into his being, piercing him to the bone. He knew that he would not have the strength to move or open his eyes.

A fear gripped him, so intense and concentrated, so consuming, that he knew his bones would melt and wither away until he lay there, a helpless blob of protoplasm. *Oh, God! Wake up! I'm going to die. Wake up!*

But he could not awaken.

The hate was implacable, merciless. He had no defense against it. There was no way he could deal with it, asleep and helpless with a down-filled pillow beneath his head.

The hateful, sibilant voice: "I warned you. I told you to leave Brooke alone," she hissed.

"You animal! Pervert! You scum!" The words were like nails being driven into his body.

"You aren't good enough to kiss her feet. You never were, never will be. I warned you. Now you are going to be punished."

She leaned forward, a shadowy, hooded figure. He knew, with a fresh surge of fear, that he was about to see her face, and he knew with equal certainty that it would be the death of him.

He felt an awful pressure on his chest and the hissing grew louder.

And then he woke up.

Felix was sitting on his chest, spitting and hissing at the empty air.

If he had not been so shaken, he would have laughed with relief. He had forgotten to put the cat out.

He was sweating like a fevered invalid. He grew aware of the dampness beneath him. At first he thought it was perspiration. Then, with a hot flush of shame, he realized that he had urinated all over the bed.

Chapter Six

THERE CAME A POINT when Gregory began to
doubt the validity of his own actions. One thing
he no longer doubted—indeed, he readily admitted it to himself now—was that his involvement with Brooke Ashley's memory was based
upon an intense infatuation. But, he realized, if
infatuation passed beyond a certain point, it
then became obsession, a state he suspected he
was fast approaching.

He had been planning to enter the study to
continue writing, but for some reason he was
unable to do so and found himself pacing the
living-room carpet. His thought processes were
disorganized to a state of frustration. The images
darting through his mind were so fuzzy and
insubstantial that he was unable to follow them
with any analytical clarity. But then, as in reading a newspaper and seeing a headline, a passing notion caught his attention, and he held onto
it. It was more a command than a thought, and
it said: *You've got to do more research—you've
got to learn more and more and more about
Brooke Ashley.*

Examining this thought, he could see no earthly reason to justify it. He was a creator and he didn't need more than a reasonable foundation of researched facts. At this stage, he could freely create a Brooke Ashley on the pages of his novel. As far as his work was concerned, he was omnipotent, dependent only upon his typewriter and the commands he gave it.

But he had to find out more about Brooke Ashley! And the shock came when he realized it had nothing to do with the novel. Nothing at all. It was simply something he had to do. There was no choice. He had taken a step on a road leading God-knows-where, and he had to keep walking if he ever intended to regain his peace of mind. The hell of it was that there were no footsteps to follow. It was almost as if, with each step he took, the road behind him disappeared, leaving a gaping chasm. No turning back.

Without further consideration, he found himself making decisions. The first thing he had to do was get in touch with people who had known Brooke. The biography, now ashes in the fireplace, had named at least three: the psychic, the studio executive she had been going out with, and the screenwriter, Michael Richardson. Richardson was dead, so that left two possibilities. He had their names written down somewhere in his notes. He would find out if they were still alive and attempt to find them. Perhaps they would be able to give him information about the Brooke he wanted and needed to know. He caught himself at that thought and marveled at how familiar she had become, this dead actress, how real in his mind. Not Brooke Ashley anymore, but just Brooke.

Sharon had gone out on a casting call, leaving his day free and open. He decided to start immediately.

Luck—or fate—was guiding him; must have been on his side, because he opened the telephone directory at the N's and put his finger on Olga Nabakov's name. It was so simple that he sat stock-still, his finger on the page, holding his breath, until he realized what he was doing. He exhaled and breathed in deeply.

He reached for the telephone and began to dial the number, his fingers shaking. He dialed a seven instead of a nine at the fifth number of the sequence and had to start again.

This time it was correct. He sat listening to the ringing, wondering what he was going to say. He hadn't even thought about it.

"Hello?"

"Uh . . . is this Ms. Nabakov?"

"*Madame* Nabakov, yes. May I help you?" The woman's voice was soft, modulated. There was the trace of an accent, undoubtedly European.

"Uh, yes, I think so, Madame Nabakov," he faltered. It had been too easy, he told himself. It was hard to believe he was talking to someone who had known Brooke. "My name is Gregory Thomas. I'm a writer, and I'm doing a book on Brooke Ashley. I believe you knew her? I'd like to talk to you about her, if I may?"

There was a long silence, and then she said very softly, "Brooke Ashley?"

"Yes, Brooke Ashley. You did know her, didn't you?"

Her voice regained its former smoothness. "Yes, of course. I knew her very well."

"Well, could I talk to you about her?"

"Yes, of course, of course. What is it you wish to know?"

"Madame Nabakov, I actually have a lot of questions. May I come and see you—now?"

There was a pause before she answered. "Yes, Mr. Thomas, I would be delighted to help you."

She gave him the address. It was in the Hollywood Hills on Sunset Drive. He knew the area well. He arranged to be there in an hour.

He put the receiver back and saw that his hand was still unsteady. He sat without moving and then impulsively looked up the name of Brooke's old companion, William Tanner. It wasn't listed. He told himself it would have been too much to expect. So far he was doing fine, just fine.

Sunset Drive winds through the hills above the Strip, and although it is not exactly paved with gold bricks, it passes through what used to be one of the most exclusive areas in Hollywood. Errol Flynn had a home up there, and the clamor of his parties once echoed down the gullies. Frank Sinatra lived there. A dozen other famous names. Nowadays, it's not exclusive, filled with a potpourri of advertising executives, lawyers, writers, actors, musicians, and expensive hookers, not to mention the nouveau-nouveau riche, the dope dealers. But it is still very expensive. One thing was clear to Gregory: psychic Olga Nabakov had done well for herself.

Her house was cut off from the road by a wall, but the gate was open and he drove up the narrow driveway. On either side was a splattered profusion of color from shrubs and flowers that he was unable to identify, interspersed among sedate circles of green lawn. It was a large lot, dwarfing the small Spanish stucco house. No more than two bedrooms and a den, he guessed.

He pulled up in front of the door and got out of the car. Looking back at the garden, he saw that it was only the grass that gave it a framework of order. The trees and shrubs grew in wild tumbles of green, dotted with other colors in native chaos. Paradoxically, the overall feeling was one of tranquillity.

He turned back to face the house and saw a woman standing in the doorway. She was looking at him, a small smile curving her lips.

"Do you like my garden, Mr. Thomas?" She spoke softly, but he had no difficulty hearing her. The accent was more noticeable than it had been on the telephone. He liked the way European women used the language. They were aware of the spaces between words and used them as a sort of punctuation that pleased the ear.

"Yes," he replied. "I do. It's much more than it appears to be at first glance."

Her smile broadened appreciatively and she gestured with a hand. "Won't you come in?"

He allowed her to lead the way. Inside, the house was an artful blend of simplicity and complexity. Much like the garden, and much like her, he suspected. Each piece of furniture was obviously unique, yet it blended harmoniously with the object beside it. There were paintings on the walls. He recognized a Picasso and a Chagall. A Tibetan Thangka hung above the fireplace, a serene Buddha surrounded by ferocious deities. The paradox again.

He followed her through the house to a patio in the back.

"I was sitting outside. It is such a perfect day. Do you mind, Mr. Thomas?"

"Not at all," he said hastily, sitting down beside a redwood table.

"I just made tea. Would you care for a cup?"

He couldn't remember when someone had last offered him tea. It was too gracious a drink for Los Angeles. "Yes, please," he said. "Cream and sugar, if you have it."

"Only honey. Sugar is the Benedict Arnold of foods, Mr. Thomas. While it pretends to give energy, it saps the body and weakens it."

"Honey is fine," he said stupidly, feeling suddenly oafish beside the sophisticated woman standing before him.

She turned and went into the house. He tried to relax by looking at his surroundings. The patio was trellised, shaded by grapevines. The back garden was an extension of the front, except he now noticed that there were pathways subtly linking the circles of grass.

Madame Nabakov returned with the tea and placed a cup carefully on the table in front of him. Then she sat down on his right, carefully straightened her skirt, and looked at him over the top of her teacup.

She was a tall, slim woman; pale, but not in an unhealthy manner. He knew from what he had read that she must have been in her sixties, but her features were fine, and her face and neck were unlined. It would have been impossible to guess her age. Her eyes were her most interesting feature, however. He'd had some hidden bias, probably from films, that psychics had fierce, piercing eyes, but hers were soft and gentle, containing a politely inquiring expression.

The irises seemed to radiate light, but he put this down to imagination.

Madame Nabakov seemed in no hurry to talk. She merely looked at him, with the unspoken question in her eyes.

He put his cup down noisily and cleared his throat. She waited, all interest and patience.

He rubbed the back of his ear with his forefinger. "Madame Nabakov," he began, "how well did you know Brooke Ashley?"

"Very well. Better than most people," she said. She put her cup down gently and folded her hands. "Back in those days, I used to give psychic readings. She first came to me in that capacity. However, we then became friends. In fact, she was probably my closest friend at the time. She was a lovely girl, you know. *Exceptionally* lovely." Her eyes wandered placidly out to the garden and he saw the memories flicker through them like short-lived flames.

He leaned forward eagerly, putting his elbows on the table. "Tell me about her. Brooke Ashley the person, not the star."

She switched her eyes back to him, but he had the feeling she was seeing someone else.

"Brooke was very beautiful, but also very modest," she said quietly. "Her beauty never obsessed her, like so many unfortunate people I know. She never thought of herself as a star. To her, acting was just a game, a game she enjoyed, to be sure, but it was not what was important to her. She played it very well, though, and she enjoyed the fruits of her success. Perhaps if she had lived longer she would have been a great star, but I think not."

"Why?"

"Because I don't think she would have stayed with her career."

"If it wasn't important to her, what was?" Gregory asked.

Olga Nabakov took another sip of tea before answering. "She had a philosophical mind. She was more interested in the why and how of things than the what. Also, she was more interested in living life than acting it. Acting, films . . . she regarded them as frivolous things compared to the spiritual aspects of life."

"Spiritual aspects?" Gregory repeated uncomprehendingly.

"Oh, life, death, love, why life, why death, spirits, things like that." She smiled suddenly, amused at herself, it appeared. "It sounds pretentious, no? Sophomoric?"

"No, no. Not at all," Gregory assured her politely.

She laughed, a throaty chuckle. "Oh, no, Mr. Thomas. You cannot hide your feelings so easily. It is an amazing world we live in. Amazing."

She grew serious and he wondered if he had imagined the laughter the moment before. "You have heard of Saul Bellow, have you not?"

He nodded and she smiled at her own words. "Of course you have. A writer yourself!" she said, mocking her question. "At any rate, in his Nobel address, he said something important. I remember it exactly. He said, 'The sense of our real powers—powers we seem to derive from the universe itself—also comes and goes. We are reluctant to talk about this because there is nothing we can prove, because our language is inadequate, and because few people are willing to risk talking about it. They would have to say, "There is a spirit," and that is

taboo. So almost everyone keeps quiet about it,
although almost everyone is aware of it.' "

"Bellow said that?" he asked incredulously.

"Yes, and it was very perceptive and coura-
geous of him to do so, because in his circles,
the subject is indeed taboo. Well, back in the
Hollywood of the forties, it was not taboo. It
seemed that everyone was interested in matters
of the spirit. Of course, the town was filled with
charlatans and fakes. And most of the seekers
were purely dilettantes, interested only in new
experiences and cocktail-party chatter. But by
the same token, there were also seekers of
truth, and Brooke was one of these."

"You mean séances . . . that sort of thing?"
Gregory asked. Again, he felt naive before this
assured woman.

"Oh, no," she said, fluttering a hand gracefully. "Of course, she attended séances. Everyone did in those days. It was very fashionable.
But it was just her entry point. She quickly
passed through that stage. Brooke was far more
interested in life than in death." She clicked her
tongue derisively. "There are so many charlatans
in that field, anyway. She was more interested
in her own abilities and perceptions than sitting
as a spectator and listening to ghostly voices.
She was not a spectator-type person."

"She was a psychic?" Gregory asked, entranced now by this glimpse of Brooke, this
other life he had never suspected.

"Brooke, a psychic? No, Mr. Thomas. I do not
like labels. They confuse what is, rather than
clarify. I stopped calling myself a psychic thirty
years ago. No, she was a person. But she had
what could be called 'special' abilities. She could
perceive things that most other people miss

because their minds are too busy traveling in useless circles. For instance, she had a highly developed sixth sense. If the telephone rang, she often knew who it was before she answered. If something bad was about to happen, she could sometimes sense it before it happened. We all have these abilities, but she was beginning to develop hers to a useful point. Perhaps I misled you when I said she was interested in spiritual matters, but perhaps not. These are all matters of the spirit. They have nothing to do with body and flesh."

Gregory drained his tea and looked out at the garden. "I find this fascinating, this side of her," he said. In truth he found it bizarre. Sipping tea in this tranquil garden setting, listening to talk of ESP and spirit, talk that made it sound as natural as the flowers he was viewing.

"We have been conditioned to think of this side of man's nature as strange—'taboo,' as Bellow put it," she continued, and he had the inane thought that she had read his mind. "It's a curious world we live in. The longer I am here, the more obvious it becomes to me that the inmates are in charge of the asylum. We spend billions on buildings and wonderful machines and devices that are destroying the world before our eyes, and nothing on researching and developing man's abilities, the true seat of his genius. The only reason it is taboo is because science has been unable to put it in a test tube, to measure and label it. By some insane logic, they have said, 'If we can't measure it, it does not exist.' This is like saying that because we cannot see the bottom of an ocean, there is no bottom! A rough analogy, but I think you see my point."

Gregory nodded. "Yes, I understand what

you're saying, but I'm not really familiar with this sort of thing."

"Perhaps you are more familiar than you realize," she said, rising. "Would you like some more tea?"

"Just half a cup, please." He picked up his cup and handed it to her. She walked quickly into the house, her steps firm. A fascinating woman, all steel behind the soft, mild exterior. Her words had rung with conviction.

She came back with the tea and placed the cups on the table. "Actually, I have not been completely fair to science," she said, light sarcasm in her tone. "For the most part it's true, scientists are fossils, dinosaurs, but there are always the exceptions, men of vision."

Gregory nodded his head. It was interesting, but this was not the direction he wanted to take. "Tell me," he began tentatively, and then decided to jump in with both feet. "The fire in which Brooke died. How did that happen?"

For the first time, those questioning eyes retreated. A cloud touched the perfect pale features. "I don't know," she said. "Nobody does, except the people who were there. Brooke, her mother, Eleanor, and Michael Richardson, a friend. They all died in the fire. God knows how it happened. I went there as soon as I heard in the morning. I was just in time to see the firemen drag their bodies out of the rubble."

Her face had grown stiff, her voice quieter.

"I'm sorry if I've upset you, asking these questions," Gregory said. "But I must."

"I know," she said. The cloud passed and she gave him a warm smile. "My memories of Brooke are happy memories. I don't mind talking about her to you. While she lived she was a joy, and that is how I remember her."

"What was this relationship she had with Richardson?"

"She and Michael were lovers."

"I see." He was running out of questions. He rubbed behind his ear. "Tell me, she and her mother died together, right? As far as I know there were no other relatives. What happened to her estate, all her personal belongings?"

"There were relatives. Oklahoma, I think. But they wanted the estate liquidated, and that was done. Many of her belongings were bought by a friend of mine, Bill Tanner."

Gregory had been doodling with his tea leaves. He looked up sharply. "Is that William Tanner, the RKO executive? The man who was her companion for a while?"

"Yes," she said. "In his way, he loved her, too, you know. Also, he was a fan of hers in the film sense. I suppose her belongings are his way of remembering."

"And he's still alive?"

"Yes. In fact, he lives just up the hill, not far from here. We see each other now and again. He's retired. A widower. But I think he never stopped being in love with Brooke. Such foolishness."

"Foolishness?"

"Unrequited love. It's such a waste."

"Madame Nabakov," Gregory said eagerly. "I know I've imposed on you already, but could you help me with one more thing?"

"You want to see Bill Tanner?"

"Yes, I would. It's a chance to speak to someone else who knew her, in a different way. Also to see some of her personal effects. It will give me an entirely different view of her."

"When do you want to see him?"

"Well, I'm in the neighborhood . . . now?" Gregory tried not to sound too eager, but he suspected he failed.

"So, I have bored you already?" she said with amusement.

"No, of course not," he protested. "It's just that—"

She interrupted him with a motion. "I understand, Mr. Thomas. But let me ask *you* a question first. What is your interest in Brooke? It is more than a book, is it not?"

Gregory looked down at his hands. He was kneading them together like lumps of dough. What could he tell her? Would she think he was crazy? More to the point, *was* he crazy? He looked up and saw her watching him, expressionless, except for the question in her eyes. He decided that she would be the one person least likely to betray him.

"I . . . I *am* doing a book, Madame Nabakov," he began. "And the heroine *is* based on her. But it's a novel, not really about her. First, though, I saw her in a film, not too long ago. That gave me the idea for the book. Now—now, I don't know. I guess I've become infatuated with her." He tripped over the words, embarrassed, pained by them. "The book doesn't seem to be the important thing anymore." He forced a chuckle he didn't feel. "Sometimes I think I might be going out of my mind. I have this compulsion to find out more and more about Brooke. I don't know why. I don't understand it, but I *must.*"

He looked up, sure he was blushing. He felt like an ungainly, lumbering teenager facing a mature, graceful woman and blurting out his shameful secrets.

Olga Nabakov looked at him understandingly. "Thank you for telling me that, Mr. Thomas," she said, and added, "May I call you by your first name? I feel as if we are friends already. Gregory, I believe you said on the telephone."

He nodded, still glum and awkward, unable to meet the limpid eyes, afraid of what they would reveal of himself.

She reached across the table and put her long, slender fingers on his hand. "Don't worry, Gregory. When in doubt, always follow your heart. What you call a compulsion because you don't understand it may prove to have a purpose. Just continue what you are doing." She patted his hand. "Now, wait a minute and I'll call Bill."

She went inside and he sat watching sparrows peck at one another, trilling in their personal code. "Follow your heart." Such simplistic advice, and yet—perhaps his mistake had been to fight it, to resist his feelings, doubting them like an idiot with no trust in himself. Maybe . . .

Madame Nabakov returned. "Shall we go, Gregory? I'm coming with you, if you don't mind. I haven't seen Bill for a while and this will give me a chance to visit."

He thought it a fine idea. It was more likely the man would open up if there was someone he knew present. He rose and made a move toward his teacup.

"No, leave that," she ordered. "I'll take care of it when we return."

He followed her through the house. They had agreed to use his car. They were going to meet a man who was still in love with Brooke, he reminded himself. Possibly, they would have a lot in common.

William Tanner was a tall, sagging man with a birdlike habit of cocking his head to one side when he listened. He wore thick glasses, which added to the birdlike impression by magnifying his light-blue eyes and making them glassy. He must once have been a large man, but, unlike Madame Nabakov, he was not at all youthful in appearance. Age had taken its toll, robbing him of much of his flesh and leaving him bald.

He welcomed them cordially, taking Olga's hands and pressing them in his, and showed them to the living room with short, uncertain steps. They both sat on the couch, declining his offer of something to drink. He stood, lost for a moment, then sat down in an armchair opposite them, carefully picking at the creases of his pants over his knees.

"I understand you are writing a book about Brooke?" he asked Gregory uncertainly.

"Yes, I am. I thought you might be able to tell me something of her. Her personality."

Tanner nodded thoughtfully. "She was a wonderful girl," he said. "A wonderful girl. Wonderful." He seemed to wander off in a dream.

"Were you a good friend of hers?" Gregory asked, hoping to pull him back.

Tanner gathered himself. "Yes," he said, his voice firmer. "We knew each other for a number of years. I thought, once, that we would marry, but it never worked out. You know what I mean?" He squinted hopefully at Gregory, then continued without waiting for an answer. "After she died, I met Mary and married her. She died two years ago. She died, too."

He quavered at the edge of a pool of self-pity, then took a mental step back. "But it's not me you want to hear about, it's Brooke," he said. "Well, she was one of the most *alive* people I've ever known. I don't know how familiar you are with the film business, but it hasn't changed much from my day, as far as I can see. Still laden with posturing, empty-headed opportunists. She was never like that. She was always herself and always a lady. She had a simple kind of dignity that some people couldn't even see—until they crossed her, and then, wham! She had a way of putting them in their place. She was always a lady, though."

When referring to Brooke, he seemed to imbue the pronoun with a religious reverence. It was clear that he had worshiped her, and still did. Gregory thought, while he listened, that this may have been the reason Tanner never won her. How do you make love to a goddess?

Tanner chuckled at some thought and hit his bony knee with a hand. "I remember one time. One time we were out at dinner, and this actor came to the table. I won't mention his name, but he was a big name, an important man. Starred with her in her second film. Tried to make a pass at her, but she rebuffed him. Hurt his ego. Anyway, he came to our table, drunk as a coot, could hardly stand, and began to insult her. He would lean on the table with one hand, then straighten up and shuffle his feet. It was kind of, you know, an . . . an . . . automatic gesture. I started to get up to deal with him, but she put her hand on my arm without taking her eyes off him, keeping her face calm, and her manner gracious.

"It was at the point where he was asking her

if she was still a virgin. She looked down at
the table and said in a perfectly even voice that
reached the farthest corner of the room—after
all, she was an actress—'Excuse me, but I believe your hand is in my soup.' Damned if it
wasn't. He was too drunk to notice. All the time
she had been looking at him, she had been
inching the soup bowl into position. And the last
time he lifted his hand, she slipped the bowl
over, right where she knew he would put his
hand down. You should have seen his face!"

Gregory and Olga laughed. Tanner slapped his
knee again, his laugh turning into a volley of
coughs.

"But she was also kind and gentle," Tanner
said, when he could continue. "Not like some
of the others. She never got a swelled head when
she began to be a success. She was nice to everybody; it didn't matter who they were or what
they did. A nice girl. And very loyal to her
friends, very loyal. . . ."

His voice drifted away and he looked down
at the carpet. He wore shiny black shoes and
he scuffed the toe of his right foot into the pile.

"I believe you have some of her belongings,"
Gregory said.

"Yes, yes, I do," Tanner said, looking up.
"Would you like to see them?"

"Yes, very much," Gregory said.

Tanner got to his feet. "Well, come on, young
feller. They're in this room over here."

They went down a dark hall, past three or
four rooms that looked as if they weren't used.
It was a big, lushly furnished house. Too big
and lush for a lonely old man who had nothing
but memories to keep him company.

"In here," he said, gesturing. They walked

into the room, which was furnished like a bed-room.

"That's hers," he said, pointing to an ornately carved oak four-poster bed.

"That's hers." He pointed to a tall mirrored dresser, teak, by the look of it, a fine dark wood.

He opened a drawer. "This is some of her jewelry. She loved turquoise, you know. It's all turquoise. I suppose I should keep it in a safe, but I never get 'round to it."

Gregory looked around the room at the objects that had once been Brooke's: the heavy quilted bedspread, the high-backed rocker, the jewelry glowing with life in the drawer. He felt a little dizzy. He touched his forehead. He was per-spiring.

"You really should put this in a safe," he heard Olga tell Tanner. "Some of it is quite valuable." Her voice seemed to travel across galaxies before it reached him. There was a sort of static in his ears. It was warm in the room. *Oh, God, what's happening to me this time?*

"This was one of her favorite pieces. She al-ways wore it." He realized Olga was talking to him. He turned and tried to focus on her. A silver chain dangled from her hand. It held a heart-shaped silver locket with a circular tur-quoise stone set in the center.

She put the locket in her open palm and held it out to him.

"It's very beautiful," he managed to say hoarsely. He hardly recognized his own voice.

Olga kept holding her hand out. Obviously, she wanted him to take it, to look at it more closely. He put out his hand, palm up.

Olga tipped her hand and the locket fell down

into his palm. It seemed like slow motion to him. He watched the locket glint with light and movement as it tumbled onto his hand.

For a moment, he was too stunned to move. Then he shouted, "Jesus Christ!" The locket was burning into his palm. It was as hot as molten lead, searing his flesh.

He flicked his hand quickly, throwing it to the floor, shaking his hand in agony, exclaiming in pain.

Tanner acted as if his guests cursed all the time. He didn't even raise his head. He was scrambling through the drawers of another dresser, looking for something.

Olga looked at Gregory calmly, her eyes giving nothing away. Even the question was absent.

"It burnt me!" he exclaimed, rubbing the palm with the heel of his other hand.

Olga reached forward and took his hand in hers. She turned the palm up. Her hand was as cool as ice.

In the center of his palm was a red, heart-shaped mark. It had already begun to blister.

Olga dropped his hand without saying anything. She bent down to pick up the locket. She cupped her hand around it and regarded it thoughtfully.

When she finally spoke, he had to lean forward to catch the words.

"How strange," she said. And he wasn't sure if she was speaking to him or not. "This locket was found in Michael Richardson's right hand after he died in the fire. It has a trick catch; it took me hours to figure out how to open it. I imagine you could open it instantly—but I'd better not put you to the test."

Chapter Seven

GREGORY SAT IN THE PATIO, viewing the splendid garden, running his hand aimlessly along the grain of the rough redwood table.

A sparrow alighted on the ground a few feet away. He looked avidly at the bird, as if trying to impress the memory of each bedraggled feather on his mind, to see the thoughts behind the glassy black eyes. He felt grateful to the bird. It was alive, real, substantial, even if diminutive in proportion. It followed the natural laws of the world. If he made a threatening gesture, it would fly away. It knew its place and it knew man's place in the order of things. Such predictability was something to be grateful for. He waved his arm to test the accuracy of his conclusions. The bird cocked its head, then fluttered away.

Gregory hardly knew how he had arrived here, back at Madame Nabakov's house. He remembered thanking Tanner for his time. Olga had taken charge. She had hustled him out in a casual way that had seemed perfectly normal.

He had driven back to her house in a daze, and when she had invited him in again, he had unthinkingly accepted.

He dared not dwell on what had happened. Which was why, when the bird left, he focused on a finely veined grape leaf, admiring its transparency in the light. His head had begun to ache. His eyes felt as if they were straining at the sockets. *I mustn't try to think about it.* Inside, the tension was building to the breaking point. Any little thing could happen now, and he would erupt, burst into a thin, high-pitched scream, try to tear the world apart with his bare hands, struggle off in the arms of men in white-cotton coats. It was too much to expect him to take any more of this sort of thing. *Why are you doing this to me?* he asked. He didn't know whom he was addressing. God? The devil?

"Here you are." The voice was pleasant, controlled. A tall glass of white wine appeared on the table in front of him. Had he asked for wine? It didn't matter. He liked the way it sparkled, the rising bubbles seeking their freedom on the surface.

Madame Nabakov stood beside him. "Drink," she commanded. He lifted the glass to his lips. The hand seemed to belong to someone else. But the cold liquid soothed his throat. Perhaps he would be able to talk now.

He turned to thank Olga, but she had gone silently back into the house. He gulped another mouthful of wine. He was glad she approved of alcohol. Alcohol had its purposes. Generally, it had just been the victim of a lot of bad PR. It was actually a fine substance. A lifesaving liquid. It was saving his life right now.

And just then, despite all his efforts, that life

of his fell apart at the seams. His world, the universe he had constructed so carefully for twenty-nine years, erupted, tilted crazily, teetered on the edge of the chasm, and fell, shattering into an infinite number of fragments.

It was Olga Nabakov's voice that did it. Olga, standing behind him, calm and sedate, except for her voice. Olga's voice that lashed out at him, whipped him, splintered his world.

"Michael!" she cried, and the voice permeated to the core of his being.

He turned, as if answering to his own name.

She stood as immobile as a statue, except for her eyes. Those light-filled eyes, they swallowed him.

Then he knew.

And knew she knew.

And felt his stomach tighten. His insides tied themselves in knots, his chest contracted. The lump of knowledge forced itself up from the stomach, past the chest, through the throat, and out as a gigantic feeling of pain and relief.

He put his head on his arms and wept. Olga touched the back of his head. And still he wept. She stroked his hair while his eyes bled tears. He did not want to stop. He wanted to cry until all the liquid had left his body. He wanted to cry all the tears he had for Brooke—and for himself. The Brooke he had lost, the himself he had lost. The pair of star-crossed lovers they had been. The dreams that had died in the flames.

"I'm sorry I had to do that," Olga Nabakov said. She sat at the table opposite him, looking concerned. "I saw you teetering on the edge. I've seen it before. It was too dangerous. You could have gone either way if I had left you alone, but I could not take the risk. I had to do something."

"Thank you," Gregory said. He felt purged now; emptied, lightheaded, relieved. All of those things and more. "How did you know?" he asked.

"I recognized you. Not at the beginning, but very soon after that."

"How could you have? I don't look the same, do I?"

"No, you don't. I'm not sure how to explain it, but each person has an *aura*, something that he projects that is uniquely himself. It's a quality of being, I suppose, the person himself, not his body, not his social personality. It's very recognizable if you look past all the other things. Then I became more sure when I saw that you still had the same physical mannerisms. For instance, when Michael was troubled, or thinking very hard, he had a habit of rubbing behind his right ear with his forefinger. When I saw you doing that, I was positive."

"Why didn't you say anything then?" he asked plaintively, as if it would have saved him all the pain.

She smiled. "Would you have believed me?"

Gregory looked at her and his mouth formed a tentative smile. It became a wide grin. And then he laughed, and laughed. It was wild and uncontrollable. Like the tears he had shed before, it was a form of release over which he had no control.

He began to get a stitch in his side, which somehow struck him as even funnier, and he had to wrap his arms around himself and bend over.

Finally it subsided; slowly, to spasmodic chuckles, and then to a foolish smile.

"I'm no psychic—no Madame Nabakov," he said after a while. "My so-called rational mind wouldn't let me even consider it. And I'm still not sure. I mean, past lives! Jesus! It's too absurd to even consider!"

Olga Nabakov cupped her glass in her hands and looked down at it. He had a sudden vision of her when she was younger. She was more serious then, but he thought he had liked her. *Brooke's friend.* She had always been "Brooke's friend" to him.

She smiled ruefully at the glass. "It is ironic that what we call the rational mind is so irrational." She looked up at him. "You will find that it is going to be your greatest enemy in the coming days."

"What do you mean?" He was alarmed. There had been no time as yet even to consider the future. He remembered his earlier thoughts, his conclusion that his life had changed. They seemed trivial in view of what had now happened.

"Your so-called rational mind will try to destroy you," Madame Nabakov said. She raised a mocking eyebrow. "Oh, I don't mean it to sound as melodramatic as all that. What I mean is that it will cause you to doubt yourself. It will tell you that this has been your imagination at work, that none of this is real. It will suggest that you are insane. Perhaps it will suggest that you seek what is foolishly called 'professional guidance.' You must not listen to it. You must believe what you see."

"Believe what I see?"

"I think your memory will return to you. The

memory of your last life—if it hasn't begun already. It may happen in stages, or it may happen whenever you put your full attention upon it. When it does happen, do not try to analyze it too closely, just accept it as true, as you would accept your memories of yesterday. Have faith in yourself."

Faith in himself? He could see why Olga Nabakov considered it important. Yes, at this particular moment, it was easy to have faith in himself. But how about the future? Right now, he remembered being Michael Richardson, what it had been like to be that person. In fact, as he sat there, the memories flooded in, almost too fast to assimilate. But would they fade later? And if they didn't, what would happen if he told his friends of all this? Would they laugh at him, be afraid of him, pity him? Would he have faith in himself then?

Gregory stood up and turned to Madame Nabakov. "I must go. I think I need to be alone for a while. It's all too new for me to absorb."

Olga nodded in agreement. "Come back tomorrow, Gregory. By then you will probably have a lot of questions. Perhaps I will be able to answer some of them, or suggest people who can."

There was a moment when he thought he saw pity in her eyes, and it disturbed him.

Her last words came just before he drove away. She leaned on the car window and said, "By the way, I would suggest you do not talk of this to anyone for a while. Their reactions may shock you. Live with it by yourself until you feel comfortable with it."

He drove to the ocean. Like a lemming, he

thought. When he was a child he had always gone to the beach when he needed solitude. It had seemed the logical thing to do then. Nowadays, and especially on California beaches, you had to step between the bodies and mark off your little patch of privacy with hostile glares. You could swim out beyond the surfers, of course, but then the lifeguards bellowed for you to return. In the city of Los Angeles, a man's most private place was the interior of his car. Modern-day man's car was his only castle.

Years before the influx, Los Angeles must have been a beautiful city. Must have been? He remembered. Even in the forties, when the first buds of growth had begun to blossom and attract the fast-buck entrepreneurs like bees to pollen, it had been beautiful. Large expanses of wild green land where there were now cities. Farmland where there were now freeways. It *had* been the promised land then, a land of milk and honey and sensual sunshine. The mistake had been to announce it to a world that was always looking for a haven, for the world had literally beaten a path to this golden city. It had beaten down the green grass, beaten down the trees, crowded the open spaces, polluted the clean air, and threatened the safe streets.

Gregory drove down the hill from Pacific Palisades, wondering why his thoughts were so somber. After all, whether for better or worse, something truly remarkable had just happened to him. He considered this as the breeze touched his face, blowing inland. He could smell its burden of salt. There was no smog over the ocean; it sparkled in the brilliant afternoon sunshine. He turned right on the Pacific Coast Highway. There was a quiet stretch of beach below the Getty Museum.

Gregory parked, left his shoes and socks in the car, and rolled up the legs of his jeans. The sand felt good on his bare feet. The horizon, unbroken except for some distant sails, suggested the infinity of the universe. There were only a few dozen people on the beach. A few young families, some joggers, residents of the area walking their dogs.

He walked down toward the sea. The harder damp sand near the water's edge exhilarated him and he broke into a trot, enjoying the sound of his breath, the effort of his body, the wind on his face. A wave came in and splashed water on his pants. He zigzagged away, slowed to a walk, and turned up into the softer sand. He sat down panting with his back against a rock, and faced the ocean.

Michael Richardson. Gregory remembered the small biography he had read at the Institute. ". . . born June 9, 1918, San Francisco, California . . ." He had been born in Oakland, not San Francisco. He was sure of it. There was a house. Victorian. White, he thought. With . . . with extravagant ornamentation protruding from every angle. The trim had been done in . . . blue. Right, blue. He closed his eyes to envision it better.

The backyard. What was it? Yes, lawn, then farther back, a vegetable patch to the left, a huge tree on the right. Oak, perhaps. He had climbed it as a child. Fell off once and broke an arm. The treehouse! Yes, he had built a treehouse with scrap lumber he had cadged off his father.

He opened his eyes. The ocean was still serene,

for all its ceaseless assault on the sands. A dog ran past, followed by a pretty girl in shorts and a halter top. She smiled as she walked past, a flash of white teeth against brown skin.

He closed his eyes again. His father. Tools. Worked with his hands. A builder? No. A carpenter! He had been a carpenter. Jason was his name. A big, bluff, hearty man with arms as thick and strong as the branches of an oak.

The workings of his mind amazed Gregory. How, after focusing on a detail, something specific, the other memories would roll by like the surf he could hear in the background. All he had to do was have faith in his ability to recall, not argue with the pictures his mind presented to him.

His father, Jason Richardson. He had prospered in business. People liked him and referred him to their friends. Yet he had never moved from the old Victorian house. Instead, he repaired it and kept it painted and clean. "It's our home," he used to say with irrefutable practicality. "There's nothing wrong with this house. No reason to move."

His mother had never argued with Jason. Her name was Miriam. A small, gentle woman who was happiest in the garden with dirt in her fingernails and mud sticking to her knees. But she never shirked her duties. She ran the house firmly, like a military installation. Breakfast at seven. Dinner at six. She never deviated. She was much younger than her husband, still almost a child when Michael had been born. But she loved her husband fiercely in her own quiet way.

Gregory remembered that they had both still been alive when he had died. The fire had been in 1949, so he had been about thirty-one when he had died. How had his parents taken it? He had been their only child, and they had maintained a close relationship, even after he had come to Hollywood and grown successful and affluent by the standards of the day. They had been proud of his achievements.

There was a scream down the beach to his left, and he opened his eyes again. It was a young girl, four or five, he guessed. The child's mother had her by one arm and was spanking her vigorously. What had the child done to offend her mother so grievously? The woman's face was livid. He couldn't hear what she was shouting over the screams of the child. They were both out of control.

The shadows had lengthened on the sand and a few people were straggling up the embankment to their parked cars.

It was strange, he thought, how his lives had repeated themselves. For how many lifetimes had he been a writer? Was it the same for everybody? Even the child crying on the beach?

What of all the other people he had known, loved, hated, been indifferent to? Where were they now?

And what of Brooke?

It was a thought he had avoided. The possibility that she too was somewhere in the world of today, with a new body, a new name, perhaps in this very city, perhaps walking along this beach right now, unrecognizable to him, unknown—it was a thought that tore him apart. Why had he, out of billions of people, fallen into a strange pattern that allowed him to remember his past life? Was it that the powers that be, whoever or whatever they were, had determined that his past life had been cut unfairly short and that he deserved another chance? Would he then be predestined to find Brooke again?

One thing was certain. Olga Nabakov had been correct when she predicted that he would have many, many questions. His mind swam with them. But would there be any answers?

His thoughts were interrupted by a *thunk!* in the sand beside him, followed by a sharp bark and the hurtling body of a dog. Triumphant at the retrieval of its ball, the dog sprayed him with sand and water.

"Red! Red! Come here!" The girl came running up. He had seen her walk by earlier with the animal.

She knelt beside him and brushed sand from Gregory's back. "I'm sorry," she apologized. "Red gets a little carried away sometimes and I never learned to throw a ball in a straight line."

"That's all right. I always expect to get sand thrown on me by a bully at least once when I'm at the beach. I didn't think the bully would be a dog, though."

He looked at her face. It was pretty. Broad forehead, a light spray of freckles around her nose, a wide mouth, and a definitive chin—all in all, a pleasing collection. She looked familiar. He frowned at her.

"Do I know you?"

"My name's Jenny Royal," she said. "You're Gregory Thomas, aren't you?"

He remembered. She was an actress he'd met at a director's party a few months before. She'd been wearing a long dress then. And her dark hair had been blond.

"You've changed your hair," he said.

She looked pleased at his memory, and her hand drifted up to touch her hair in a uniquely feminine gesture.

"That was just for a part," she said. "I don't normally bleach it."

"Do you live down at the beach?"

"Just over there," she said, pointing in the general direction of a group of houses. She added uncertainly, "Would you like to come up for a drink?"

"Love to," he said, without hesitation. He got to his feet and brushed himself.

She had long slim legs and matched his stride as they walked along the edge of the waves. The dog ran ahead, dashing in and out of the water and barking playfully. Gregory asked about her work.

"I'm doing quite a lot right now," she said, with just the right touch of modesty in her voice. "I'm starting an Altman movie in about a week. How about you?"

He told her vaguely that he was working on something, and then she pointed at some wooden steps. "Up here," she said.

He followed her up the stairs, admiring her lithe figure. They went into a small two-bedroom house. It was sparsely furnished, but bright and comfortable. She seemed to suit the house. A direct, no-nonsense girl, a rarity in his circle. He asked for white wine and she brought him a glass of cold Chablis. Then she sat beside him on the couch.

"You were looking very thoughtful on the beach," she said.

"Just stunned by the sun," he replied, trying to laugh it off. Then he had an impulse to talk.

"Do you know anything about reincarnation?"

She blinked at the question. He noticed that she had long, naturally curly eyelashes. "Not much. Why?" she asked.

"I'm doing a story that involves it," he said. "But I'm just in the research stage right now."

"I've seen some articles and talked to people who are into it," she said. "But I've never studied it."

"Do you believe it's possible?"

She smiled and shifted on the couch. "I don't know. A lot of wilder things have been proven true. I just take each day as it comes. I can't be bothered thinking about what happens after I'm dead. It's hard enough trying to get through the week without worrying about the next thousand years or so."

"Don't you find it hopeful, though," he persisted, "the thought that we all get another chance?"

She thought about it and grimaced sourly. "I suppose that's one way of looking at it. But you could also say that we have to live with our mistakes. And live with them, and live with them. Nothing hopeful about that. If that were true, death wouldn't be the escape that we all hope for, would it? What's the point? We just have to keep coming back and coming back? Till what? It's sort of a depressing thought."

"Well, there might be some plan to it that we don't know about," Gregory said thoughtfully, more to himself than her. It sounded inane, put that way, but he wondered if there might not be some truth to it.

"What a drag! That would make us puppets," she said derisively.

That wasn't necessarily so, Gregory thought

to himself, but he felt the subject was getting out of hand. They talked about other things for a few minutes, and then he looked at his watch.

"I must go," he said, rising. "Thanks for the drink."

"Why don't you stay a while? I'll cook us something, if you like," she said with a direct look.

The invitation was unmistakable. He looked at her wide mouth, parted now in a slow smile, and considered it, tempted to escape for a few hours into a stranger's warmth. He felt himself respond to her physical presence. But then he thought of Sharon, waiting at home. And Brooke. What of Brooke now? And what would that do to his relationship with Sharon?

"I have an appointment in town," he lied pleasantly. "Let me take a rain check."

Disappointment crossed her face, but she quickly recovered. "Any time," she said, still smiling. "I'm listed in the book under J. Royal. No address."

He walked back slowly along the beach. The sun had dropped over the edge of the sea and there was a chill in the air. A gray-haired man walked past him in the opposite direction, pulled on a leash by a Great Dane.

Gregory realized he had hardly thought of Sharon at all during the day. It sobered him. What should he tell her? How much? Should he tell her at all? He didn't know. Then he remembered Madame Nabakov's parting words— "Do not talk of this to anyone for a while." It was good advice.

He picked up a stone and flicked it out at the waves. It skipped twice and disappeared below the swirling water. His life *had* changed.

The realization hit him again. It was no small change, like getting a new job or buying a new house. It had changed sweepingly, drastically, and there was no way to change it back. That damn road again! He had now taken another irrevocable step along it.

Chapter Eight

GREGORY WAS UNAWARE of the dampness seeping into his trousers as he sat on the sand. The air had become chilly, but he was impervious to the change. The sun had long gone, replaced by a moon that somehow deepened the whiteness of the foaming ribs of water rolling into shore.

If anybody had stopped and asked him what he was doing, he would have replied, "Remembering."

It had been a fairy-tale romance from the first moment. All the elements were there: the instant recognition, the immediate affinity, the feeling of finally finding her.

He had intended to go home after leaving Jenny Royal's house, but instead he had sat in the twilight, embraced by memories. It had all come back to him with remarkable clarity. The first time they had met . . .

It was 1948 and the film industry was in a slump. America's changing postwar lifestyle and

the bogeyman in the box combined to under-
mine the old habits of entertainment. Columbia
Pictures, after showing an all-time profit in 1947,
made only half a million dollars in 1948. Louis
B. Mayer wasn't as lucky. In 1948, his studio
dived more than six million below the red line.
Altogether, film profits plummeted from ninety
million to fifty-five million between 1946 and
1948. There were hard realities to be faced.

But Michael Richardson didn't care. The in-
competent would be the first to suffer, and he'd
cry no tears for them. Next would be the new-
comers and the novices, and although he regretted that part of it, he didn't see how it could
affect him. He was one of the most successful
screenwriters in the business. In the past ten
years he had worked for almost every major
studio in Hollywood, acquiring both a reputation
and a considerable amount of money. He figured
that the worst that could happen to him would
be a decrease in assignments. And that he could
afford.

Tonight was going to be special. He buttoned
his jacket and patted his hair. Then he slipped
into a cream-colored topcoat. A quick look in
the mirror and—perfect, he thought. He was a
tall, wide-shouldered man with a face that had
seen the floors of a few rough bars, but he was
handsome in a rugged way that women found
alluring. With a final quick motion he straightened the collar of his coat, thinking it was lucky
he looked as he did, because the way he was
attracted to women, he needed to be attractive
to them.

The party was at the home of Dolly Crocket,
a Beverly Hills socialite with whom Richardson
had had a minor fling a couple of years before.

As with all his affairs, they had parted on good terms and often saw each other socially.

He drove down the Strip in his black Mercury convertible, with the white top down, enjoying the lights and the warm breeze. Some kids in a stripped-down Ford zipped past, leaving a trail of whoops. He slowed down to watch an elegant young woman make a tantalizing long-legged exit from a Cadillac. When the show was over, he sped up and followed the curve of Sunset into Beverly Hills. After a mile, he turned off into the broad, dark avenues.

Dolly's house was ablaze with lights. The huge, curved driveway was littered with Cadillacs and Lincoln Continentals. He parked among them and walked briskly up the steps past the towering decorative pillars.

Richardson allowed the butler to take his coat and deftly captured a drink from a fast-moving tray carried by a liveried waiter. Dolly charged over, a pink gown setting off a bundle of dark hair, arms wide in welcome, a hostess smile plastered to her face.

"Darling! I'm so glad you could come. The party would have been *devastated* without you." She took his arm and tiptoed to kiss his cheek, clouding him in perfume. "There are so many interesting people here. Just *everyone* has come. I'm sure you'll have a *wonderful* time."

He looked around the room while she prattled on. She was right. Almost everyone was there. He looked at the women first, of course. Rita Hayworth, divorced the year before from Orson Welles, was enjoying her freedom, surrounded by a circle of admiring men. Deborah Kerr looked gracious, as always. On the other side of the room he saw Lucy Ball, Greer Garson, a flash of Loretta Young disappearing into another room. The press corps was represented by arch-rivals Hedda Hopper and Louella Parsons. They were not talking—at least, not to each other, only *about* each other. David Niven, Broderick Crawford, Bill Holden, and a few other head-liners drifted through the crowd. He saw that L. B. Mayer was there with Lorena Danker. The word was that they would soon marry, or not marry, depending upon whom you read and listened to.

The band in the ballroom next door stopped drinking and picked up their instruments. They started a rhumba, but they hadn't yet warmed up and it sounded halfhearted. A few couples drifted through the large open doors and began to dance.

Richardson chatted with English actor Brian Murphy and screenwriter John Sherman. Murphy, an impeccably tailored and well-spoken English-man of seemingly mild disposition, was best known for his unique method of handling a studio mogul the year before, an ogre of an executive who had refused to release him from his contract. During a high-powered business meeting, Murphy had crashed his way into the man's office, stood up on his desk, pulled out his penis, and pissed on the paper-covered oak antique. He was released from his contract and barred from the studio for life.

Sherman, a small, intense man who chopped his hands nervously about when he spoke, was telling the latest Harry Cohn story when the actress Virginia Upman joined the circle and raised her eyebrows. "I hope you men aren't telling dirty stories," she said.

"Just the latest Harry Cohn one," Michael told her.

"Then you *are* telling dirty stories," she said, turning up her pretty nose. She took Michael by the arm and pulled him aside. "I must steal Michael for just a teenie-weenie minute," she told the others over her shoulder.

"I dunno how that bastard does it," Sherman complained when they were out of earshot.

Virginia took Richardson to a corner and pouted up at him delightfully. "Michael, you haven't called me," she reprimanded.

He tried establishing innocence: "I heard your husband was in town, Ginny."

"That creep!" Her face momentarily lost its benign expression. "We're in the middle of divorce proceedings."

Michael ran a finger down her bare arm. "I was just thinking of you, Ginny. If he's having you tailed by private dicks, it wouldn't do your settlement any good to be seen with me, now would it?"

Her eyes narrowed maliciously while she inspected his logic. Then she brightened up. "Oh, how clever of you. I would never have thought of that. You're probably quite right. Silly me." She threw her head back artfully, exposing an abundant area of uncovered bosom, and placed one hand lightly on his chest. "He's leaving in about a week and the divorce should come through by then. Call me?" She pinched his breast delicately with forefinger and thumb.

"Of course."

She walked away after kissing him on the cheek. He felt irritable suddenly and captured a fresh drink. Perhaps it all went with turning thirty. He walked back to the others, scowling at his thoughts.

"What-ho, old chap," Murphy said cheerfully. "Toppled off your white horse?"

Richardson grinned back at him, but he didn't feel at all cheerful.

And then he looked up.

She was standing on the stairs, one hand on the banister, looking down at the party. Knowing the women he did, he was an expert on posed entrances, and he could have sworn that this was not one of them. She seemed totally unself-conscious. And, oh, so beautiful! He'd never seen anything so perfect in his life.

She wore a white gown that deepened the golden glow of her skin. Long blond hair fell to her shoulders. Deep red lipstick emphasized her mouth. The specifics were blurred by distance, but the overall effect was stunning.

His upturned face must have attracted her attention, because she looked in his direction. Murphy, who was recounting one of the more notorious Errol Flynn exploits, lost half his audience. Richardson left his two friends and began to walk toward the stairs.

"Oh-oh," Murphy said softly. "I think he's been smitten."

They looked up at the girl. "That's Brooke Ashley," Sherman said. "A doll, isn't she?"

Richardson walked through the crowd, oblivious to its presence, his eyes never leaving her face. A woman plucked at his arm as he passed. "Darling!" But he ignored it.

He stopped at the bottom of the stairs, resting a hand on the rail, and looked at her. She was about ten yards away and now he could see that she had a full mouth, an obstinate chin, a slim waist, long legs. But even then the details meant nothing. It was the entirety of her that held him there. She had watched his approach and she stood looking calmly down at him, her mouth unsmiling.

He walked slowly up the stairs, and stopped at the step below her.

"I'm Michael Richardson," he said.

She inclined her head to one side in gracious acceptance. "Brooke Ashley." Her voice was low, contained. She had deep blue eyes and he felt they were seeing everything there was to see about him.

Then she smiled, and it was like plunging into a calm, refreshing sea. He smiled back at her. They stood, transfixed in the moment.

Finally he held out his hand. She placed hers in it. "Dance?" he said, and his voice sounded as coarse as raw leather to his ears.

Mercifully, nobody stopped them as they walked through the room. He led her to the dance floor and took her in his arms. Normally he prided himself on his dancing ability, but tonight, holding this exquisite creature, he felt clumsy, as awkward as a teenager. Her arm was light, but it burned on his shoulder. Her hair smelled as fresh and untainted as newly mown grass.

They danced silently. He didn't know what to say to her. Intuitively, he knew that all his usual ploys and sophisticated ice-breaking witticisms would be inadequate. He cringed as he thought of the sort of dialogue he normally used when he met a new girl.

She was wearing a faint, subtle perfume. He lifted his hand and touched the skin on her back. It was smoother than silk.

He couldn't stand it any longer. "I think I love you," he blurted.

She stopped dancing and looked up at him, her mouth slightly parted, her look penetrating him.

"Do you say that often?" she asked.

"I've never said it." His palms felt clammy, his collar too tight. But it was the truth, and he knew that he could never speak anything except the truth to this woman.

"That's good," she said, resting her head on his shoulder and moving again.

The music stopped and they stood looking at each other, both waiting for the roof to fall in, the heavens to fall, a shooting star to cross the room and illuminate the feelings they couldn't express.

"Can we leave?" he said. "I don't want to lose you."

She didn't hesitate. "Yes." She looked around the room. "But first I have to tell the man I came with."

"Will he understand?"

"Yes."

He took her back to the other room and stood near the door while she went over to a group of men. She put an arm on the shoulder of one and spoke into his ear. It was Bill Tanner, a man he had met once or twice. She turned and pointed in his direction. He felt like a bear standing there as the other man's surprised eyes raked over him.

She walked back unperturbed and collected her coat from the butler.

"What did you tell him?" he asked as they stood on the terrace. He helped her on with her coat.

She smiled at him. "I told him I've just fallen in love with you," she said.

He bent his head and kissed her. He expected rockets and clashing cymbals, but all he felt were lips as soft as petals and an aching tenderness that made him want to crush her to him.

He opened the car door for her and went back to the driver's side. He started the engine. "How about . . ."

"The beach," she finished for him. It was what he had intended to say.

They talked as he drove. He had lost his earlier feeling of discomfort. Miraculously, he had also lost the tough, flippant exterior he usually used to deal with people. It was an easy, flowing conversation, like talking to an old friend. He told her things he'd never told anyone. She asked about his work.

"I can't say the traditional thing . . . that I feel like a whore," he said. "I like what I'm doing, for the most part, and I get well paid for it. It's creative within certain limitations, and if you're willing to work within those limitations, it can be great—most of the time. Of course, I've had to fight every studio I've ever worked for, but that's part of the game. But what I'm trying to say is that there are other things I'd like to do. There's this novel I started. The problem is I never seem to get the time to finish it."

"Tell me about it," she said.

He told her, and when he'd finished, he told her of his ideas for two more. "I've got about a dozen of them running through my head. All I really need, I guess, is to do them."

"I think they're all wonderful stories," she said enthusiastically. "You *must* do them. In fact, *we* must do them—if you'll let me help you."

"How?"

She held up a dainty fist. "I'll punch you when you need punching, and I'll push you when you need pushing. You could have been working instead of going to this party tonight."

"But then I wouldn't have met you," he protested.

"Yes. But now you have."

He thought about it for a moment. "That means we'd have to spend a lot of time together if you're going to be my slave-driver, doesn't it?"

She smiled happily and touched his cheek.

It was too much to expect there to be a full moon, but there it was, shimmering over the ocean and casting a supernatural glow on the sand. To Michael, the whole night seemed supernatural. He told her so. She had taken off her shoes and he had done the same. They walked, hand in hand, down to the water.

"It's magic," he said.

"Well, don't you believe in magic?" she asked.

"Now I do."

"I do too. Perhaps we create our own magic, though. Maybe we created this moment a long time ago and it's only now being fulfilled."

He asked about her career. "I've heard your name once or twice, but I've never seen anything you've done."

She linked her arm in his. Her head came up just past his chin. "I've had a lot of small parts, and recently I got two starring roles. It looks as if I'll be doing another lead soon. I'm being what they call 'groomed for stardom.'"

"You don't sound happy about that. Plenty of girls would give anything for a break like that."

"I like my work," she said quietly, "but it's not the most important thing in my life. It's funny. I've been working for years, preparing for that break. Now that it's almost here, I'm finding that it doesn't mean that much to me. I've always had this strange feeling that acting has just been a way to pass the time while I waited."

He stopped and they both looked out at the waves. The surf was only about two feet high and the waves rolled in lazily. "Waited for what?" he asked.

She turned and looked up at him, her face painted with ivory moonlight. "I think I might have been waiting for you."

After he had taken her back to her apartment on Fountain, just below the Strip, and arranged to meet her for dinner the following night, he went directly home. He parked the car, but instead of going inside, he walked aimlessly for a while, scuffling his feet through the lavender jacaranda flowers that carpeted the sidewalks.

He had never felt so elated in his life. He felt as confused as a schoolboy. In a sense, it was almost too much, the strangeness and the intensity of his feelings. This was a brand new emotion for Mister Love-'em-and-leave-'em. It was as if all his emotions had been on hold, as if he had just awakened after thirty years of sleep.

The streetlights seemed brighter, outlines crisper, the night smells headier. He thought about what she had said about waiting for him. Surely that was all he had been doing too: waiting for her.

Gregory's long reverie was broken by the hushed voices of a couple as they strolled by a few feet away from him. They didn't see him there, sitting on the sand; they were too intent on each other. The man was in his forties, tall and thin, with thick red hair. The woman was shorter, slender. Their laughter drifted back to him.

Tears pricked at his eyes. That could have been him with Brooke all those years ago. They could have had a long, happy life together. Their children would have been adults by now. If only . . .

He tried to remember the fire. His mind remained blank. What had happened? A warm sensation started at the base of his spine and rose slowly up his back. He tried to picture it in his mind. The flames, the panic? Nothing. He just grew hotter. He touched his forehead. He was sweating. He suddenly became unreasonably fearful and stood up quickly. He had to get home. Sharon would be worried. These were things he shouldn't be thinking about. It was too dangerous, no matter what Madame Nabakov had said.

Chapter Nine

"GENIUS IS EXPERIENCE. *Some seem to think that it is a gift or talent, but it is the fruit of long experience in many lives. Some are older souls than others, and so they know more. . . .*"

The quotation didn't come from the revered writings of some Hindu holy man or Himalayan sage; the words were Henry Ford's, and they were reported in an interview published in the *San Francisco Examiner* in 1928. Gregory was astounded to discover that Ford was but one of many notable public figures who believed in reincarnation.

Gregory was in the Hollywood Public Library on Ivar Street. He glanced at the man beside him, a bearded old derelict in ragged clothes, his hands and face black from dirt and sun. The man had a book open on the desk before him, but he hadn't turned a page in almost two hours; he just sat there, his pale, rheumy eyes filling with water. The library was one of the few places of refuge for Hollywood's bums. They crept in at opening time and often sat there until the doors closed at night and it was once more safe for them to go out onto the streets and forage.

Gregory hadn't returned to see Olga Nabakov. Instead he had decided upon a crash research project and gone to the library. He had found more than a dozen books dealing with reincarnation and he sat in the reference room skimming through them, taking notes on a ragged yellow foolscap pad. Although his understanding of the theory and mechanics of reincarnation hadn't increased considerably, he was pleased to discover that his interest was shared by exalted company.

The list wasn't limited to poets and philosophers, people whose ethereal lives and thoughts might bias them toward such views, but included statesmen, generals, hardheaded businessmen, and others. Bonaparte believed that he had been Charlemagne in a former life; General George Patton remembered battles he had fought in past lives. Such illustrious men as Ralph Waldo Emerson, Benjamin Franklin, Walt Whitman, Oliver Wendell Holmes, Edgar Allan Poe, Henry David Thoreau, Flaubert, Tolstoy, and Mark Twain had all expressed a belief in reincarnation at one time or another.

In more recent times, the list was even more astounding: Thomas Edison, Charles A. Lindbergh, Hermann Hesse, William Butler Yeats, David Lloyd George, Jack London, Aldous Huxley, J. D. Salinger.

As far as the general theory of reincarnation was concerned, Gregory couldn't find much of significance to which he could relate. Nearly all the various schools of thought on reincarnation seemed to believe in some variation of the Hindu concept of Karma, the moral law of cause and effect which, in simple terms, means that each individual's present situation is a direct result of his past.

Gregory closed the last book in his pile and sat there, thinking. Reincarnation could also explain a number of other phenomena that had puzzled man, Gregory thought. The feeling of *déjà vu*, the appearance of child prodigies, dreams in which people found themselves speaking in strange languages, the religious experience of "speaking in tongues."

But this line of thinking, fascinating though it was, was unproductive. He took the books back to the shelves. His real questions were still unanswered. Who was he? Why couldn't most people remember their past lives? Why could he? What was the source of his nightmares? How could he find Brooke?

When he'd arrived home from the beach the night before, he'd been full of questions. Luckily Sharon had already been asleep, body rigid on the far side of the bed. He was thankful, for he had expected a scene. He knew he should have called and told her he would be home late. But what could he tell her? That he had just discovered that he had lived before?

In the morning, Sharon had been distant and polite. She asked where he had been, but he was evasive, merely telling her that he had been doing research. She had snorted disbelievingly and said, "Till midnight?" Then she left, without waiting for an explanation. It was lucky, even though it made things uncomfortable between them, because there was nothing he could really tell her. He didn't dwell on it, however.

He had left for the library shortly after her departure.

Gregory now stood on the library steps, undecided. He needed to talk to someone. But he decided to go home first, have something to eat, and call Olga from there.

When he got home he found a message from Steve Sherman. He called back and Liz answered.

"Steve's gone out," she said. "But he wanted you to know that Bob Lion is giving a party tonight. He says you're invited and it'll be a good chance for you to meet him."

She gave him the address, and while he wrote it down, he asked if they would be there.

"Of course. If it gets boring we can cuddle in the corner," she said.

"You've given me something to live for," he replied.

Perfect, he thought. Maybe he'd get some answers there. Next, he called Olga. She asked how he was, a trace of concern in her voice.

"I'm fine. Just bewildered by a lot of questions —as you predicted," he said. "I'd like to come over, if I may."

She replied, with the graciousness he had come to expect of her, that she would be delighted.

Olga met him at the door. "Gregory," she said, taking his hands in hers. "I am so glad you could come."

For one split-second, time spliced.

He remembered the first time he had met her. Brooke had introduced them. "Michael, this is my friend, my *very* good friend, Olga Nabakov.

Olga, this is the man I love, Michael Richardson.
I hope you two like each other as much as I
do." He had liked her, although she had been
more intense when she had been younger, lack-
ing the maturity and sense of fulfillment she
now projected.

They sat on the rear patio as before and she
brought the tea out, although this time she did
it in the English manner, pouring it at the table
before him from a silver kettle.

"You were right," he said, when the ritual
was complete. "I'm full of questions."

"Are you managing all right, though?" she
asked obliquely.

"Yes. Yes, I think so. I mean, it's a shock,
of course. It's just eradicated everything I ever
believed in, and I'm as confused as hell, but I
think if I just take one step at a time, I'll be
all right."

"That's very sensible," she said approvingly.
"You know, in a way, you're very lucky. Thou-
sands of people would give anything to find out
about their past lives, but they never do."

"Have you?" he asked. "Remembered your
past lives?"

"Yes, some of them," she said.

"How?"

"Through meditation. There's a system where,
by focusing on the self, the ego-consciousness,
and blocking out everything else, certain scenes
from past lives come to view. But it's admittedly
a hit-and-miss method, and some people can
study for a lifetime without ever attaining that
state."

"I see." Gregory drummed his fingers absently
on the table. "That brings up one of my ques-

tions. What is the Self, as you call it? Who and what am I?"

The question made him feel a bit foolish. It sounded pretentious. You're into your third decade of life and suddenly you ask someone a question that sounds absurd even from an adolescent.

Olga smiled tolerantly. "You're asking a question that's been asked by philosophers throughout the ages, and there are as many different answers as times the question has been asked. Buddhism believes you are an individual soul that is a part of the World-Soul. Hinduism also believes that it is your soul that is trapped in the cycle of rebirth. Christians, as you know, believe that the soul goes to heaven or hell. Some groups believe that the soul or 'I' is an illusion and that there is no personal identity."

"And you?"

"I believe that there is an eternal part of us, a self or ego, that is unchanging and immortal. It is not our personality or social patterns; it is perhaps consciousness itself."

Gregory was disappointed. "That's very vague."

Olga shrugged. "I'm sorry. Yes, it is. But there is a basic difficulty in trying to talk about something infinite in finite terms."

"All right. Why have I been able to remember my past?"

"I can't give you a definite answer to that, either," she said resignedly. "You know about the law of Karma?"

Gregory nodded. "Yes, I read about it just today."

"Well, it seems that your Karma has dictated these events that have happened. In a manner of speaking, you are on a path of destiny that is a direct result of your past experience. Exactly what it is, I don't know. Where it will lead you, I don't know. I just know that you are the result of everything you have ever thought or done, and what happens now is an outgrowth of that."

Gregory felt a growing sense of desperation. These concepts were like grains of sand slipping through his fingers. Consciousness, what the hell *was* consciousness? And Karma? It sounded like fatalism to him. Where did his free will fit into it? If he was a puppet, who was pulling the strings, and why?

Olga sensed his disturbance. She put a hand on his arm. "I'm sorry I can't express it in a more comprehensible manner," she said. "But I have been studying metaphysics all my life, and there is much I do not understand either. It is said that only when you lose the desire to know, can you know. Finding only comes to those who no longer seek. One must lose all desire to be free in order to achieve freedom."

"What can I do? How can I use the knowledge I have now? How, for instance, can I find Brooke again?"

Olga looked distressed by his questions. "I don't know, Gregory. You are in the middle of a cycle of events and you just have to see where it takes you."

"Dammit, Olga! I'm *not* a puppet. I have will. I have ability. I can't subscribe to fatalism."

"Whether you subscribe to it or not doesn't change things," she said gently.

"All right." His voice was heavy. "What about Brooke?"

"I have often wondered where she was. I think if you are meant to find her, you will. In the past, I have tried to use my abilities to see where she is in this life, but all I have been able to sense is a large ocean, a wide expanse of water."

Gregory pounced on her statement. "Then she might be across an ocean? In Europe?"

"Perhaps. I don't know. There is more ocean than land on this planet. It could be any ocean."

Gregory was deflated. The brief flare of excitement deserted him. "Or Africa, or Asia, or Australia, or some little island," he said hopelessly.

Olga was silent for a long time before she spoke again. "Gregory, there is one thing I believe," she said finally, her voice resolute. "I believe that there is a purpose to everything that happens. Call it fatalism, if you will. But it should not cause you to lose hope. Follow the path you are on. This return of memory has miraculously happened to you, and it has happened for some reason that you are unable to perceive at this time. Have faith."

"Maybe the reason it happened is just to torture me," he said.

"No," she said firmly. "This regaining of memory is an increase of awareness, not a decrease. It must lead to something positive. Have faith in that."

Faith again. Olga was a great one for faith. Maybe it could move mountains and part oceans, but somehow the thought didn't console him.

"All right," he said, after a pause. "There's another thing you might be able to help me with. I've been having dreams, nightmares in fact. They're very real, and to put it bluntly, I'm afraid of them. I don't understand what's happening."

Olga raised an eyebrow. "Tell me about them."

He told her about the ugly cowled figure, the threats, the hate, the helpless feeling of surrender, the strange state of half-wakefulness he had experienced.

Olga was shocked. "Have you ever seen the face of this woman?" she asked.

"No. Never. It's always covered by the hood."

"So, you have no idea who it is. . . ."

He felt a shred of that black cloud of fear touch him again. "You talk as if it's someone real."

"It is real." Olga's tone was casual, but he could sense the effort in her voice to make it seem that way.

"What do you mean?"

Olga didn't answer immediately. Instead she poured more tea into her cup. There was a minute tremor in her hand. She finished pouring her tea and said, "You are being attacked. Someone is attacking you on a psychic level."

"But they're just nightmares," he protested incredulously.

"Don't be obtuse," she said sharply. "You suspected they were more than that, otherwise you wouldn't have brought the subject up. These dreams have all the earmarks of a psychic attack. The feeling of presence, the helplessness, the sense of reality. I have had experience with this before."

Gregory slumped limply, unbelievingly, in his chair. "I'm lost," he said weakly. "Please explain this to me, Olga."

"There are many methods," she said, "but what they all come down to is that, on a mental or psychic level, someone is trying to destroy you."

"Who would do that?" Gregory whispered.

"I don't know. Obviously it has something to do with Brooke Ashley. Someone who knew her. It might even be a ghost or spirit. You have heard of people being haunted, have you not?"

Gregory was stunned by her words, but his rising fear accepted their truth where his rational mind could not.

"What can I do?" he asked.

She narrowed her eyes at him, as if trying to measure his worth. "First, you must not panic. Fear breeds fear. The next time this vision comes to you, you must realize what it is and fight it. Realize that it is an enemy attacking you, that it is not a figment of your mind. Remember, its only power over you is the power you grant it. Will it to show its face. Order it to. Once you know who it is, you will be better able to defend yourself."

"This is incredible! This is too much!" Gregory's face had lost its color. "I'm supposed to have a battle of wills with a ghost!"

Olga leaned toward him across the table, her expression grim. "Not only must you battle it," she said, "you must win."

Chapter Ten

THE ANGER BEHIND Sharon's words twisted her face into a mask.

She stood, leaning down hard on the kitchen table as if trying to crush it, her face pushed forward pugnaciously. Gregory sat opposite her, attempting to maintain a calm exterior, a cigarette in one hand, a mug of coffee in the other.

"You already accepted the invitation to Horowitz's party," she said tightly. "You can't cancel out now."

"But I don't want to go to Horowitz's party, and even if I did, I *need* to go to Lion's."

"But *I* do want to go to Horowitz's. Who the fuck's Lion? The next thing to a nobody. I can meet people at Horowitz's. Useful people."

"There'll probably be 'useful' people at Lion's party," he said resignedly. "Look, I have to talk to Lion about this book I'm doing. He has data I need, and this is the best chance for me to get it."

He knew he'd said the wrong thing even before he completed the sentence. Sharon's face was red, her knuckles white on the table.

"Research, research, research!" she yelled. "I'm getting goddamned tired of your research and your book and your stupid self-centered life. What about me?"

"What about you, Sharon?" he asked wearily. He stubbed his cigarette forcefully into the ashtray. He was tired. He had enough problems without the addition of a major upset with her.

Sharon rolled her eyes up in a theatrical gesture of bafflement. "What about me, he asks," she said to the ceiling. She looked down, her eyes flashing angrily. "I'm the girl you're supposed to love, remember? We're supposed to share things, do things together. Remember? In case you've forgotten, we're also getting married."

"Well, if we look at this logically, you want to go to Mike's party on business, to meet the 'right' people. I want to go to Lion's party on business, to meet him. Right? So let's be honest and admit we're both being selfish. Don't lay it all on me."

"But you promised we were going to Horowitz's party," she wailed.

"I didn't promise," he contradicted. "I said we were going. That's a different thing. Now I've changed my mind."

"But I haven't changed mine," she said menacingly.

"All right, all right," he said. "Let's do this— you go to Horowitz's party, I go to Lion's party, and then, later, after I've talked to him, I'll come to Horowitz's and meet you there. How's that?"

"That's just beautiful," she said icily. "Just wonderful. I've got a better idea, though. You go to Lion's party and I go to Mike's. And fuck you!"

She hit the table with her hand, then turned and stalked out.

"Sounds good to me," Gregory shouted after her, finally losing his temper.

He lit another cigarette and sat frowning at the smoke. Dammit, if this was an indication of what their married life would be like, he'd better think again. They had never even argued before . . . before what? Before he had started work on the Brooke Ashley project. What would happen if he told her the truth? Total disaster, no doubt. "Sharon, the reason I'm so wrapped up in this is because in my past life I was Michael Richardson, Brooke Ashley's lover." Oh, great! It would go over like a lead balloon.

He looked up at the kitchen clock. He'd better get ready to leave—without her, if that was how it had to be.

When he reached the bedroom, she had already showered and was sitting in front of the dressing table. She was braiding her long black hair into a plait, a style he'd never seen her use before. She ignored his entrance, continuing her task with even more concentration. He thought about talking to her, saying something light to snap her out of her mood, but he didn't have the stomach for it, and went into the bathroom instead, cursing her and berating himself for letting the situation deteriorate.

After his shower, she was still sitting there, carefully applying make-up to her face, still acting as if he weren't in the room. Screw her, he thought, injured pride getting the better of him. If she wants a truce, *she* can take the initiative for a change.

The silence continued as each prepared for their separate parties.

Gregory's host met him at the door and shook his hand enthusiastically. Lion was a short, slim young man with alert brown eyes and a quick, decisive way of talking.

"Come in, come in," he said. "Steve and Liz are here already, somewhere around."

Lion gestured toward the crowd of people milling about in two large rooms, steering Gregory into the main one by the elbow. A James Taylor record was playing just below the level of conversation. The laughter was easy and relaxed.

"Steve said you wanted to talk to me," Lion said.

"Yes, I'm doing research on past lives for a book, and I hear you're an authority."

"Hell, I'm no authority. But I'll be happy to pass on whatever I do know." The doorbell rang. "Let's get together later in the evening when I'm through playing host. Help yourself to a drink," he said. He slipped off to answer the door, leaving Gregory at the side of the room.

Steve and Liz weren't visible. Gregory saw a few people he recognized, however, and nodded greetings. Brett Corydon, a director who had made several successful motorcycle flicks, came up and shook his hand.

"Congratulations on your nomination," he said, pumping Gregory's arm.

Gregory had to think twice. The nomination. During the events of the past few days he had almost forgotten his new celebrity status. Academy nomination for the Best Original Screenplay.

Corydon introduced him to a couple of other people, prefacing his name with the information that he had won an Oscar nomination. The ensuing respect and awe heaped upon him began to make him feel uncomfortable.

He was rescued from behind by a pair of svelte arms that snaked around his middle. Soft breasts pressed into his back.

"Liz!" he guessed. She wiggled against him. "I'd recognize your boobs anywhere." He turned around and kissed her.

"Where's Steve?" he asked.

"In the other room," she said, taking his hand. "Listen, you want to meet a prime, A-one asshole?"

"What do you mean?" he said, bemused. Liz was wearing tight blue jeans and a T-shirt that said "100% Organic."

"Steve's talking to this guy who's the biggest asshole I've ever met. He's a walking Hollywood cliché. Your life just won't be complete until you meet him."

"Well, I guess I've got nothing better to do," Gregory said, and followed her into the next room.

Steve was sitting on the couch among a small group of people. His eyes were glazed, and he was nodding on full-automatic. A short, stocky, dark man was holding court.

Steve introduced Gregory to the man, Mike Glover, an executive story consultant on a television series. Glover had a thin-lipped feral mouth and a loud, abrasive voice, totally out of proportion to his size. He was saying how he loved being in Hollywood. He and his wife, a tiny, dowdy woman who was as meek as he was brash, were both from New York.

"I love the lifestyle here," he said. "In New York, I was as poor as a pauper and lived in a run-down apartment. Now we've got a fantastic house in Woodland Hills, a pool, a sauna, a barbecue pit outside, a maid . . ."

He continued to run down his list of possessions and Gregory began to understand why Steve had that vacant look on his face. Maybe he could save Steve—and himself, he suspected —from terminal boredom by steering Glover toward more interesting subjects. The man's show, he remembered, dealt with underwater adventure.

"Do you do a lot of research for each script?" he interrupted Glover, mid-list.

"Hell, no!" Glover exclaimed, ready to launch into another favorite subject. "Research is the dirtiest word in my vocabulary. Writing," he pontificated, "is the art of lying. The better liar you are, the better fiction you can write. Besides, if I did research I might come up with some good ideas and the network wouldn't stand for it."

"What exactly is your job?" Gregory asked, ignoring Glover's attempt at humor.

"I assign stories to the writers, then when they bring them in, I throw them out and do them myself," Glover said, a shit-eating grin on his face.

Gregory's hackles rose. "You have a high opinion of writers, I see."

Glover was undeterred. "Well, I did when I was a writer," he said smugly. "But now I can't afford to."

At that point Gregory gave up. He dropped out of the conversation and sat listening. The man was an egomaniac. Amoral, avaricious, cynical, insensitive, a whore who had sold himself to the highest bidder and who proclaimed loudly to everyone who would listen how much he loved his new slavery.

Finally Gregory stood up discreetly, intending to move away. A finger poked into his back. A hoarse voice close to his ear said, "Don't move, pal."

He turned and looked into the face of the girl he had met on the beach, Jenny Royal. Her wide mouth was parted in a smile.

"Hello," he said, pleased to see her. He walked with her to where he wouldn't have to listen to Glover.

"Are you enjoying yourself?" she asked. "You looked like you wanted to throttle someone when I saw you." She looked pretty in a long, loose dress with short sleeves.

"Yeah," he said, inclining his head toward Glover.

"I've met him before," she said knowingly. "Hooray for Hollywood."

They both laughed. "Come on," she said. "I'll buy you a drink."

They went over to the cabinet and he poured them each a glass of wine. She clicked her glass against his and asked, "Where's the girl friend?"

"Elsewhere," he said curtly. Sharon had left the house before him with a screech of tires on the gravel driveway. They hadn't spoken to each other.

"Mmm, that's good," Jenny said.

"Are you here alone?"

"Uh-huh."

"Mmm, that's good," he said.

She smiled and moved closer. He touched her cheek softly. Her skin was warm.

"Maybe I'll cash in on that rain check," he suggested.

"I said any time." She scratched the palm of his hand lightly with a long, pink fingernail, her eyes fixed on his.

Bob Lion walked up to them. "Hi, Jenny," he said, hugging her. "Can I steal this man away from you for a while?"

"As long as you bring him back," she said.

Lion turned to Gregory. "We can talk now, if you like?"

Gregory nodded and Lion said, "Let's go to my study where we won't be interrupted."

"Fine," Gregory said. He turned to Jenny. "Don't go anywhere I can't find you."

They went into Lion's study, a warm, paneled room with hundreds of books, a desk, an old manual Remington typewriter and a long, comfortable couch. Lion gestured to the couch and they sat. Lion put an ashtray between them and they each lighted a cigarette.

"Do you have specific questions?" Lion asked. "Or is it just the general subject?"

Gregory looked into his glass. "Specifics. One authority says that people can't remember their previous lives because of painful incidents. How is it then that some people can? I mean, there are people around who can remember."

Lion nodded in acknowledgment. "Yes, that's true, of course. And there are probably a number of reasons. One of the main ones, I think, is that people suppress their memory, or they let other people suppress it. Children are a good example of that. Some children remember past lives. The mistake is that they say something about it to their parents, who immediately tell them to stop 'pretending.' In fact, when I was a kid, I told my parents once that I had been in England 'before I was born this time' and even described my previous parents. It scared the shit out of them! They told me it was impossible, and said it so strongly and so often that I lost all ability to remember for a while. I couldn't even remember what I'd done the day before.

"Well, in spite of this, people will sometimes get into a situation where they see something— a place, a person, something from their last life —and they'll suddenly blow the so-called rule that it's not okay to remember. And bingo! They'll remember. Sometimes people are also helped by the fact that they were lucky enough to have parents who didn't suppress them when they were children.

"There's another possibility—that during some past life, when he had knowledge of the fact he had lived before, the person might have made a decision to remember in his next life. He might just have postulated his memory into existence."

"I'm not sure I understand," Gregory said. "What do you mean by 'postulated'?"

Lion coughed harshly and put out his cigarette.

"Well," he explained, "a postulate is a self-fulfilling assumption. Whatever is happening to you is happening because you postulated it to be so."

Lion looked at Gregory, inviting a question, but Gregory just said, "Go on. Go on."

"Well," Lion continued. "A guy, when he's a little barefoot, dirty-faced kid, will make a postulate that he's going to be a failure in life. Some years later you see the guy working like crazy to be a failure in life. He doesn't know why. He's forgotten the postulate by this time, but by God he's still operating on it and making

it come true. In order to change conditions, for
better or worse, you have to make a postulate
that they will be changed before you can change
them."

"Jesus! That's something!" Gregory exclaimed.
"Each time, before you make a move toward an
objective, you actually get the end result in your
mind first. It's just that sometimes it happens
so fast you don't even notice you're doing it."

"Right," Lion said. "The postulate is first made
in your universe, by which I mean the universe
of thought, your mind. Then, through action, it
becomes a reality in the physical universe. But
it's always the end result that is postulated.
That's why you see people who never get anything done. They can never postulate the end
result of a cycle of action. Instead, they say,
'I'm going to do this,' or 'I'm thinking about
writing a book.' Each one of those statements
is not the end result, and therefore the postulate
floats in time and never becomes real."

"So," Gregory said, "when you say a guy postulated his memory into existence, you mean that
in a past life he got the idea of having his memory back, actually made the decision that in a
later life he would remember."

"Yes, he must have, otherwise it wouldn't
happen. Everything that happens is the result of
postulates."

"Why don't all our postulates work, then?"

"Because we also make counter-postulates,"
Lion said. "Our counter-postulates are just as
powerful as our postulates. A guy says, 'I'm
going to do this,' and then postulates it. Then
somebody tells him it's impossible, and he buys
that guy's opinion. Well, the next thing he does

is make a postulate that he can't do it, so nothing happens."

They sat in the study for another hour. Gregory asked every question he could dream up. There were many Lion was unable to answer, but he always admitted it immediately and differentiated between what he thought was true, based upon his own experience, and what was out-and-out speculation.

Gregory also found himself telling Lion about Brooke and his experiences in the last few days. Lion accepted it all in his matter-of-fact way.

"Well," he said, getting up to go back to the party, "if you both decided to find each other again this time around, there's nothing surer than that's what will happen. So don't worry about it."

"Easy to say," Gregory complained.

Lion smiled mischievously. "Yes, I guess if you're going to worry about it, you're going to worry about it, no matter what I say."

The volume of the party had increased since they had left the room. Laughter was louder, conversation more competitive, faces flushed. Couples were dancing in the room where the stereo was located.

Gregory saw Liz and Steve and waved. He looked around for Jenny and couldn't see her, so he went to the bar cabinet and refilled his wineglass. He strolled into the next room and saw her standing beside the big bay windows. She was talking to a couple and watching another pair stimulate each other erotically under the pretext of dancing, hips and chests sliding against each other, eyes gleaming, teeth bared.

He walked over and put his arm around her

waist. She jumped at his touch, then leaned against him.

"Taken care of business?" she asked.

"Most of it," he said, pulling her closer.

She introduced him to the people she had been talking to, but he never heard their names, too intent by far on the warmth of her body and the curve of waist and hip.

She inclined her head at the dancers beside them and said, close to his ear, "Shall we go do the real thing?"

He felt her breath, a wisp of her hair against his face, and sensed the healthy animal waiting to burst out of her flesh.

At the door, she said, "Your place?"

"Heavens, no! Yours, definitely yours," he said hastily, and was rewarded with a mocking smile. "I'll follow you in my car," he added.

He tried to imagine what Sharon would do if she walked in and found Jenny at their house. It would be high drama, that was for sure. Screams, threats, tears, name-calling, the full gamut of emotions, a part any actress would love. On the drive to the beach he relived his argument with Sharon, regaining the cold anger he had felt at the house. It would serve her right if he didn't go home, he thought. Give her something real to worry about. Finally, when he parked outside Jenny's beach house behind her red MG, he realized what he had been doing, and laughed softly at himself for attempting to justify his impending unfaithfulness.

Jenny fumbled for her key in the shadow of the door, and he used the opportunity to kiss her. It was a carryover from an old teenage habit when he had always used what he called the "door-key fumble" as an invitation. Jenny's lips were soft. They tried to devour his and she searched the inside of his mouth with her tongue. He could hear the surf rolling down on the beach and the mixed rhythm of their breath.

As soon as they got inside, they kissed again, hungry for the sensation. When they pulled apart, her face was flushed, her eyes bright with excitement.

"I've wanted to fuck you since I first saw you," she said.

"How fortunate for me," he said.

They went into the bedroom and she turned on a small bedside lamp. Then she drew her dress over her head, standing on her toes, presenting her body to him. He sat on the edge of the bed and began to remove his shoes.

Her breasts were large and they swayed as she walked towards him. Her legs were sleek, well-shaped. Her mouth was wet against his, her skin brown and smooth. She unzipped his pants and his penis sprang free, already hard. She began to lick it, then changed her mind.

"Wait," she said, lifting her head. "Wait a minute."

He lay there passively while she left the room. It was how he wanted it, to be ravished by a beautiful carnivore. Helpless for a while.

She came back, carrying two ice cubes in a glass.

"What's that for?" he asked.

"Take your clothes off and I'll show you," she said. She watched him as he undressed, and when all his clothes lay on the floor, she told him to lie back.

She gripped his distended penis worshipfully with one hand. "Oh, lovely, gorgeous thing," she said. With her other hand, she popped one of the ice cubes into her mouth. Then she lowered her head.

He sucked in his breath quickly. "Oh, God!" he groaned. "Oh, my God!"

Chapter Eleven

GREGORY WAS LYING in bed smoking, as satisfied as a sultan in his harem. Jenny had finally fallen asleep, satiated and exhausted, one long leg stretched out, the other drawn protectively up to her stomach, her hair a dark, glossy spray on the pillow.

She had been an intensely passionate and demanding lover, innovative, exciting, an unabashed hedonist, childlike in her eagerness to give pleasure and accept it. The uninhibited reminders of her passion had pierced his flesh—a bite here, a scratch there. Gregory wondered how he would explain the marks to Sharon.

He seemed to attract demanding, sexually masterful women. Sharon was the same, not as exciting as Jenny, he found himself admitting, but savagely intense in bed, totally committed to the gratification of the moment, all thought and action dedicated to it. It hadn't been that way for him, though, with either Sharon or Jenny.

He rose quietly from the bed and walked to

the window. He stood there naked, smoking automatically and watching the luminous sheets of water pummel the sand.

There was the first time with Brooke. Now *that* had been something special. That had really been something. . . .

He had picked her up for dinner as eagerly as a novice. She had answered the door herself and stepped out quickly. To his adoring eye she seemed cloaked in a rarefied atmosphere. Since he had met her the previous night, he had done nothing except think of her, unable to work, eat, or sleep, his mind fixated helplessly on a series of images that it had faithfully recorded during their first meeting.

When they reached his car, he kissed her like an impatient adolescent, smearing her lipstick, then apologizing.

"It's all right," she said. She took the silk handkerchief from his breast pocket and dabbed at her mouth. "Lipstick's replaceable. Kisses aren't."

While he drove, she elaborately applied fresh lipstick, peering into the mirror of a small compact, greatly exaggerating the make-up bit and making him laugh with her clowning.

At one point he tried to explain how he felt about her, but for a writer he did badly, impeding his thoughts with clumsy words.

"It's hard to explain," he said, darting quick, sidelong glances at her while he drove, resisting the temptation to sink helplessly into the depths of her eyes and let the car manage its own affairs. "But with you sitting beside me, I feel complete. No, that's the wrong word. I feel right. Hell, that's not it either. It's like looking at a painting with a gap in the canvas, a hole obliterating one of the main figures. When you're not with me there's an absence, a hole in the painting. Do you know what I'm trying to say?"

"Of course I do. I'm feeling the same thing, although I'd put it more succinctly. Until I met you I was half-alive. When I'm away from you I'm half-alive. When I'm with you I become totally alive."

"Well, I'd be a fool not to concede defeat in the exchange of metaphors," he said cheerfully.

They had dinner at Fazzi's, a small, unfashionable, neighborhood Italian restaurant in the Los Feliz area. There were red-and-white checkered tablecloths, carafes of wine, and there was sawdust on the floor. Michael went there frequently, whenever he wanted a quiet evening away from the Hollywood crowd.

The proprietor, a slim, morose man, welcomed Michael and allowed his swarthy face to break into a rare smile when Brooke spoke Italian, telling him how happy she was to be there.

"I didn't know you spoke Italian," Michael said when they were seated. "Ernesto is looking at me in a new light. Now he's thinking that maybe he was mistaken about me. Perhaps I'm not such a bum, after all. He's going to love you until judgment day. He's also going to try to make you fat."

"Don't tell him," Brooke said, "but I dealt him one card in my total vocabulary of four phrases."

"We could have gone somewhere more fashionable, but I don't want us to become a gossip-column item. It's too special for that, Brooke.

I'd prefer if we kept our time together our own. Agreed?"

"Of course I agree. I loathe the whole celebrity bit. 'Are wedding bells in sight for starlet Brooke Ashley and studio executive William Tanner?' That was one of the latest, literally. Apart from the syntax, I hate any part of my life being thrown to the lions."

She was even more beautiful tonight than she had been the night before, if that were possible. Her skin seemed to glow with a soft light, her eyes danced with life, her laughter was a bubbling, captivating thing. Her glances at him were so warm, so embracing, it was as if there were no distance between them. Yet behind it all was a contented calm, like a deep, still pool. The thought came that, just maybe, she was especially lovely tonight because she was happy to be with him. He sat there feeling proud, and a little foolish.

"What are you thinking?" she said.

"Oh, hell. Now you're going to make me say something trite. Naturally, I'm thinking you're the most lovely creature I've ever seen in my life. And I'm not talking about superficial beauty."

She took his hands and leaned across the table to kiss him lightly on the lips. He lifted his glass to her, still feeling that strange, special pride. He noticed that other people in the restaurant were looking at him surreptitiously, smiling embarrassingly when he caught them at it. Everybody loves a lover, he thought. One slightly overweight man in a rumpled gray suit couldn't keep his eyes off Brooke. He darted hungry looks at her between every mouthful of his spaghetti, but Michael was surprised to note he didn't feel any resentment. They belonged to each other. Other people's thoughts didn't matter. Nothing else mattered.

Ernesto hovered over them. Brooke captivated him with two more of her Italian phrases, and he couldn't do enough. He even brought out a special bottle of fifteen-year-old Barola and told them it was on the house, an unprecedented act of generosity.

They talked of nothing in particular, laughed a lot, gazed at each other during long periods of silence.

Brooke mentioned her studio boss, Harry Shankman. "He adores me—as long as I do what he says. In fact, when I first arrived at the studio and went into his offices, he sat behind that god-awful teak desk and said, 'Young lady, if you do vat I tell you to do, every time I tell you to do it, I vill make you into a star.' Do you think it was a recording?"

"Has he ever made a pass at you?" Michael asked uncomfortably. Like all the studio moguls —Cohn, Mayer, the others—Shankman made small distinction between his female stars and his personal property.

"He's always been a perfect gentleman," she said. "Should I feel rejected? Most of the other actresses haven't been so lucky."

Michael knew why. She wasn't someone who encouraged familiarity. That self-possession of hers would cow most men.

After they had eaten, they sipped thick espresso from small cups, lightheaded from the wine, dizzy from each other.

"Where would you like to go now?" he asked.

She toyed with a silver spoon and didn't answer. He was unable to see her eyes.

"Brooke?"

She looked up. There were tears in her eyes.

"I want to go home with you," she said.

He touched her hand. "Why is it so sad?"

She gripped his fingers with hers. "Because I'm afraid. Everything has been so perfect."

He didn't understand. "Yes, it has," he said urgently. "There's no reason to be afraid."

She smiled bravely and stroked his hand. "I know, Michael. Don't worry. It's just a silly woman thing. Everything is fine."

When they reached his house, she stood in the center of the living room, looking lost for a moment in the setting. Then, while he hung up her coat, she began to walk around, looking at the pictures on the walls, the bookshelves, his desk in another small room.

"This is where you work?" she said, pointing at his typewriter.

He was standing behind her, leaning against the door. "Yes," he said.

She turned and walked up to him. There was nothing to say. They kissed, surprising each other with their hunger, bruising each other with their lips, fighting with their tongues, each seeking to merge with the other.

They went to the bedroom and he made a move to turn off the bedside lamp.

"No," she said. "Leave it on. I want to see you."

He watched her while she undressed. She put a hand behind her back, then rolled the dress off her shoulders. It dropped to the floor and lay like a shroud at her feet. With another quick movement she unhooked her brassiere and it fell too. Then, gracefully lifting her legs, she slipped off her pants, and stood there, naked, unembarrassed.

She was perfect. Slim, rounded, her stomach flat, her breasts high with pink nipples which hardened beneath his stare.

He stood up slowly and dropped his trousers. She looked down at him, her eyes wide, and he grew as he stood there. She walked slowly toward him, the insides of her thighs brushing against each other like butterfly wings.

He pulled her to him and they kissed again, bodies burning against each other. He fell back onto the bed and she lay on top of him, rubbing her body against his, hoarse sounds in her throat. He wanted to lick the fine golden down from her body, the flesh from her bones.

She was not an experienced lover by his standards, but she made up for technique in ardor and curiosity, eagerly exploring his body, leaving nothing untouched, and demanding he do the same. The first time she climaxed, she screamed her love and thrashed against him like a wild filly, almost unable to bear the sensation that gripped her body. He groaned and heaved with pleasure above her, and when he finally let himself collapse alongside her body, completely spent, he felt proud and triumphant and sad and happy, all at once.

Gregory still stood at the window staring out at the ocean. He shivered slightly. The early-morning chill had set in and his cigarette had died out in his hand. Each time they had made love it had been better. Always fresh and exciting and new. That first night they had made love four times, unable to get enough of each other.

He looked down and saw that he had grown hard with the memory. He turned back to the bed. Jenny was still sprawled out, one leg uncovered by the sheet.

He walked back to the bed, his desire awakened again, leaned down, and kissed her on the neck. She stirred and turned over, looking up at him through slitted eyes.

"More?" she murmured, incredulous. "More?"

"Yes," he said. "More."

Chapter Twelve

SHARON'S CAR wasn't in the driveway when Gregory arrived home at seven A.M. He had refused Jenny's offer of breakfast and driven back slowly from the beach, his thoughts wooden. He'd had too much sex and drink and not enough sleep. He was tired.

He parked the car in the garage and walked through the back garden toward the house. Instead of going in, however, he detoured impulsively and sat on a rock beside the goldfish pool. He lighted a cigarette and listened to the soothing trickle of water. The sun was not yet warm enough to increase his lethargy, but it already glinted off the surface of the pool like shattered jewels. Below, the golden perch lazily circled the periphery of their small world. He envied them their mindlessness. Their decisions were limited to a very small environment.

Guilt had begun to send out its tentacles. He cursed himself for it, saying he'd done nothing that Sharon hadn't deserved; her behavior had demanded betrayal. Yet he couldn't rid himself of the guilt. He seesawed back and forth, mocking himself on one hand for his naiveté, on the other, for his faithlessness. It had been a mistake and he would have to pay the consequences. Tell her about it, talk.

And then what? In a sense, his preoccupation with Brooke's memory was also a betrayal. If, by some miracle, Brooke turned up on his doorstep today, he would have Sharon out of the back door so fast, she wouldn't have time to pack. Wasn't that betrayal? Even just to consider it? And even if that never happened, how could he marry a woman he wasn't sure he loved, standing at the altar, knowing she could never compare to Brooke? And what if the whole thing with Brooke was some kind of delusion, what if he really had snapped? No, he told himself, it's real and it happened, and I still love her, wherever she is.

He had asked Lion if she would still be the same Brooke he had loved. "Of course," the actor had replied. "Beings don't change. Her social background, education, mores, all that might be different, but that's not what you fell in love with. You fell in love with a being, with her individuality, and that never changes. You'll recognize that being when you see her."

Oh, God, would he? The hope, and the fear of having it unrealized, was almost too much to bear. How could he begin to look for her? She could be anywhere, anyone. He wished fervently that he could remember that last night, the night of the fire, what they had said to each other in those last moments. He had a feeling that it was important, that it contained some key. He tried again to dredge up the memory. Blank.

Jesus! Here he was again, plotting further be-

trayal of Sharon. Should he tell her about it?
She'd never believe him. She'd laugh him out of
the house. Either that, or leave, herself, running
as if pursued by the hounds of hell. And yet, it
wasn't fair not to tell her.

He was startled out of his thoughts by a sound
in the bushes to his right. There was a yowl and
Felix jumped out, his glossy coat covered with
twigs and leaves.

Felix was ecstatic to see him. He miaowed
and rubbed his back on his master's leg, his
head on his shoe. When Gregory brushed the
debris off his fur, Felix arched his back and
purred loudly.

"You must be hungry to give me such a welcome," Gregory said cynically. "Come on then,
let's get you some food."

He stood up and walked toward the house.
Felix followed, still miaowing energetically.
Gregory fumbled at the back door and finally
unlocked it. He opened it and stood there, waiting for Felix to slip in ahead of him as he
usually did.

There was a hiss from the cat. He had stopped
about six feet away from the door.

"Come on, boy. Come and get some food."

Felix didn't budge. He faced the house in a
fighting crouch, hissing and spitting at it.

"Come on, Felix, dammit! I'm not going to
stand here all day."

The cat wouldn't move any closer.

Gregory bemusedly looked inside, half-expect-
ing a large dog to come bounding out. There
was nothing, no obvious reason for the cat's
behavior.

He tried again. "Ksssss, kss, kss, come on,
Felix."

The cat just continued to look ferocious, fully prepared to attack the entire building.

"Shit!" Impatiently he walked back and bent to pick Felix up. As soon as he turned to face the house and take the first step, the cat shrieked, twisted violently, and slashed at Gregory's hands with its claws. He let him drop, now thoroughly puzzled. The animal had never behaved that way with him, not even when he force-fed him medicine. Well, he decided, he'd try again later. Right now he was too tired. He'd leave the door open in case Felix changed his mind.

Gregory entered the house, went to the kitchen, and put some water on the stove. Coffee would help. A shower would be even better. He turned the heat down low and went to the bedroom.

He took his shirt off, threw it on the bed, and stepped toward the bathroom. He stopped with his foot in midair and swung around. The bed. It hadn't been slept in!

He hadn't even thought to wonder why Sharon had not been here. He'd just assumed that she had gone to the store or something. Jesus! While he'd been playing out his remorse in the garden, she'd been playing in someone's bed. He warned himself not to jump to conclusions.

There was the sound of a car in the driveway. It went back to the garage where he had parked. Well, he'd soon find out. He sat on the edge of the bed and waited.

The back door slammed shut. Footsteps. Sharon appeared in the doorway. He noted with some satisfaction that she looked almost as tired as he felt.

"Where have you been?" he said belligerently.

She hardly looked at him. She walked over to the dresser, put her bag down, and peered into the mirror.

"Sharon, where have you been?"

She turned and looked at him, her eyes cold. "I've been out with a guy," she said flatly. "I had a good time for a change."

Then she noticed the bed. And the marks on his chest and shoulders.

"Bastard!" she shouted.

He was taken by surprise. She was on him before he had time to lift his hands and protect himself. She slapped his cheeks twice, stinging him, bringing tears to his eyes.

She pushed him back onto the bed and sat on top of him. He lifted his arms to guard his face. She pummeled his chest wildly with her fists.

He was more shocked at her ferocity than hurt by the blows. He tried to grab her arms. "Sharon, stop it! For God's sake, cut it out!"

She drew her lips back in a grimace. "Bastard! Bastard! Bastard!"

He got hold of her arms and swung her off him onto the bed. She tried to bite his hands. He spread-eagled on top of her, using his weight to hold her down. She bucked beneath him, but he was too strong. She began to sob, grief disfiguring her face and signaling the end of the battle.

Gregory rolled off and lay on his back beside her, panting with exertion, his eyes closed. Jesus Christ! He heard her get up and stumble to the bathroom, still weeping. The sound of running water. Her sobs growing farther apart. He sat

up slowly, wondering what would come next—
a bloodbath or a truce.

She came out of the bathroom and started
to cry again as soon as she saw him. "Oh, Gregory!" she wailed, and ran toward him. She
buried her face against his chest.

He patted her head. "It's okay, Sharon. Come
on, stop crying now."

She lifted her face up, still sobbing. "It's all
my fault, Greg. It's all my fault. I've been such
a bitch. I don't know what got into me. I'm
not like this. I'm not like this."

He kissed her dryly on the forehead. "No, it's
okay, Sharon. It's not all your fault. I've been
a bastard, too."

"Oh, Greg." She kissed his chest and sniffled
against him. "It's just that I need more of you
than you've been willing to give."

Now was his chance. He could tell her what
had been happening. Explain the pressures he
had been facing. Tell her about Brooke. Everything. Now, as they both sat defenseless in the
aftermath, resting in the eye of the storm.

Instead he stroked her hair. "I know, love. I
know. Let's try and work it out, okay?"

She rubbed her eyes with the backs of her
hands, looking like a forlorn puppy. "Yes, we
can work it out," she said, her smile feeble.
She stopped crying and went back to the bathroom. When she came out, she sat beside him
and ran a finger over one of the scratches on his
chest.

"Was she any good?" she asked.

He grinned. "Yeah. And yours?"

"Yes," she said.

They both broke into laughter and fell back

on the bed giggling helplessly as the adrenaline ebbed away.

"Oh, God, it's so silly," she said when she could talk. "I get so jealous about nothing, and now that something real happens, I'm not jealous at all. It's not that I don't care," she put in hastily. "It's just that now it doesn't seem all that important."

She leaned on one elbow and looked down at him. "Lately there's been such a distance between us. And it's been growing and growing and driving me crazy. There's been that feeling that something horrible was about to happen. Do you know what I mean?"

"Yes, I do," Gregory said. "Let's try to spend a little more time together from now on. I think that'll help."

"I wish you'd stop work on that book," she said. "Then we could just take off for a while."

"I can't do that," he said. "I'm committed to finishing the project."

He felt her stiffen against him; then she relaxed. The book again. It stood between them like a wall. He wondered if she knew, on some subconscious level, that this—and what it represented—was the thing that threatened their relationship.

"Well, we couldn't get away, anyway," she said, finally. "I've got a shooting this week."

He grew aware of a noise in the background. It was the kettle whistling shrilly in the kitchen.

"Hey, I forgot," he said. "I put the water on. Would you mind making some coffee while I shower?" Instinctively, he knew it was time for the practical realities.

"Instant okay?" she asked.

"Yeah, that's fine."

By the time he was out of the shower, she was back with the coffee. He took a mouthful, scalding his throat. She was looking at his chest again.

"Would you like me to dress your wounds?" she asked mockingly.

"Maybe I'd better keep them as a reminder to tread the straight and narrow," he said. He smiled, but he was relieved when she changed the subject.

"Did you check to see if there were any messages on the phone?" she asked.

"No, not yet."

She left the room and he went to the closet to select a shirt. He chose a thin blue cotton one with short sleeves. It looked as if it would be a hot day.

"Greg!"

There was a quality to her cry that sent a shiver through him. He hurried from the room and met her in the hallway.

"What's the matter?"

"Have you been in the study?" Her voice was shaky.

"No. Why?"

"Look," she said, taking his arm.

He followed her to the den and stood at the door.

His desk lay on the floor on the opposite side of the room from where it had originally stood. It was upside down. The armchair was overturned, his typewriter was on the floor. Papers littered the room.

"What . . . ?"

He walked in quickly. It was a disaster. Books had fallen or been thrown out of the shelves, the lamp was shattered, cigarette butts were strewn about like confetti.

He did a quick inventory. Nothing seemed to be missing. His typewriter was still there. Surely, he thought, if thieves had done this, they would have taken that first.

"Anything missing in the living room?" he asked.

"I don't think so. I didn't really notice."

Gregory stood and looked around the room, perplexed. What had happened? Why had it happened? And above all, why had it happened to him?

Sharon had wanted to call the police, but Gregory had talked her out of it. After a thorough search it became obvious that nothing was missing. Television, video unit, stereo, tape deck— all there. No windows were open or broken; no doors unlocked. It seemed senseless.

Gregory was unable to confront even the idea of cleaning up the room. Instead, they sat in the kitchen and ate breakfast. Gregory pretended to be engrossed in the newspaper.

Sharon picked at her food. "What could have happened?" she said for the third time.

"Look, I don't know," Gregory said testily. "Let's forget it. Maybe it's just somebody's idea of a joke. Anyway, there's no real harm done. Nothing's missing."

"No harm done? With your study looking like that?"

"It's all right. I'll fix it up later after I have a nap. It won't take long."

She went back to picking at her food.

"Listen," he said, "I'm going up to Oakland tomorrow."

"What for?"

"I've got some research to do up there."

Her mouth tightened. "For the book?" The words hung dangerously in the air.

"Yes," he said.

She stabbed at a sausage with her fork, clanging it against the plate. "That damn book! After what we just went through."

"Hey, it's only for a day," he said placatingly. "It's necessary, or I wouldn't do it. I'll take an early-morning plane and be back by dinner."

She didn't say anything; she just poked another four holes in her sausage.

He put the paper down on the table. "Sharon, we *are* going to try to do better together, aren't we?"

She looked up. "I'm sorry, Greg. You're right. I'm going to be working tomorrow, anyway. I don't know why I got so uptight."

He looked at her carefully. She sounded sincere and contrite. But she was an actress. He tended to forget that sometimes. Somehow, there was just a touch of the theatrical in the loving look she sent his way. It occurred to him that perhaps she was enjoying the whole situation. One never knew with actresses. Reality and fantasy sometimes merged unrecognizably in their lives.

He picked up the paper again. Sharon stood.

"Let's go to bed," she said. "I think we both need some sleep."

He put down the still-unread newspaper and got up. Yawned and stretched. Maybe everything would be clearer after a rest. It usually was.

He padded toward the bedroom. Halfway down the hall, he stopped. Turned. There were goose bumps on his arms.

He had to look.

He walked back to the study. Went in. The typewriter. He had to look at it.

It lay on its side on the floor. There was a piece of paper in the carriage.

He bent over to see better. There was writing on it. He pulled the sheet out and held it up. The message was neatly typed in capital letters.

It said: *I WARNED YOU TO STAY AWAY FROM BROOKE.*

Chapter Thirteen

GREGORY LOOKED OUT of the airplane window at the hypnotic blur of tarmac. There was a slight bump and then they were smoothly airborne. The businessman beside him settled heavily into his seat and took a *Wall Street Journal* from his briefcase. It was early morning, yet Gregory saw that smog had already begun to obscure the San Fernando Valley.

He felt well rested. After sleeping most of the previous day, he had cleaned up his study in the evening. He'd decided that the destruction there had been a formal declaration of war—laid down in terms he couldn't possibly mistake. Whoever or whatever his enemy was, he or she had decided to leave the plane of dreams and victimize him on a more material level. Yes, he told himself, it was an irrational conclusion, but one not incompatible with the other irrational things that had happened to him. Besides, what other explanation was there?

He hadn't mentioned to Sharon the message he had found in the typewriter. The domestic bliss of their early-morning reunion had already eroded by the time they parted. Although she hadn't said anything more about it, he knew she disapproved of his trip. "More research on that stupid book," he imagined her thinking. He'd discerned it from the increasing chill in her attitude.

To be sure, he had also had arguments with Brooke in his last life, but they had been different. Stormy while they lasted, but once they were over, there had been a purity to them, a "clean" feeling, a clearing of the air. He looked out of the window of the plane. They were over clouds—a mad, stormy sculpture of cotton.

He remembered the first and the worst argument he had had with Brooke.

It had been quite a tempest, blown out of proportion by aggravated emotions. The beginning had been simple enough. He had called her and her mother answered the telephone. She told him Brooke wasn't in. Later, he had discovered that Brooke *had* been home at the time.

He brought the subject up with her one day. They were sitting in the living room of his apartment.

"You've got to move away from your mother and find a place of your own to live," he said moodily. It had been on his mind for a number of days.

Brooke looked shocked. "I can't just walk out on her like that. It would hurt her terribly."

"What happens when we get married?" he asked peevishly. "Is she going to come live with us?" It was a subject they had discussed before. They hadn't formalized it by setting a date, but they both took it for granted they would get married.

"Of course not," she said irritably, responding to his tone. "That's entirely different. It's not the same as walking out on her now, for no particular reason."

"Brooke, she's coming between us. I can feel it," he said flatly. "I'm not going to stand for it. We agreed not to let anything like that happen."

She twisted her hands, pained by his words. It was a subject she preferred to avoid. "I don't think that's really true, Michael. Just because of that one telephone call."

He shook his head stubbornly. "No, not just the phone call, Brooke. She doesn't think I'm good enough for you. I admit she has a point—but it is not just that she dislikes me—she positively hates me."

Brooke reacted angrily. "That's unfair. She's never said anything like that to you, nothing to give you that impression!"

"She hasn't needed to. I can feel it every time I see her. I want you to move away from her."

"You want me to move away from her," she repeated icily. "Since when did you begin to stage-manage my life?"

"Since I've loved you," he said. "Since you're too dumb to see what's best for you, for both of us. I'm telling you, she'll destroy what we have. I know it."

"So now I'm too dumb!" She rose to her feet and stood over him, her hands on her hips, eyes flashing warnings, chin jutting out defiantly. "I owe my mother a lot. Everything I have."

"You owe her your career, which you don't particularly want anyway. The most important thing you have is me. And she had nothing to do with that."

"God! The conceit of you!"

He slapped his leg in exasperation. "Brooke, you're twisting my words. You know what I mean. All I'm saying is that I want you to move out. If you really want what's best for us, you'll do as I say."

"And if I don't?"

He didn't want to answer. It had gone too far already. Her cheeks were flushed, her mouth trembled. She was beautiful. He wanted to kiss her and forget he had ever brought it up. But his pride would not allow it.

"Then I'll doubt your intentions as far as we're concerned," he said stiffly.

She threw him a look that would have shriveled a lesser man. "You bastard!" It was doubly effective because she rarely cursed.

She grabbed her coat and bag and threw them violently over her shoulder. "Don't bother seeing me to the door," she said frigidly, and stalked out of the room.

They didn't speak for two days. Michael felt miserable, physically ill, foolish, sad, right, wrong, confused. And then, on the morning of the third day, the telephone rang.

He picked it up eagerly, knowing it was she. "Brooke?"

"Michael, I . . ."

"Brooke, I'm sorry too," he interrupted. "I really am. I had no right to talk to you that way, to dictate to you like that. No right at all. I don't own you, God knows. In fact, I love your independence. I'd kill myself before destroying it. I'm sorry. I . . ."

She broke in. "Michael."

"Yes."

"I've thought it over. You were right. I just hated being forced to face it. I moved out yesterday."

"Yesterday?" he said stupidly.

"Yes. I've got an apartment near yours."

"I'm glad, darling. But I was still wrong to speak to you that way. Forgive me?"

"Oh, Michael, of course. Do you forgive me for the things I said? I didn't mean them."

"Hell, forgive you? I love you."

She sounded doubtful, girlish. "Are you sure?"

"How do you want me to prove it?"

He heard the smile in her voice and knew it was all fine. "Send me some roses," she said. "A dozen red roses. No, three red roses, three white ones, three pink ones, and three yellow ones. Then I'll know you forgive me."

"Where are you living?"

She gave him the address and told him she'd be at the studio until dinner time.

"The key is under the doormat."

"I'll see you when you get back," he said. "I love you, Brooke. I can't tell you how miserable I've been these last two days."

"Me, too," she said.

After she hung up, he made a couple of telephone calls and then left the apartment.

When she arrived at her new place that night, he met her at the door.

"Close your eyes," he said, blocking her path.

She closed her eyes and he led her into the center of the room.

"Okay, open your eyes now."

She opened her eyes and gasped. One hand

went to her mouth. Her eyes were wide as they roamed the room.

There were roses on the tables, roses on the couch, roses on the chairs, roses on the floor. There were red roses, white ones, pink, and yellow roses. They covered everything. Hundreds of perfect roses.

She began to cry and laugh at once. "Oh, Michael. Michael."

He took her arm again and led her to the bedroom. It had taken him painstaking hours to prepare everything.

"There's one more thing," he said. "We're going to do something nobody's done before."

She stood transfixed at the bedroom door, not believing what she saw. Red and white petals, pink and yellow petals, laid out like a blanket. The bed was completely covered with rose petals.

Chapter Fourteen

GREGORY PICKED UP a Ford Pinto from the Hertz girl at the Oakland airport and took the Nimitz Freeway into town. He turned off at the Broadway exit and stopped at a small corner diner for coffee and a chance to plan his next move.

He intended to find the house that he had lived in as a child during his last life as Michael Richardson.

In a sense, it was a herculean task, and he surprised himself with his own audacity. He didn't know what part of Oakland he had lived in, couldn't remember the street name, had no idea if the house would even still be standing. And yet, he was compelled to try. If he could find the house as he thought he remembered it to be, and if his "memory" proved correct, that last disquieting ember of doubt in the back of his mind would finally be extinguished. It would prove beyond a doubt that he had been Michael Richardson, that he was not the victim of some strange, frighteningly realistic delusion.

Gregory entered the diner and sat at the

counter. The waitress stopped chatting with her regulars long enough to ask him what he wanted. She sloshed his coffee into the saucer when she poured it. The diner was like a thousand others, fading Formica tops, vinyl-covered stools, the cracks optimistically taped over. But the coffee was good, better than the prepackaged muck on the plane. He sipped at it thirstily, considering his options.

There were several approaches he could use to find the house. He could go to the county courthouse and search through Probate and Vital Records, even go to the telephone company and look in a thirty-year-old directory for Jason Richardson's listing. Chances were that it would probably carry an address. Yet these methods did not appeal to him. When he had left Los Angeles, he'd had a quixotic feeling that he should be able to find the house on his own, that once in Oakland, the sight of familiar landmarks would revitalize his memory. Now he wasn't so certain. So far, nothing had looked familiar. It was just another dirty city he hadn't visited before.

He tried to remember when he, as Michael Richardson, had last been in Oakland. It had been about six months before he had met Brooke. That was the last time he had seen his parents. He had told them about her in his letters, but he had never seemed able to find the time to bring her up to meet them, although it had been something he'd wanted to do. He regretted it now. He had told her about his folks and knew she would have liked them. He'd also told her about his childhood, and especially about the treehouse and the wonderful adventures he had created there in his imagination.

Piedmont! The thought came to him out of nowhere. Their house had been in the foothills just below it. A middle-class belt that had acted as a barrier between the poorer homes on the flats and the great mansions up on the hill.

He called the waitress over.

"Anything else?" she said, reaching for a menu.

"No, thank you. I wonder, could you tell me, is there an area called Piedmont in Oakland?"

"Yeah." She pointed a pudgy finger. "Up in the hills that way. Snotty neighborhood, ya know what I mean?"

He said he did and paid for his coffee. He left the waitress a large tip, hoping she wouldn't think it snotty.

Gregory drove down Broadway toward Berkeley and then turned right at a large intersection, figuring the road would take him up into the hills. It did, but he saw nothing he recognized. As was the case in most cities, the houses just grew progressively larger as the elevation increased. The rich, he thought, liked to look down at the world, and everybody else in it.

It occurred to him that the road he was driving on could be relatively new. Perhaps he should leave it and travel some of the side streets. He saw a hitchhiker and stopped to ask him where Piedmont was.

The youth, bearded, disheveled, and dull-eyed, shrugged his thin shoulders. "Dunno, man. How about a ride?"

"Where are you going?" Gregory asked.

"I'm just splitting, man. Whichever way the wind takes me."

Gregory left him waiting for the wind and

stopped a few blocks farther when he saw a group of orange-vested workmen trimming trees. He opened his passenger window and leaned over the seat. "Excuse me," he said.

A tall black man ambled over. "Yeah?" he said suspiciously.

"Could you tell me how to get to Piedmont, please?"

The man glanced at the car and its driver. He threw a thumb over his shoulder. "You're just about in it. Go a few blocks that way."

Gregory thanked him and drove off. He swung right at the next corner. The houses soon grew larger. It was mansion country. Big fences, big yards which were probably called "grounds," tennis courts, sweeping driveways, towering trees.

He stopped at the crest of a hill and got out of the car. He stood beside it and looked around. Somehow it began to feel familiar. San Francisco was to his west, Marin County northwest across the bay, and Berkeley directly north. And he had lived somewhere down the hill.

He began to travel downhill laterally, sweeping along the parallel streets, peering to each side for landmarks, some beacon to throw light on his shadowed memory. He drove past Victorian houses, bungalows, stucco duplexes, apartments, but the childhood of another life remained elusive. He did remember, however, that there had been no apartments in his old neighborhood. It had been strictly residential. Times had changed. Perhaps nothing remained of the past but his memories. The house he had lived in and those surrounding it may all have been torn down, replaced by concrete, glass, and aluminum matchboxes, greened by plastic bushes. Modernized and sanitized for a brave new world.

And then the clangor of a memory bell sounded in his mind.

It was a corner grocery store, fronted by fading, scarred wood and smudged glass. The neon "Liquor" sign didn't look at all familiar, but the store itself did. He parked outside and looked at it. There had been a corner grocery at the end of the block he had lived on. Its candy counter had contributed heavily to the tooth decay he had experienced later in that life. Was this the same place? He couldn't swear to it, but he thought so.

He started the car and drove slowly down the street. Apartments on either side for about a hundred yards, then old houses. Houses he remembered! He was sure of it. He gripped the wheel in excitement. This was it! Where was the house?

He almost missed it. The blue trim had gone now, replaced by the white paint which now covered the building. But it was the same house, two-story, peaked roof, gingerbread cropping out, the wooden porch overlooking the street. There was no mistaking it.

He parked and sat there for a while, feeling a bit dizzy. It was the same house he had remembered. It hadn't been his imagination, it couldn't have been. He had never been here before in this life.

There was a faint row of letters on the mailbox. He got out of the car and walked over to it.

Richardson, it said.

The thought that either of his parents, the

parents of Michael Richardson, might still be alive had never occurred to him. After all, he had died. How could his parents, so much older than he, still be alive? Yet it was entirely possible. He was only thirty-one when he had died and his mother had been only in her early fifties then. His father had been about ten years older, which would put him in the late eighties or early nineties now.

The situation had its fantastic elements. What would it be like to meet people who had been your parents in a previous lifetime, people you remembered loving dearly? Meanwhile, you still had a mother who had given birth to your present body. Yet, even as these thoughts passed through Gregory's mind, he also considered the possibility that the new occupants had simply never removed the faded name from the mailbox, or that some distant relatives lived there now; or, wilder still, that through some coincidence, the people now there merely had the same name.

There was only one way to find out. He tucked in his shirt and walked up to the house. The steps creaked beneath his weight. The boards on the porch had been warped by rain and age.

He pressed the bell and waited, his stomach contracting in knots. There was no sound inside the house. He pressed it again, this time with his ear against the screen door. Still no sound. Perhaps it didn't work. He pulled back the screen and knocked loudly on the door. There were footsteps in the hall, and then the door opened slowly, uncertainly.

The woman who stood there was old, well into her late seventies, he guessed. Her body had been bent by the passage of the years; the skin hung in thick folds around her neck, and her face was furrowed with deep lines.

But the limpid brown eyes were still alert, still the eyes of Miriam Richardson—his mother.

"Yes?" she said, resting one arm on a cane.

"Are you Mrs. Jason Richardson? Miriam Richardson?" he asked.

"Yes, I am." She looked surprised to find somebody asking for her.

"Mrs. Richardson, my name is Gregory Thomas. I'm a writer and I'd like to talk to you, if I may?"

This was his own mother who stood looking placidly at him, her voice quivering with age. "A writer, you say? My son was a writer."

"I know, ma'am. I'd like to talk to you about him."

"About him? He's been dead for many years."

"Yes, I know. Do you think I could come in?"

She inspected him slowly. Old people don't invite strangers into their homes in Oakland. Then she rapped her cane sharply on the floor. "Yes, come in. Come in. Excuse my manners."

He followed her into the house, slowing his steps down to match her shuffle. They sat down in the living room. It had hardly changed in forty years. The piano in the corner, the same pale-green couch, even the picture above the fireplace, its glass now browned with dust. *Birds in Flight*, it had been called. This had been his home.

She took a long time settling into a comfortable position on the couch. Finally, she crossed her legs at the ankles, and looked over at him.

"Mr. . . . Mr. . . . er . . ."

"Thomas," he supplied. "Gregory Thomas."

"Mr. Thomas, would you like some coffee?"

"No, thank you," he said, eager to talk, yet apprehensive.

"Are you sure?"

"Thank you, yes," he said, imagining how long it would take those arthritic hands to prepare a pot of coffee.

"Well, what, er, what was it you wanted, Mr. Thomas?"

He wanted to take this frail old woman in his arms and hold her. To tell her that the lines that grief had plowed into her face were not necessary, that nothing of value ever really ended, that she would once again be a laughing young girl with soft, smooth skin, glowing with new hopes, that she should have stopped mourning for him years ago, that he was fine, just fine, Mom.

But he could only look at her, and feel for her. There was nothing he could say.

"Mr. Thomas?"

He had been staring at her and seeing not this old woman nearing the end of her days, but the earnest young mother he had known, pretty in her own prim, serious way.

"Uh, yes, Mrs. Richardson," he said quickly. "I'm doing a book on Brooke Ashley, you see, and in view of the fact that your son almost married her, I wanted to get some information about him."

"Brooke Ashley . . . about him," she repeated. "Yes. Yes, he almost married her. Would have, but they died together in 1949 in a fire. A horrible fire. My husband and I, we never met her, but Michael said she was a lovely girl."

"Your husband? Is he still alive?" Gregory asked.

"No, he passed on in nineteen fifty-five," she said. "I'm alone now."

"Tell me about your son, please," Gregory prompted gently.

"Oh, yes, Michael. He was such a good boy, a writer in Hollywood. He wrote some fine films, did very well for himself. We were both very proud of him. He used to come and see us when he could. Even when he couldn't, he would write to us without fail. He was such a thoughtful boy. I still have his letters upstairs, you know." She smiled to herself.

"Do you think I could see those letters?" he asked eagerly. "It would help me get a better idea of what kind of man he was. Perhaps he mentions Miss Ashley in them?"

She thought about it briefly, then creaked to her feet. "I don't suppose it could do any harm. If you could come upstairs with me, I wouldn't have to carry the box down. I don't get around as well as I used to."

"Of course," he said. He moved beside her and held out his arm. "May I help you?"

She smiled gratefully, pleased by the attention, and took his arm. "It's nice to see a young person in this old house," she said. "I don't see very many these days."

"You have no relatives?"

"There's my brother Willie in the East, but he's getting old now. Haven't seen him for ten years or more. I still have a few friends in the neighborhood, though. But, of course, most of them have passed on or moved away, and the youngsters these days don't want to talk to an old lady who has nothing but memories." She sighed. "But I have no right to complain about my lot. All things considered, it's been a good life."

They reached the top of the stairs and went into her bedroom. She rapped her cane on a closet door. "In there," she said.

He opened the closet. It was filled with fine old dresses and dozens of pairs of shoes.

"It's on the top shelf," she said. "That brown box. Would you get it down, please?"

The box was heavy. He put it down on a chair, wondering how she could have carried it. She pointed to the bed, and he carried the box there. She sat down beside it and leaned her cane against the bedpost.

"My box of memories, I call it," she said, rummaging through it with a frail, liver-spotted hand. "Here."

She lifted out a stack of letters, held together with a frayed ribbon. He took it from her and looked around for a place to sit.

She patted the bed. "Sit on the bed, young man. Sit on the bed."

He carefully removed the ribbon and began to leaf through the letters. They were all type-written and signed, "Your Loving Son, Michael." Descriptions of Los Angeles, news of his work, and of some of his friends. The prose was of a type reserved for parents, the kind that makes one sound like a naive, good-natured child, still attentive, still trying hard at school.

He found the letter in which he had first told them about Brooke. There were the familiar consoling phrases about how well he was doing, and then, "... *and I recently met a wonderful girl. Her name is Brooke Ashley and she's an actress. One day she will be very famous, I think. You'll be surprised to know that I love*

*her very much and although it's premature right
now, I think we shall get married in the not-too-
distant future. I think you'll both like her a lot
and perhaps we'll come up to visit you one of
these days so that you can meet her."*

The memory of writing the letter came back
to him. It had been about a month after he had
met Brooke, although by then it seemed that he
had known her forever. He had felt very pleased
to be writing to his parents about her, for although they had never bothered him about it,
he knew they both wanted him to give up his
freewheeling lifestyle and settle down.

His thoughts were diverted by her voice. *My
mother's voice.* She was scrambling deeper into
the past. "I have some things that belonged to
Michael here. Most everything he owned was
burned in the fire, but they sent me the few
things that survived."

She pulled out some cuff links, a tie pin, a
watch, a small clock, a ring. Gregory picked up
the ring. It was heavy, thick gold. In its center
was a black stone carved in a *fleur-de-lis*.

It was the ring he had seen in his dream!
The dream where he stood on the hill with
Brooke, looking down at Los Angeles, his hands
on her shoulders, a ring on his finger.

The old lady chatted on, although she had
lost her audience. Brooke had given him the ring.
"It will always remind you of my love for you,"
she said. "And whenever I see it, it will remind
me. It's our magic ring," she had added laugh-
ingly. She had slipped it onto his finger, her
hand so cool, her face intent.

Something the old woman was saying jerked
him back into the present. ". . . and although
I never met Miss Ashley, I'm sure she was a

lovely girl, which is more than I can say for her mother."

Her mouth was pursed in disapproval. Gregory asked what she meant.

"She never liked my son. She wanted us to discourage him from marrying her daughter."

"She spoke to you about this?"

"She wrote us a letter." She delved into the box again. "It's in here somewhere still, I think. Here it is. I don't like to speak ill of the dead —but that woman! There must have been something wrong with her."

Gregory took the letter from her hand and opened it. The handwriting was small and somehow spiteful in its cramped style.

"Dear Mr. and Mrs. Richardson," it said. *"As you probably know, your son Michael has been seeing my daughter, Brooke Ashley, a great deal. It is my belief that continuation of the relationship between them is in neither of their best interests. I would like to come and visit you in Oakland to discuss the situation with you. I am sure that once we talk you will both understand why it is best that they discontinue seeing each other. I look forward to hearing from you. Yours Sincerely, (Mrs.) Eleanor Harvey."*

"Did she come and see you?" Gregory asked.

"Oh, dear, no. I wrote back to the lady and told her I'd never before interfered in my son's personal life and I didn't intend to start then. We never heard from her again."

"That was very loyal of you," Gregory said.

"Well, Michael was a good boy. Oh, he was a little wild, but then all the young people were pretty wild after the war, weren't they? I felt sure that he would do the right thing."

At last, Mrs. Richardson began to put her mementos back into the box, her hands lingering on certain items, her eyes shuttered by the past. When she came to the ring, she held it in her hand and looked at it fondly.

Then she looked up at Gregory and smiled, her face curiously coy for a moment.

"It's a shame that this ring just sits in this old box. You've been very nice to a lonely old woman, young man. I'd like you to have Michael's ring. Perhaps you will remember our visit when you look at it."

He walked over and hugged her. "You're a lovely lady, Mrs. Richardson. I promise, I'll never forget our visit."

When they got back downstairs she offered him coffee again. This time he accepted. While she put the pot on in the kitchen, he walked out onto the back porch.

The yard was smaller than he remembered, little more than a patch of overgrown grass now. He went back into the kitchen and asked if the yard had always been that size.

"Oh, no," she said. "It was much bigger. There was a big oak tree in one corner and I had a large garden planted. But after Jason died, I sold it, and that house in the back now sits on the land."

So much for tradition, he thought. In adult life, everything is supposed to look smaller than remembered as a child. But this time the yard was smaller. It no longer contained the huge oak, and, most important of all, his treehouse.

They sat in the kitchen, drinking coffee and chatting. Gregory was relieved to find that Jason had left her well provided for. The sale of the land in the rear had been an added bonus. He had been casting around for an acceptable way in which he might contribute to her support. But still, she was lonely and old and he promised that he would visit her as often as possible and write regularly.

When he was leaving, she stopped him at the door with a hand on his arm and asked him again what he did. "You said you were a writer?"

"I'm actually a film writer," he explained, "but I'm doing a book on Miss Ashley first. Then I'll write the film script."

"My son Michael was a film writer," she exclaimed, then chided herself. "But, of course, you know that. How silly of me." She looked up at him then for a long moment, her eyes soft. "You know, there's something about you, young man, that reminds me of my son. He was such a fine boy. And I'm sure you are, too."

Chapter Fifteen

"WHAT DO YOU DO, if I may ask?"

The man in the plane returning to Los Angeles leaned toward Gregory, a friendly smile on his face.

Gregory told him what he did and the man allowed himself to be impressed. He'd seen Gregory's last film, it turned out, and wanted to talk about it. "I'm in the import business; electronics. Stereos, television, that stuff. But I like films," he said, as if art and life were two incompatible entities.

Gregory didn't want to talk, he needed to think. He managed to refuse the man's offer of a drink without offending him by announcing his desire for sleep. Adjusting his seat, slipping a pillow behind his head, he closed his eyes and retired to inspect his private memories.

Brooke's mother. Reading the letter Eleanor Harvey had written to his mother had jogged his memory. Something he had forgotten. The time she came to visit him . . .

He had just moved into the new house above Franklin Avenue earlier that week. He had chosen the brightest room in the house to use as his study, an airy space lined with windows that were brushed by blue sky and tangled shrubbery. He was working there when she came.

He had completed the script for *The Flight of an Eagle* a few weeks earlier. It had worked out well. Harry Shankman had liked it, bought it, and chosen it as a vehicle for Brooke to star in, just as they had intended. Now he was using the time to work on one of the novels he had always wanted to do. Brooke had pushed him into it, although, in truth, he hadn't needed much encouragement. For the first time in his life he felt confident enough to take it on. Knowing Brooke had evened his life out into controllable segments, given him some order, eradicating most of the confusion that had driven him and tossed him around like a leaf in a whirlpool.

He stopped in mid-sentence when the doorbell rang, stubbed out his cigarette, and went to answer it.

Brooke's mother stood there. He was surprised to see her. Since Brooke had moved into her own apartment, he hadn't seen her at all. Before that, after the initial interrogation when he had started to take Brooke out, their conversation had been limited to the mildest social intercourse.

"May I come in, Michael?" she said.

"Of course," he said, recovering from his surprise. "Come in, Mrs. Harvey."

He took her coat and led her into the living

room. "Would you like a cup of coffee or a drink?" he asked.

"No, thank you." She chose an armchair and sat with her knees together, her hands resting on its arms.

He went to the couch and leaned forward with his elbows on his knees. "It's nice to see you again, Mrs. Harvey," he said politely. "What can I do for you?"

She took her time replying, crossing her legs to get comfortable, and showing a slim calf. She was still a good-looking woman, with pitch-black hair pulled back into a long plait. She was totally unlike her daughter, with broad, Teutonic features that gave her face a flat, watchful look. Although her figure was still good, she had begun to thicken around the waist and neck. Brooke had once described her to him as "totally selfless." Brooke had added, "She gave me everything. Gave up her life because she wanted me to become a star." Michael, instinctively distrustful of all forms of altruism, had wondered if her conduct had been selfless, or motivated by a much deeper selfishness. He hadn't made up his mind.

"I want to talk to you about Brooke," she said.

"What about Brooke?"

"I want you to stop seeing her."

Michael struggled against a rising flush of anger.

"Would you care to explain exactly what you mean?" he said carefully.

She looked coolly over at him, her face impassive, her voice even. "We are both adults, Michael, and we both want what is best for

Brooke, so I will assume that we can speak freely to each other."

"By all means," he said, still maintaining a facade of politeness and control.

"The simple fact is that you are not what is best for her. You are not what she needs," she said.

"What right have you to judge who is best for her?" he asked tersely.

"A mother's right," she said, imbuing the phrase with divine authority. "So far, I have guided her well, don't you think? Soon she'll be one of the best-known actresses in the world. She has a great career ahead of her, and I don't intend to allow her to jeopardize it in any way. Least of all for a common screenwriter."

Michael managed to ignore the insult. "Don't you care about Brooke's feelings in this? What she wants?" he asked, awed by her singleminded callousness.

Her composure slipped a notch. Her mouth tightened and the muscles of her jaw flexed. "My only thought is for her true interests. Her long-range interests. I have always known what is best for her. For some reason, where you are concerned, she has lost her judgment." She gave a derisive little laugh. "Love! Marriage! These are indulgences she can't afford. Not even with someone worthy of her. These are things for ordinary people. She is hardly an ordinary girl. Brooke has a destiny to fulfill. Do you think I am going to allow such a thing as animal sexual attraction to spoil that destiny?"

Michael got up and stood in front of her. He was furious, but he spoke calmly. "No, Mrs. Harvey. No. I agree that Brooke is not an ordinary girl. But that's about the only thing you've said that I agree with. Brooke is totally extraordinary and unique. Too extraordinary to be manipulated by you for the rest of her life. She knows what she wants, and if it doesn't happen to coincide with your desires, you'll just have to step aside. She's a big girl now, with her own hopes and plans. You can't even see the real Brooke anymore—all you see is your own dream. Well, she has *her* dreams now, and you'd better recognize them, or you'll lose her completely."

She pointed a trembling finger at him. "You . . . you've poisoned her mind, changed her values. Before she met you, everything was perfect. Now she's talking about marriage . . . becoming a mother. It's all your doing."

Michael cut her off with a movement of his arm. "Listen to me," he said. "This will probably come as a shock to you, but Brooke wasn't really happy before she met me. You were just too blind to see it. Yes, we've talked about marriage and children, but I've never tried to influence Brooke to give up her work, and never will. If she decides to do that, it will be her own decision. But if she *does* decide to do that, if that's what she really wants, I'll back her every step of the way. And nothing you do can change that!"

Mrs. Harvey rose to her feet. Her face had paled, giving her rouged cheeks a crimson glow. She didn't bother to hide the malice in her eyes. "I can see there's no point in talking to you," she said stiffly. "But you haven't heard the last of this. I'm going to stop this nonsense any way I can. You're not good enough for my daughter and never will be. I'm going to do everything in my power to see that you don't get her."

She turned and stalked toward the door. Michael put his hands on his hips and smiled grimly. "Lady, if it's a war you want, you've got it. I warn you, though, you're going to lose it."

She turned in the doorway and looked at him contemptuously, her lips drawn back. "Michael, as you'll find out, I *never* lose."

Gregory opened his eyes and straightened up in the seat. The man sitting beside him looked over.

"Well, back to the land of the living, hey?" he said jocularly. "Have a good sleep?"

"Yes, thank you," Gregory said. He looked out of the window at a cloudless sky. In spite of Michael's brave exterior, he knew that the scene with Brooke's mother had been a nightmare. Michael hadn't underestimated the seriousness of her declaration. Even now, Gregory realized, his stomach was knotted up exactly as it had been when Mrs. Harvey had trounced out of the house, slamming the door behind her.

He turned to the man beside him and forced a smile. "I'll have that drink now, if the offer's still open," he said. "On second thought, I'd better pay for it myself. I'm going to make it a double."

Chapter Sixteen

IT WAS ALL SUDDENLY too much for him to take. It was three in the afternoon when Gregory arrived home from Oakland. Instead of parking in the garage, he pulled up in front of the house and sat there for a while with his back hunched and his hands tight on the steering wheel. He felt an icy chill permeating his entire being.

He closed his eyes and rested his forehead on the wheel. It was too much for an ordinary man to bear. And yes, perhaps as one among a million, he had been destined to remember his immortality; yet, by God, he told himself, he was still just an ordinary man. He had no special qualities that would lighten the load he was carrying. Wouldn't he be better off if he could somehow deny his experiences? How comfortable it would be to return once more to a state of ignorance, struggling through each day the same as everybody else and winning just enough to keep from losing.

What were his chances of winning this strange new game? Winning meant finding Brooke and regaining what they once had. No guarantee of that, even if he did find her. But finding her! That in itself seemed a hopeless quest, impossible for an ordinary man with his feet in the mud, his head in the stars. And even if he found her, would that mean playing out the game to the same horrible ending?

At the party the other night he had asked Lion a leading question. *The* leading question, as far as he was concerned. God knows, enough men had cried it out through the ages. "Who am I?" he had said.

Lion had tried to explain his beliefs, and at first it had sounded like the same concept Olga had conveyed to him. But then Lion had taken it to a more practical level.

"Now close your eyes," he had told Gregory.

Gregory closed his eyes.

"Good. Now get a mental picture of an orange cat."

Gregory nodded that he had done so.

"Okay. Now, who's looking at the cat?"

"I am," Gregory said.

"Right," Lion said. "That's who you are. The entity that perceives, understands, decides, creates. Ask any of today's materialistic scientists the same question and they would claim that the cat was being viewed by the brain, the computer's circuitry. But their thesis is neglecting an important fact, and that is that someone had to be programming the computer of the brain. And that's you, the programmer."

"But what am I?" Gregory had asked.

"Well, one thing's for sure. You're not your leg, your arm, or any other part of your body, including your brain. You're a spiritual entity, not a material entity. You *have* a body, but you aren't that body."

Gregory had still looked puzzled. "Listen," Lion said. "The reason it's so hard to understand something so basically simple is that we think of 'things' in material terms. You say, 'What am I?' and you mean 'What thing am I?' You mustn't look at it in that frame of reference. You are not a material thing, you are a creator of things, an immortal being."

Gregory loosened his grip on the steering wheel. His knuckles had turned white. Yes, he said to himself, I concede that I'm an immortal being. How does that help me now? How does it help me find Brooke?

Gregory climbed slowly out of the car, straightening his legs like an old man. He was overwhelmed by the length of the road to Brooke. He tried to tell himself that this mood was a temporary thing, probably brought about by remembering the scene with Brooke's mother. He shouldn't allow himself to get so discouraged. He had no other choice but to see it through, and he shouldn't allow his own thoughts to cripple him. He was progressing slowly enough as it was, without creating artificial limitations.

He unlocked the front door, picked up the mail, and put it on the hall table. The house seemed gloomy and oppressive. It had never struck him that way before. He got a beer from the kitchen and then whistled for Felix from the back door.

The cat came bounding from the shrubbery. Suddenly, Felix stopped about six feet away from the door and looked up with a plaintive expression. He still wouldn't come into the house. Gregory shook his head and left the door open anyway.

He went to the living room and checked the telephone. There was a message for Sharon, which he scrawled on a note pad, and a message for him to call his agent, Willmer. He dialed the number and the secretary put him through immediately.

"Hey, babe," Willmer said buoyantly. "I'm having a party tomorrow night. Just a few people. Can you and Sharon come?"

It was the last thing in the world he felt like doing, but he said yes, remembering his promise to spend more time with Sharon. She would probably enjoy it. Make a lot of new contacts, he thought sarcastically. Willmer's idea of "just a few people" was anything under fifty.

He took a long swallow of beer from the bottle. The mail. He carried his bottle into the hall with him and leafed through the bundle: bills, circulars, flyers—a letter addressed to him. He flipped it over. No return address, front or back.

He carried it back to the living room and sat down. Placing the bottle on a table, he tore the envelope open.

His heart stopped. Then it started again and raced at twice its normal speed. But the blood still didn't reach his face, which was as white as the paper he was holding.

The letter was neatly typed. It said:

I warned you to stay away from Brooke. This is the last warning. Stop trying to find her. STOP NOW BEFORE IT IS TOO LATE! You were responsible for her death. Do you want to destroy her again?

The letter was signed in ink. *Eleanor Harvey*.
The paper fell from Gregory's hand and landed on the floor. He couldn't move to pick it up.

When Gregory could function again, he tried to compare in his mind this signature to the one he had seen in Oakland. He thought they were the same, but he couldn't be sure. The small, neat script looked exactly as he remembered, but he needed to know positively.

He went to the telephone.

"Mr. Tanner? This is Gregory Thomas. I came to your house the other day with Olga Nabakov."

"What's that? Oh, yes. Yes, Mr. Thomas," Tanner said eagerly, another lonely old soul starved for communication.

"You might be able to do me a favor, Mr. Tanner. Among Miss Ashley's possessions, do you have any letters from her mother?"

Tanner hesitated. "Uh . . . yes, I think I do. I think there are some letters she wrote to Brooke while she was on location somewhere."

This was exactly what Gregory had hoped. "Mr. Tanner, could I come over now and see them? It would be a great help to me. For my book, you know?"

Tanner was more than willing to help. He told Gregory to come right over.

Gregory ignored the speed limit. He leaned on his horn, took chances passing cars, forced pedestrians to wait at crosswalks, a cardinal sin in California. He didn't care. He had to know.

He told himself again and again that it was impossible. Dead people don't write letters, not even in this crazy twilight zone he had stepped into, where everything was not only possible, but likely to happen. How in hell did he know what was possible, anyway? He was like a blind man in a maze of mirrors. But the letter *was* real.

What was it Olga had said? "Fear breeds fear and creates weakness." Right. So, if the signature was genuine, he'd at least know who the enemy was. He slowed down as he entered the Strip, calming himself a little. Anyway, a letter couldn't hurt him—even if it was written by a ghost.

He almost passed Tanner's house and braked sharply just in time. Tanner answered the door, wearing the same gray pants and glossy black shoes he had worn before. He half-bowed in a courtly, old-fashioned manner. "Come in, young man, come inside."

He ushered Gregory in, patting him on the shoulder. "I found the letters you wanted. I have them all ready for you in the living room. Would you like something to drink?"

Gregory declined and Tanner motioned toward an armchair where he could sit. He scuffled over to the mantel and picked up three yellowing envelopes.

"These three are all I could find," he said. "I hope they're what you want."

"I'm sure they are," Gregory said, taking them. He needed to get Tanner out of the room. "By the way, could I see the silver locket I saw the other day, the heart-shaped one with the round turquoise stone in it?"

"Yes, I'll get it for you," Tanner said. "Just make yourself comfortable."

Tanner left the room and Gregory quickly took the paper he had received in the mail from his pocket and spread it on his knees. He opened one of the envelopes Tanner had given him and took out a single brittle sheet. He didn't bother reading it—just opened it and placed it next to the sheet on his knee.

"Mother." It was signed "Mother"! Damn, of course! He should have thought of that. The handwriting looked the same, but he needed to compare an actual signature to be sure.

He hurried down the passage to the room where Brooke's belongings were kept. Tanner was bending over a drawer, looking for the locket.

"Mr. Tanner?"

"Eh?"

"Actually, I need to see a paper with Eleanor Harvey's signature on it. I have a document and I want to see if it's genuine. These letters were signed 'Mother.' Do you have anything that might have her full signature on it? A birth certificate? Something like that?"

He handed Tanner the three letters. The old man said, "Now, where did I get these?" He went to another drawer. He pulled out a cardboard box and handed it to Gregory.

"There might be something there," he said. "I think Brooke's birth certificate is there. I know I have it somewhere. Why don't you look through all this while I find the locket."

Gregory pawed through the papers. Contracts, letters, pictures. No birth certificate. But there was a check. It was made out to Brooke for $110 and it was signed by her mother. It had never been cashed, but he didn't waste any time trying to figure out why; he just whipped the paper from his pocket and compared the signatures.

There could be no doubt. It was her signature. They were the same, right down to the last little curlicue.

Eleanor Harvey had written the letter he had received. It wasn't possible. But it had happened.

He folded the note slowly and put it back into his pocket. Then he put the check back into the box and closed it. His mind refused to function. It couldn't come up with any explanations, logical or otherwise.

Tanner walked over with the locket. Gregory took it from him gingerly, remembering what had happened when he had held it the time before, but now the silver felt cool and smooth against his skin. He thought of what Olga had said about the trick catch. He pressed a tiny lever, but nothing happened.

Tanner chuckled.

Then it all came back to Gregory. He pressed simultaneously at two points which lay at about two and eight o'clock on each side, and the locket snapped open. Tanner was astonished.

The locket contained a small photograph— and the face staring back at him with a slightly sardonic smile was his own. Not his as he knew it now, but the face of his previous identity, Michael Richardson. Rugged features, lazy brown eyes.

"That's Michael Richardson, the man she fell in love with," Tanner said sadly.

Gregory snapped the locket closed. "Mr. Tanner, would you consider selling this locket? You see, it has great sentimental value to me. Michael Richardson was a distant relative of mine." He was becoming a convincing liar these days, Gregory thought. But he consoled himself that it wasn't really a lie.

Tanner looked undecided. He licked his bottom lip tentatively. Obviously he hated to part with anything belonging to Brooke. The man had his own obsessions.

"Look, Mr. Tanner," Gregory said persuasively. "You've got a drawer full of jewelry. One piece won't make any difference to you. What's more, it has a picture in it of a man you surely didn't like, the man who took Brooke away from you. I'll pay you a collector's price for the piece."

Tanner's brittle eyes flickered. Gregory suspected he could use the money.

"Well, I suppose so," Tanner said.

"How much do you want for it?" Gregory asked, throwing finesse to the winds. He hadn't expected Tanner to respond to an offer of money.

"No, you can have it, Mr. Thomas," Tanner said. "As a friend of Olga's, I couldn't charge you for it."

Gregory reminded himself never to jump to conclusions. "Mr. Tanner, I appreciate that very much, but you paid for it when you bought it from the estate, so at least let me reimburse you. Really."

Tanner shrugged his bony shoulders helplessly. "I've no idea how much it cost. It was so long ago."

"Does five hundred dollars sound fair?" Gregory persisted.

"I suppose so, but . . ."

"No. I'm going to write you a check for that amount. I insist, Mr. Tanner. I wouldn't feel right about it unless you let me pay."

Tanner gave in and Gregory wrote him a check.

"Will you send me a copy of the book when it's done?" Tanner asked, taking the check.

In spite of his waning resolve to finish the book, Gregory assured him he would send an autographed copy. He did attempt to explain, however, that it was actually a work of fiction only loosely based on Brooke.

His words went straight through Tanner. Perhaps the only word he heard was "Brooke," because he looked at Gregory with moist eyes and said, "She was a great and wonderful woman, you know, and the world should know it. You must tell them how remarkable she was. Such a wonderful girl, such a . . ."

His voice trailed off and he stood there, breathing heavily, his eyes turning inward, not seeing Gregory or anything else in his present environment, his mouth relaxed in a strange half-smile, a victim of his past.

On the way down the serpentine road, Gregory decided to see Olga. He turned off into her driveway and pulled up in front of the house. The sprinklers were on, creating dozens of miniature rainbows. Birds circled the lawn, searching hopefully for careless worms.

Olga smiled in surprise when she opened the door. "Gregory! I didn't expect to see you. Come in."

He sat with her at the kitchen table. "Sorry to drop in unexpectedly like this, but I was up at Tanner's house and I decided to see you."

"I'm glad you did," she said. "What were you doing at Bill's house?"

"I wanted to check a signature." He pulled the note from his pocket and tossed it across the table.

She picked it up and read it, lifting one eyebrow. She put it down and looked at him. "My God!" she exclaimed.

"Yes. It's her signature."

She didn't speak, just frowned, and moved the sheet of paper in circles with her finger.

"What does it mean?" he said.

"I'm not sure," she replied carefully. "When did you get this?"

"It was in the mail today. I don't mind telling you it scared the hell out of me. I mean, it's totally impossible."

"It's not impossible. It's here."

"How?"

His question stumped her. "Tell me what you've been doing since I last saw you." She stood up. "Tea?"

"Yes, that would be good."

He talked to her as she moved around the kitchen preparing the tea. He left out his indiscretions, but he told her about some of the things he had remembered, about what had happened in his study, and the note there; his trip to Oakland. She interrupted with a few questions, but generally she was content to let him talk.

When he finished, she sat down and poured the tea, her movements delicate and sure, calming. She handed him his cup. "Well, let us see what we do know and then analyze things," she suggested.

She counted off the fingers on her left hand. "First, we know that you have been attacked on a psychic level. Second, we know that, more likely than not, this presence is Brooke's mother. Third, that she is also attacking you on a physical level. Fourth, that she hates you desperately and blames you for Brooke's death."

Gregory winced inwardly. It was a thought that hurt, one he hadn't been particularly willing to examine since he had received the letter. Maybe that was why he was unable to remember the night of the fire—his guilt had clouded his memory. If he had indeed been responsible for Brooke's death, he wondered whether he could live with the knowledge.

"So, where does that get us?" he asked, putting the thought away.

"Not very far," she said with a thin, humorless smile. "It still leaves a lot of possibilities."

"Like what?"

"Well, you are either being victimized by a disembodied ghost, or by someone that she has possessed. And it is more likely the latter, I think."

"How do you figure that?"

"A ghost could attack you on a psychic level, of course. But I find it hard to believe that a ghost could use a pen to sign a letter, seal it in an envelope, stamp it, and mail it. No, it looks as if a person did that. Somebody as real as you and I." Olga leaned toward him earnestly. "Strange things have happened to you, Gregory, terribly strange. But there *are* limits. Ghosts don't write letters, as I said. But a live person possessed by a ghost could."

"Possession?"

"Well, that's what I said. But not necessarily. There is another alternative. Just as you remember who you were, she could, too. She may be walking around in another body, male or female. Just as you did, she could have remembered what had happened and be acting out the same role."

"But that doesn't explain the powers she has."

"True. But I knew Eleanor Harvey, too. She was a strong woman. I have to admit that, even though I never liked her." Olga tapped her finger on the table and frowned. "Still, it does seem unlikely that her new incarnation would have developed these abilities so suddenly. Unless, of course, she was doing it on an unconscious level."

"How would that work?" Gregory asked.

"There have been cases, well documented, of children who had the ability to move objects around without touching them, particularly when in a highly emotional state. More often than not, they weren't even aware they were doing it, but they were doing it, nevertheless. Eleanor Harvey, now another person, could be doing something like this. Or, as I said, she could be doing it by possessing another person's body. The person involved might not even know it was happening."

"What defense do I have?"

"I don't know," Olga said. "You just have to meet each thing as it comes. Remember, you now know whom you are dealing with. That may be useful."

"Any way you look it at," Gregory said, "whether possessed or reincarnated, she must be insane."

"That," Olga said, "is the one thing we can be sure of. To carry on a vendetta like this is not rational. But remember, it is probably her hate for you that has driven her insane. Don't underestimate her."

"And on that cheerful note," Gregory said, rising with a grin, "I guess I'd better leave."

It was a show of bravado and they both knew it.

Driving home, Gregory felt somewhat reassured. It's the twentieth century, he thought; these things don't happen. He reached into his pocket for a cigarette and his fingers touched the letter. Suddenly sobered, he drove quietly, his eyes fixed on the road ahead.

Gregory had been home an hour when he heard Sharon drive up and park in the rear garage. Then he heard the scream.

It was shrill—so penetrating that it jerked him upright in his armchair. He bolted up and ran for the rear door, flicking on the outside light as he passed the switch.

He opened the door and Sharon came stumbling out of the shadows, screaming and sobbing hysterically. She threw herself at him. "Oh, God! Oh, God! Thank God you're here!"

"What happened? Sharon, what happened?" he held her to him and searched the dark with his eyes. He could see nothing out of the ordinary.

He led her, still crying, into the house. Her arm was wet. He took his hand off her and looked down at it. Blood.

"What happened?" he asked again.

"It was Felix," she said. "Felix attacked me."

"Felix attacked you?" he said stupidly.

"I was walking down the path and Felix attacked me. Oh, God, it was terrifying!" She broke into a fresh flood of tears.

Gregory held her closely, trying to soothe her, rubbing her back ineffectively. "Come on," he said. "Let's go to the bathroom and get you cleaned up."

There were three deep lacerations and a cluster of smaller scratches on her arms. He washed the cuts, poured disinfectant on them, taking care not to miss even the smallest mark, and bandaged them.

Sharon calmed down slowly, but he suspected she was in shock. Her eyes were wide and vacant, and every now and then she broke into uncontrollable spasms which shook her body.

He made her lie on the bed, covered her with a blanket, and left the room. He came back with a glass of whiskey. "Here, drink this," he said, sitting beside her.

She gulped it down eagerly and coughed and spluttered before falling back onto the pillow.

"First thing in the morning, we'll have a doctor dress those scratches properly," he said, trying to remember if cats carried rabies. He didn't think so, but it worried him.

She nodded. "Jesus, that was the freakiest thing that ever happened to me," she said. Her voice had regained some of its strength.

He was glad to hear her talk intelligibly. "Tell me what happened."

She moved onto her side and flinched. "Light me a cigarette."

"But you gave up smoking."

"I just started again."

He lighted two cigarettes and gave her one. She took a deep drag. "I parked the car in the garage and walked down the back path. It was dark, you know. All of a sudden, I heard a hissing sound. It scared the shit out of me, it was so sudden and unexpected. Next thing, a shape hurtled out of the bushes at my legs and attacked me. It was Felix. I tried to beat him off with my hands—like a dummy, not realizing what would happen to my bare arms." She shuddered. "Thank God, he didn't get my face!"

"Are you sure it was Felix? I mean, it sounds nuts. Felix wouldn't do anything like that."

She grabbed his arm tightly. "Of course, I'm sure. I saw him and you can see what he did. Greg, you've got to get rid of that cat. Put him to sleep. Anything."

He patted her hand consolingly. "We'll see in the morning. Right now I want you to get some rest." He pulled the blanket up over her shoulders. "I'm going to the den. I'll be back to check on you in a little while. Okay?"

He went back to the study and sat down, lighting another cigarette. Restlessly, he got up, went to the back door and opened it, whistling for the cat. He called its name, "Felix! Felix! Come here, boy."

There was a miaow, and he saw Felix approach the house. The cat stopped about six feet away and sat on his haunches, regarding him complacently.

Gregory took a step out onto the path toward his cat, watching for any threatening motion, feeling both nervous and foolish. He reached him and stopped, looking down at the animal.

Felix moved.

He rubbed his head against Gregory's leg. Gregory realized he had been tensing up; he exhaled slowly, allowing his body to relax. He bent down and put his hand on the cat's head.

He could feel the soft vibrations. Felix was purring.

Chapter Seventeen

THAT NIGHT, in spite of the seeming "reconciliation," Felix had still refused to enter the house. Gregory slept fitfully. In the morning, he and Sharon exchanged only monosyllables. He hadn't yet decided on what to do about the cat's attack on Sharon. The thought of having it destroyed repelled him. It would be like murdering an old and trusted friend. Sharon hadn't relinquished her demand, however. She'd mentioned it again in the morning. So he went into the garden to find Felix, to talk to him in their own manner and, finally, to reach a decision.

The cat didn't answer his whistles or his calls, and he walked around to the front of the house.

From a distance, the mass on top of the fence fronting the road looked like a pile of garbage someone had tried to throw over into the garden. But as he approached the fence, it slowly became obvious to Gregory that it wasn't garbage. He broke into a trot, and as he grew closer, he realized with mounting horror that it was a cat, and then that it was his cat.

He'd read somewhere that cats always land on their feet, and Felix had evidently tried. One spike had speared the soft underside of his belly, another his chest. Blood had run down the rods, gathered on the crossbar, and then dripped down to the concrete foundation where it formed a red stain.

Gregory stood, unable to move, his expression desperate. There was no way Felix could have jumped onto the spikes. The fence was five feet high. He must have been thrown by someone, something.

He climbed up onto the concrete and tried to pull the cat off, ignoring the blood as best he could. But the spikes were firmly embedded and it required an effort to pry the body loose. With a final tug, he pulled it off and jumped to the ground, holding the dead animal by the neck.

It must have required considerable force for the spikes to have penetrated this deeply. He examined the body objectively. The blood looked darker than normal, a fact that struck him as curious. Looking closer, he saw another oddity: the entire coat of fur seemed to have been lightly singed.

Gregory shook his head, dumbfounded. At last, he carried the cat over to the garage and grabbed a spade. Finding a soft patch of garden soil, he laid Felix down beside it, and began to dig. A cold fury gripped him as he bit the spade into the ground with short, powerful strokes. It had been a senseless atrocity and he wished with all his heart that there was something he could do, some vengeance he could inflict upon the person or thing responsible.

Sweat was pouring down his face and neck by the time the hole was deep enough. He dropped

Felix in and shoveled the dirt back without ceremony. He stamped the dirt down with his feet.
Then he took the spade back into the garage
and went to the house to clean up.

He washed the blood and sand off his arms,
wiped the perspiration from his face, gazed at
his reflection in the mirror. He looked a little
mad, he thought. His mouth was a hard, straight
line; his eyes wild and determined. If this was
intended to cow him, it had not achieved the
desired effect, for it had only intensified his
desire to strike back. If only there were a tangible enemy to attack.

Sharon came into the bathroom. "What are
you doing?" she asked. "Did you find the cat?"

"Yes," he said curtly. "I just buried it."

She lifted a hand to her mouth. "You killed
it yourself?"

"No. Somebody else did the job for me."

She was mystified by the tightness in his face,
the tautness of his voice. The skin on his face
was drawn back like a mask and he looked ready
to explode.

"What do you mean, Greg?" There was trepi-
dation in her voice, as if she was already afraid
of the answer.

He swung round and faced her, his voice con-
necting them like a wire, holding her in place,
his fathomless brown eyes boring into her. "I
found Felix impaled on the front fence. Somebody had thrown him down on top of it."

"What . . . who?"

"I don't know," he said. "But I'll get . . ."

"Who?" she said. "Get who?"

"I don't know. Forget it. It's over, done.
There's nothing we can do about it now."

"But that's terrible," she said. "That's the

most vicious thing I've ever heard of."

"Well, you wanted the cat dead, didn't you?"
He knew he shouldn't have said it. It was unfair,
but he had to lash out in some direction.

Her face flushed and she glared at him angrily.
"Yes, I did. But not like that. And you know it!"

"Of course I do. Please forgive me."

Sharon looked at him narrowly. "As long as
you're okay," she said uncertainly. Then she did
one of those quick-changes that always amazed
him. "Listen, I've got to go on a call. I'm late
already. But I'll be back for dinner. Then we're
going to Richard's party, right?"

Gregory wanted to describe the tangled mess
of Felix's guts to her, shock her, scream, "This
isn't a movie, goddammit! This is life!" But
there would be no point to it.

"Yes, we're still going to the party," he said
heavily. He smiled sardonically. "You might
make some valuable contacts there."

She tried to read his eyes, but there was
nothing there except some deep resolve that
made her feel vaguely frightened. She dropped
her gaze and kissed him on the cheek. "See you
later, Greg," she said.

He nodded. After she had gone, he leaned on
the sink and dropped his head. If only there was
something he could do. The waiting was chipping
away at his reserves—waiting for the next thing
to happen and then not being able to do anything about it except wait for more. It was
chipping at him. Chipping.

Gregory spent the rest of the day working.
He'd decided to continue the book in spite of
everything. It was the ideal palliative. Brooke
could be lost in eternity, the devils could be

knocking his walls down with battering rams or torturing him with spite, but he knew that as long as he could work, he could maintain some control over his life.

By night, he felt more able to face the party. The work had gone well and cheered him considerably. He even surprised Sharon with a show of affection. It wasn't hard for him to do; she looked ravishing in a long red dress, her black hair braided in a plait down her back, her face flushed and excited. The long sleeves of her dress covered the marks on her arms. It was as if nothing had happened.

Gregory felt both admiration and affection toward her for her resilience. If all it took was a party to get her out of a slump, it was perhaps nothing but self-indulgence that allowed him to wallow in the depression and doubt that had been seizing him recently. That realization, together with his newfound resolve to somehow give back as good as he was getting, combined to elevate his mood, not to a point that equaled Sharon's, but at least to where her high spirits did not irritate him.

Richard Willmer lived in Pacific Palisades on a hill overlooking the ocean, and during the long drive down Sunset, Gregory managed to sustain an amusing conversation, delighting Sharon and surprising himself.

Their host greeted them at the door, hugging Gregory warmly and kissing Sharon while complimenting her on her appearance. When he inspected Gregory, however, he grimaced, and told him he looked as if he had been working too hard.

"Don't complain," Gregory joked. "I do it just so you can keep up payments on this house."

Willmer laughed, showing teeth that looked as if they had never been used before. He looked as trim as a shark in fashionable blue jeans and a white silk shirt with a wide collar.

"I won't talk shop again tonight, but how's the book coming?" he said to Gregory in a low voice.

"I'm a little behind—did more research than I'd expected," Gregory said blandly. "But it's coming along fine now."

"Good! Good!" Willmer said, rubbing his hands together energetically. He led them to the bar. "This barman can mix everything you've ever heard of," he said.

Gregory ordered a margarita, Sharon a screwdriver. The party was already well under way. There were about forty people so far, most of them in the living room, although a large group had swirled out to the patio for a view of the ocean and to sit around the lighted pool.

Gregory found himself talking to Willmer's girl friend of the moment, a vapid blond actress named Gloria with a beautifully bounteous body that oozed sex. Willmer had dragged Sharon across the room to "meet some people you should know."

"You don't look as if you've been working too hard," Gregory said, "so I imagine you have been."

"Ooh, yes," she said breathily. "I hardly have any time to play with Richard these days. I just did *The Return of the Ant Men* with Blake Connors. It was such a demanding part, I was just exhausted afterward and had to go to Acapulco for a week to recover." She gushed on, gathering steam, jumping from one subject to the next, now touching his hand, now his elbow, never missing a moment of the action in the room around her, yet trying to give the impression that she was entranced by his sparkling company.

After running through her Acapulco trip, her list of credits, her tastes in music, food, drink, and men, she asked him what films he had produced recently.

"I'm a writer," he said.

She turned blank eyes on him. "A writer?" She gave the word a connotation that ranked it with waiters, film editors, union cameramen, insurance salesmen, and other occupations that couldn't possibly assist her career.

He began to tell her what he did, but he could see he'd lost her. Her eyes drifted off, calculating her next move with predatory finesse. It came when she saw somebody across the room. She waved enthusiastically, throwing her head back in what was intended to be a joyous smile of recognition and welcome. She put her hand on his arm one last time. "There's Billy and Dee, such nice people. You do know them, don't you? I must go over and say hello to them," she said, wriggling her fingers at him and darting across the room, all flash and glitter.

Gregory wandered back to the bar and ordered another margarita. He sauntered out to the patio. He leaned on the railing and looked out at the blackness of the ocean, momentarily filled with that longing the sea always gave him. There was no fog, for a change, and an ocean liner traveling north along the horizon looked like a Chinese lantern with its winking crystalline lights.

There was a soft footfall behind him, a hint of familiar perfume, an amused voice.

"Have you been following me?"

He half-turned and saw Jenny Royal. "No, I thought you were following me," he said.

She leaned on the rail beside him and looked out into the darkness. Dressed in tight slacks and a casual turtleneck sweater, she looked trim and athletic, her tanned face glowing under the patio light.

"How've you been?" he asked her profile.

"Fine. And you?" she said self-consciously.

"Let's not pretend," he said. "I guess you expected me to call."

She bit her lower lip and half-smiled. "Not expected. I hoped."

"There's no future in it," he said. "I told you I was tied up with Sharon." He realized he sounded defensive.

"Oh, I know!" she exclaimed, swinging her head to face him. "I'm sorry. I didn't mean to imply that you had any commitment to me. It's just . . . we had fun, and I . . ."

"I like you a lot too, Jenny," he said, finishing the thought for her. "It sounds corny, but I like you too much to treat you to a series of one-night stands." He smiled. "Besides, I'm a lousy liar. I guess I'm not cut out for infidelity. I get guilty and regretful and into a bad scene with myself."

"Did you tell her?"

"Not that it was you."

"And you regret what happened?" she asked, her voice heavy.

He looked away from her and thoughtfully inspected his glass. The least he could give her was an honest answer. He thought back to the night they had spent together. He lifted his head and grinned.

"No. Not a bit," he said. "I loved it."

She clinked her glass against his in a silent toast, her sparkling eyes laughing above the rim of her glass.

"Well, I'd better split," she said. "If your girl friend spots me with you, she might jump to some nasty conclusions."

"I'll see you later, Jenny," he said.

"Is that just a figure of speech?"

"Let's see how time treats us, okay?"

She nodded, then turned quickly and walked back inside.

A few seconds later Sharon came up to him. She must have been sitting out on the patio, and he wondered guiltily how long she had been watching him. But he was relieved that she still sounded cheerful.

"Hey, party-pooper! Don't stand there by yourself. Come and meet some people."

He allowed her to drag him away, stumbled once, and realized that the margaritas had begun to go to his head. It was a sneaky, treacherous drink. She took him over to a large table where Richard Willmer was sitting with two couples.

"I was wondering where you'd disappeared to," Willmer said. He stood up and introduced Gregory to the others at the table. It was still fairly early in the evening, but a few minutes later, Gregory found an opportunity to draw Sharon aside and suggest to her that they leave. To his pleasant surprise, she agreed instantly.

On the way home, Gregory discovered soon enough that Sharon's amiability was nothing more than party manners. Sharon was indeed furious with him. At first, she hardly spoke. Then came a quick, lashing outburst.

"You bastard!" she said.

"What do you mean?" he asked innocently, armored by his margaritas and their cozy glow.

"You know what I mean. I saw you with Jenny Royal."

"Yes," he said. "I suspected that you did."

"She's the girl you spent the night with, isn't she?"

He ignored the stridency that crept into her voice. "Hell, Sharon. I'm a gentleman. A gentleman never tells."

She didn't speak again.

It was a dream like the others, and yet it was different.

The woman was there, but he was unable to see her. There was just the voice, that same harsh, malicious voice, grating at him with jagged edges.

"You were never good enough for Brooke, never good enough, never good enough, never good enough, never . . ."

The chant hammered remorselessly at him, its power and rhythm echoing through his being, bearing down on him and pushing him further and further into some deep abyss.

Then he became aware of more than the voice. A woman was standing over him beside the bed. Her hands were raised above her head and they were gripping the handle of a long, silver-bladed knife.

Soon, he thought fatalistically, it would descend in a flashing arc, and everything would be over. If only he could wake up. But he had never been able to awaken during these dreams.

And then he realized that the dream was over. He wasn't sleeping!

His eyes were open. The woman holding the

knife above him was Sharon. The voice, although it wasn't hers, was coming from her mouth. The knife was real, and if it entered his body, it would be thrust by the force of Sharon's arms. He lay paralyzed as the blade swung down.

But I'm not dreaming!

He rolled frantically to the other side of the bed. Heard the knife slash into the sheet. Felt his feet hit the floor. Watched Sharon move with slow purpose around the side of the bed toward him, the knife now gripped firmly in her right hand.

"Sharon! What the devil are you doing?"

But the voice wasn't Sharon's. "Never good enough, never good enough," it continued.

Her eyes were wide, empty, the eyes of a blind person. His horror increased when he saw that her face was smooth, peaceful, undistorted by the hate tumbling from her mouth.

She was trying to kill him!

The blade slashed at him again. He sucked in his stomach, backed up.

She began to swing it level with his stomach, like a machete.

"Sharon!" he screamed again. But it was useless. She could not hear him.

There was only one thing to do. He let her close in, backing up slowly, praying that he was judging the distance accurately.

She made one more swing with the knife and he felt the wind against his belly, saw her body twist to one side with the force of the blow.

He lifted his fist and hit her as hard as he could on the point of the jaw. There was a dull sound and her eyes turned glassy. The knife fell from her hand and her knees began to buckle. Slowly she toppled backward and fell.

He meant to take a step toward her to check if she was all right, but he couldn't make it. His legs had turned to jelly and were unable to support him. Instead he leaned back against the wall and sank to the floor beside her. Two rag dolls: one unconscious, the other petrified.

Chapter Eighteen

THE ROOM SEEMED CLOAKED in drama. Half of it was highlighted by the bedside lamp and the other half drifted into insubstantial shadow. Outside, close to the window, an owl hooted a forlorn message.

Sharon was as still as death. Her face looked as if it had been carved from white wax. When Gregory could finally move, he lifted her up onto the bed and felt her pulse. He had hit her hard, but her pulse seemed to be normal and she was breathing regularly. He sat on the side of the bed and waited for her to regain consciousness.

He looked down at her quiet features, wondering who would be there when she woke up, Sharon—or Brooke's mother?

After five minutes her eyelids began to flicker. Her hand moved to where he had hit her jaw and she groaned. Her eyes opened in cautious stages and focused slowly on his concerned face.

"What happened?" she said faintly. "What am I doing here like this?"

It was her normal voice, he noted with relief.

Another battle would have pushed his resources beyond the limits.

"You're okay," he said.

"What happened?" she repeated, her voice stronger now. She felt her face with tentative fingers and grimaced. "Why am I hurting, Greg?"

"I hit you," he said.

"What? Why? What happened?" She struggled up onto her elbows. "You *hit* me?"

"Yes. You tried to kill me." He bent down and picked up the knife from the floor. It was a kitchen carving knife about ten inches long, with a point as sharp as a needle. He showed it to her. "With this," he said.

She began to laugh painfully. "Come on, Greg. What sort of joke is this? What happened?" She pulled herself up and looked at him perplexedly.

"What's the last thing you remember?"

"We got back from the party. We went to bed. Why are you asking? Why in the hell is my face so sore?"

He looked at her without answering. Was she that effective an actress? He doubted it. She really didn't remember. Where did that leave him? What would she think?

"Gregory!" she demanded, her voice containing the first stirrings of fear.

"I already told you," he said evenly. "You tried to kill me."

Her eyes widened and her hand moved uncertainly up to her jaw again. The faintness reentered her voice. "You're crazy," she said, almost in a whisper. "What are you trying to do to me?"

He twisted the knife in his hands. It would have done a lot of damage.

"What's more to the point is what you tried to do to me," he said.

The attempt to question Sharon proved useless. She remembered nothing from the moment she had fallen asleep to when she had awakened with a swollen jaw to see Gregory looking down at her.

He told her what had happened, not mentioning the fact that she had been speaking in a strange voice. It would have involved laborious explanations that, more likely than not, she would not believe. It was already too much for her mind to accept. So he told her that she had come at him with a knife and attempted to cut him. After a while, facing the evidence of a rapidly darkening bruise on her jaw, she seemed to believe him, and indulged in a bout of self-recrimination. She had never before walked in her sleep, she said, but that must have been what had happened. He didn't dispute her. Finally he had given her a sleeping pill and suggested that she see a doctor in the morning to see if her blackout, if that's what it had been, had a physiological basis.

It was close to two-thirty in the morning when Sharon fell asleep. Gregory decided to take a walk. He was too agitated to sleep and he never used pills. He got as far as the front gate before changing his mind. The quiet tree-lined streets of Los Feliz weren't the panacea he needed. Solitude was filled with pitfalls. Better, he thought, to be among a comforting group of anonymous people.

Sharon's attack had shaken him up more than he had admitted to her. *She tried to kill me!* Perhaps on a lonely shadowed street he would not be able to resist the urge to scream it out. In the anonymity of a crowd there would be other things to occupy him and the full force of thought now buzzing through his mind would diminish.

He drove down to Hollywood Boulevard, parked a block above it on Las Palmas, and walked down. The boulevard was dotted with stragglers.

A tall black man, as skinny as a lamp post, stepped out of a doorway and asked him for a light. Gregory cupped a match in his palms and the man bent over, lighting his cigarette with one puff. He looked up, his eyebrows raised, his skin yellowing in the orange flame, eyes as black as volcanic rocks. Gregory started, moving back a half-step, certain for a moment that he was looking at the face of evil.

"Hey, man, you lookin' for some action?" the man asked in a hoarse, unnecessary whisper.

Gregory shook his head and dropped the match. He turned and walked away, not asking the nature of the action that had been offered. It could have been women, drugs, gambling, bestiality, sodomy, or murder—any of the myriad activities men indulged in when they were lost in a senseless city.

Two uniformed policemen walked by and gave him a hard look. They knew that normal people didn't drift through the streets at that time. A few yards behind them, a pair of homosexuals minced by, snickering, looking Gregory over boldly, causing him to scowl down at the star-studded pavement.

He entered an all-night restaurant, sat down in a booth, and ordered coffee and a toasted muffin. The coffee came from the bottom of the pot. It was too strong, bitter, as black as his thoughts. He sipped it without pleasure, eyeing the collection of late-night freaks gathered there like flotsam in a backwater.

She tried to kill me!

The threat no longer consisted of dreams and notes and overturned furniture. It was as real as cold steel. There was little doubt in his mind that Eleanor Harvey had somehow caused Sharon to act. Perhaps Sharon's enmity toward him after the party had made it easier for her to use Sharon's body for the attack, or to plant some kind of hypnotic suggestion. In the morning, after he had slept, he'd call Olga and tell her what had happened. Perhaps she would have some answers. He'd call her if he was still alive, he corrected himself. If the old bat could do that with Sharon, she might be able to do it with other people. It was a horrifying thought. Anybody in the restaurant could walk up to his table, pull out a gun or a knife, and kill him. He had to stop thinking like that, remain calm. Nothing would please her more than to know that he was trembling in his boots. There wasn't anything he could do about it now. He'd put it out of his mind as best he could until morning, he decided. Then he would speak to Olga.

Gregory realized that a man sitting at the opposite side of the aisle was looking at him strangely. There was an expression he couldn't read in the man's eyes. Was it recognition? Hope? The man dropped his eyes as if embarrassed when he saw Gregory looking at him. He seemed out of place in the restaurant: burly, mid-thirties, crew cut, neck beginning to turn flabby. Gregory guessed that he'd just gotten out of the armed services. Looking for a new life in the big city and finding the same crud he'd run away from in the first place. Gregory didn't care. He had problems of his own. He looked away disinterestedly.

What did Brooke's mother have against him, anyway? What had he done to earn such hate? Was he really responsible for the fire that had killed them all? *Please, God, don't let it be*. He couldn't remember. He tried again. That night, that night of flame and fury. Blank. What was the last thing he could remember of that life? He looked back. Brooke going away. The airport. A restaurant like this . . .

Brooke had refused to use the studio limousine so that Michael could drive her to the airport. She was going to New Orleans for a week to redo some location shots, the final work on the film, and they were both apprehensive. It was their first real separation. Yet they had never been closer. Michael had told her the day before about the visit from her mother, and this had served only to weld them together all the more. Brooke had immediately stormed over to her mother's apartment and warned her never to interfere with them again, unleashing her anger and, in the process, redefining their relationship. When she came back, she told Michael that her mother was not likely to give them further trouble. Silently, he doubted it. He remembered Mrs. Harvey's words when she had left his house: "I never lose."

On the Sunday of her departure, Brooke spent the afternoon at his house and they made slow, delicious love, sweetened by the impending separation. After a light dinner, they left the house early for the airport. He drove slowly, not wanting their time together to end.

When they arrived, he carried her bags to the counter and checked them in. There was almost an hour to spare, so they walked the long, tubular corridors together, holding hands and talking softly, two lovers, almost still against a backdrop of hurried, intent passengers and visitors.

They went to a restaurant and sat at the window. The landing lights looked like colored marbles thrown haphazardly onto a giant playing field.

Brooke was forlorn. Each cup of coffee brought them closer to good-bye. She wore a long fur coat, very little make-up, and her hair was pulled back with a silk scarf. It made her look five years younger, and terribly vulnerable.

"I'm going to miss you," she said.

"Mmm," he replied, eyes glinting. "That's too bad. I'm not going to have time to miss you."

"What do you mean?"

"Oh, you know. Parties up at the house almost every night. Naked broads running around. One in the closet while another's in the bed. You know, the usual."

She reached out and pinched his cheek softly. "You're terrible, Michael. I'm never going to be able to change you."

"Would you want—"

"No," she interrupted quickly. "I wouldn't want to. I love you the way you are."

"Ah," he said with a satisfied grin. "There's a woman with impeccable taste."

He continued the banter for a while and then suddenly broke off. He bent forward and cupped her face in his hands, staring with glum eyes at the portrait of her face. "I'm going to miss you desperately. God, I'm going to miss you! I don't know how I'll survive without you. In fact, it makes me wonder how I lived before I met you."

"I'll call you every night." She lowered her head and kissed his palm.

They got up and walked grudgingly toward the boarding area. He stopped when it came into view.

"Listen, I'm going to say good-bye right now. The whole film crew's there. It'll be pandemonium. Call me when you arrive at your hotel."

She nodded, her eyes silvery with tears. They kissed hungrily and he could feel the dampness on her face. He savored the sweetness of her mouth and then broke away.

"It's going to be all right. I love you, Brooke."

She nodded again, not chancing words.

He turned and walked away quickly, not looking back. He'd gone about twenty yards when her voice halted him.

"Michael!"

He turned. She stood where he had left her, hands in the pockets of her coat, a waif.

"Good-bye again," she shouted clearly.

He lifted a hand, then turned. This time he did not stop.

Gregory shook his head. He had to blink to realize he was still sitting in a restaurant on Hollywood Boulevard. That was his last memory of Brooke. From that point onward, the past had been erased. It might well have ended there, but the record told him differently. There had been a terrible fire. Other things must have happened.

He sighed and picked up the check. He started to slide out of the booth, but stopped when he noticed the man on the opposite side of the aisle.

The man was crying.

He sat there, as stiff as a totem pole, hands cupping his coffee, staring down at the Formica table top, unmoving, while the tears streamed down his face.

God knew what his problem was. Loneliness, a death, hopelessness. Perhaps, Gregory thought, he, too, had lost something very, very precious.

Gregory continued his passage into the aisle. First lesson in the city: Don't interfere. You mind your own business, keep your hands clean, your nose clean, and anything else you can think of clean. Guide to Survival. He walked away.

And yet. He turned impulsively and walked back. Put his hand on the man's shoulder.

"Listen, fellow. It's going to be okay. Everything's going to work out all right in the end."

The man lifted his head and looked blindly up at Gregory. His eyes were red with anguish.

He reached over, gripping Gregory's hand for a brief moment.

Gregory left. It was all he could do for either of them.

Chapter Nineteen

GREGORY'S HEAD FELT HEAVY, weighted down in a black fog. His tongue clung to the sides of his mouth, two scaly surfaces trying to sand each other down. He'd only had about four hours of restless sleep.

By the time he got up, Sharon had already left for the doctor. He found a note on the kitchen table, saying that she would call and let him know the results after she had been examined.

He made the coffee stronger than usual and brooded over the paper while he drank it. World news was grim as usual, but the entertainment section provided interesting relief. A local critic was announcing his selections for the Oscars, and Gregory's script was his choice for the best screenplay. It wasn't particularly encouraging; the man was notoriously wrong almost every year.

He got up and poured himself more coffee. The sun was casting its glow indiscriminately on the world below. A hummingbird hovered outside the window, trying to stare Gregory down, but as soon as he moved his head it darted away in a zigzag pattern. Its feathered cousins were making short work of the fig tree, cluttering the path with debris. He went back to the table with his cup and tried the sports pages.

As soon as the fog in his head lifted enough, Gregory tried to call Olga. The recorded message said she was out of town and wouldn't return until the following day. It asked him to leave his name and number. He complied irritably. No answers today.

No sooner had he replaced the receiver than the telephone rang. He picked it up again.

"Gregory Thomas," he said.

"Hi. How's the head today?" It was Richard Willmer.

"All right. I'm sorry I had to leave your party so early."

"Ah, that's okay," Willmer said. "How's the story coming?"

"Just the same as it was when you asked me yesterday," Gregory complained.

"Well, something's come up. Do you have an outline or anything to show? Bert Wolfe wants to see it. He's all fired up about the idea."

Wolfe was an independent producer, well known in the industry. He'd already optioned one of Gregory's earlier scripts.

"Yeah, I have a rough outline for working purposes," Gregory said dubiously. "But I thought we were going to wait. I'd do the book first and *then* you'd start hustling it?"

"Oh, you know me," Willmer said. "It won't hurt the book to hype it now."

"I have to type it up, smooth it out."

"Fine. Just get it to me as soon as possible. I'm meeting with him next week." Willmer was never one to miss a shot. "Did you see the paper this morning?"

"Yeah," Gregory said. "He's probably wrong again."

"Hell, what kind of attitude's that? Think positive, man. It's a good omen. The word is you can win. Right now you're front runner, babe."

"Well, I'll believe it when I see it. I'll have the outline to you in a couple of days," Gregory said, and hung up.

He was irritated, not with Willmer in particular, but with the entire system. Talk. The normally verbose industry reached new heights of loquacity during the period approaching Oscar time. The lobbying was as intense as anything going on in Washington. Awards meant fame, and fame meant money. In the weeks before balloting, the studios poured enormous sums into promotional campaigns designed to generate excitement for their products. Gregory didn't underestimate the importance of it. A nomination was an honor, but an Oscar was also worth its weight in gold, a bankable commodity. Still, he considered it a long shot in spite of Willmer's enthusiasm. No matter how fine the work or how expert the lobbying, the wild card was always sentiment, particularly among the older Academy members. The industry that had deluged the world with sentiment by the bucketful was not immune to it itself.

He would wait and see. No high hopes.

Sharon called at noon.

"I'm fine," she said.

"That's good," he said, even though he knew she wasn't. "What did the doctor say?"

"He took a bunch of X-rays and stuff. Other tests, you know. Some of the results won't be back until tomorrow. But he said that so far I looked fine—as healthy as a horse. No tumors, blood clots, anything like that to account for a blackout that he could see."

"So how did he explain it?"

"Well, he didn't really. He said it could be sleepwalking. Anyway, he just said I should eat better and get more rest." She sounded relieved at the mild cure.

"That's great."

"Well, I'm glad. You had me worried."

Not as worried as she'd had him, and the doctor's report didn't help. It only validated what he'd known all along. There was no physical reason for what had happened. And it sure as hell hadn't been sleepwalking. No way.

"Going to be home for dinner?" he asked.

"Yes. I'm going to do some shopping now. I need some new clothes. Everybody's seen me a dozen times in what I have."

"Okay, have a good time."

"I will," she said. "I'm celebrating my good health. See you later."

He heard the telephone click in his ear and hung up. Celebration seemed quite inappropriate to him. She had tried to kill him.

Olga wasn't around to help him, so Gregory did the next best thing, and called Bob Lion.

Couching the incident of the night before in hypothetical terms, he told Lion about it.

"Would you say it was some kind of possession or hypnotic trance?" he concluded.

"No, I don't think so," Lion said. "First of all, a trance, unless drugs are used, has to be induced knowingly by oneself or by another person. In your example, it doesn't seem likely. As for possession—hell, I don't know. I'm pretty much of the opinion that there's really no such thing. It seems to me that what they call possession is really being done by the person himself, although he may not be aware of it. He's just acting out something that happened in the past, maybe in another lifetime, but it's something that's still influencing him on a level below his present awareness."

"Well, how about the amnesia afterward?" Gregory asked.

"That's just an extreme example of a person saying that the buck doesn't stop here."

"How do you mean?"

"Well, the person is trying not to confront his actions. He finds it so difficult or abhorrent to take responsibility for them, he just blacks it out and pretends it never happened."

"So it's a self-caused thing?"

"Hell, yes," Lion said emphatically. "Listen, there's no such thing as loss of memory. Everything that's ever happened to a person is indelibly recorded. All that loss of memory means is that, for some reason or another, the person is refusing to look at it. God, even when a person is unconscious that little recorder is winding away, taking everything in."

"Yeah, I see what you're saying."

Lion's voice dropped a notch. "Listen. It's none of my business, but is there something you need help with? Trouble, I mean?"

Gregory suppressed the urge to blurt it all out, but the fact that Olga knew the story was

enough. It was not something he wanted to
spread around.

"No. No trouble, Bob. You've been a great
help. Thanks."

"All right," Lion said. "Call if you need me."

After he'd hung up, Gregory thought about
what Lion had said. He had to be wrong. Either
a trance had been induced somehow, by some
hypnotic method, or it was an out-and-out case
of possession. There were no other alternatives.
He knew as certainly as he felt the floor beneath
his feet that Eleanor Harvey had been responsible for Sharon's attempt to murder him.

He hadn't really intended to get to it for a
day or two, but it was an easy task, so Gregory
prepared the outline for Willmer. He needed an
easy task, one that didn't require a great deal of
thought or effort.

It was a simple matter of retyping the rough
outline he'd already written, and he finished it
in about an hour. The emptiness of the house
made him uncomfortable. He decided to drive
down to Willmer's office in West Hollywood and
drop it off.

It was a beautiful day. High thin clouds and
a light ocean breeze kept the temperature in
the comfortable seventies, and the smog had
been pushed out to Glendale and Pasadena, leaving Hollywood citizens nothing to complain
about. Without the intense sunlight, the colors
fronting the road lost their offensive glare and
dropped to more serene hues. Gregory allowed
the atmosphere to pervade him, relaxing as he
drove.

The girls on the street were pretty. His car
stalled at the traffic light near Motown Records

while he was watching a tall, majestic African queen cross the street, ass high, unhindered breasts swinging, really proud of the effect she was creating. A revelry of car horns spurred him on.

Willmer's office was at the foot of the Strip, on the tenth floor of a high-rise. It was surprisingly sedate and professional, considering Willmer's character and that of his peers. No giant posters on the walls, STOP signs on the receptionist's desk, exotic plants, or funky antiques— just a suite with thick carpeting, comfortable furniture, and dark wood paneling, giving it a rich feeling.

Willmer's secretary, Maggie, a short, stout redhead in her late twenties, was surprised to see him.

"Gregory! Hi. Was Richard expecting you?" she said uncertainly.

"No, Maggie, not at all. I'm just dropping something off. Is he tied up?"

"Well, yes, he has someone in with him right now, but he should be free in five or ten minutes. Can I get you some coffee?"

Gregory sat in an armchair while Maggie went to an alcove behind her desk to pour his coffee.

"Two sugars and cream, right?" her voice sang out.

"Right," he said.

She reappeared and handed him a mug of coffee.

"Richard told me about the story you're working on. I think it's a fantastic idea," she said.

"Thank you. I hope so."

"You're basing the female character on Brooke Ashley, aren't you?"

"Yes, I am."

"I just saw her in *The Flight of an Eagle*. She was really some actress. And what a beauty! What a tragedy that she died so young."

"Yes, a tragedy." Gregory looked at his watch.

"Let me buzz Richard and let him know you're here," she said conscientiously.

"No, don't bother," he said, getting to his feet. "Why don't you just give him this?" He handed the outline to her.

"You're sure? He'll just be a few minutes."

"Yeah, I'm sure. See you later."

"Okay," she said. "Have a nice day."

Gregory walked down the passage to the elevators. He pressed the DOWN button and waited. Such a tragedy that she died so young, Maggie had said. He marveled at how glibly people could treat real-life tragedy, as long as it happened to someone else. That, he supposed, turned it into make-believe tragedy, as if it were taking place on the stage or a motion picture screen. He didn't blame her at all; it was the way things were. It was just that it made him realize once again the full emotional isolation of the lonely bubble each person travels in.

Gregory dreaded the thought of sleep. He couldn't put his finger on the reason. He wasn't really afraid of a second murder attempt, he assured himself. Sharon had come home for dinner, then dashed off again to attend the screening of a new film at Universal Studios. She had tried to get him to go with her, but he had begged off, entering a plea of fatigue. It wasn't just an excuse to avoid a bad movie, for he was genuinely tired, exhausted, in fact. Yet when he went to bed at eleven, he found himself tossing and turning like a small boy being forced to take an afternoon nap.

He got up, slipped on a robe, and went to the kitchen. After examining the refrigerator and the well-stocked cabinet shelves, he decided on hot chocolate. He poured a cup of milk into a saucepan and put it on the stove, turning the heat on low point so the milk wouldn't scald.

Sharon's car crunched up the driveway and a couple of minutes later he heard her come through the back door.

"I thought you'd be asleep," she said, entering the kitchen. "What's happening?"

"Too restless," he said with a shrug. "I went to bed, but it didn't work."

"So what are you making?"

"Hot chocolate."

"Oh, make me a cup too, will you?" She kissed him on the cheek. "I'll go and change."

He poured another cup of milk into the pan and sat at the table while it heated up again. Sharon returned wearing a dressing gown and sat opposite him.

"How was the movie?" he asked.

"Yech!" she said disparagingly. "Two million dollars of yech."

"See anyone I know?"

"Richard was there. Oh, yes. He said to tell you he got the treatment and it was fine. He'll let you know how it goes. What treatment was he talking about?"

"Outline, actually," he said. "Bert Wolfe wanted to see the outline of the book I'm doing. He's interested."

"Hey, that's great," she said, with what seemed to be genuine enthusiasm.

Gregory got up and turned off the stove. He

spooned hot chocolate into two mugs and poured in the milk. "Too early to tell yet," he said. "You know all the talk that goes down."

"No harm in hoping," she said, taking the cup he handed her. "Anyway, didn't Wolfe buy one of your other properties?"

"Well, he took an option on it. But he hasn't done anything with it except pay me money."

"Poor Gregory. Crying all the way to the bank."

"How'd you like to get paid for a bit part and then have that scene cut out of the movie before it reached the screen. Real good for your career, huh?" Gregory retorted.

"True, true," she admitted.

The conversation safely changed to a discussion of her career. There seemed to be an unspoken agreement not to discuss the events of the previous night. Yes, thought Gregory, here we sit, silent witnesses to the mendacity of the human mind.

He chided himself for the uncharitable thought immediately. She had no understanding of what had happened and it probably terrified her almost as much as it did him. An explanation of sleepwalking was probably stretching it, even for her. Her only solution would be to try to forget it, or to deny it. A denial, however, would entail discussion, so forgetfulness was her best answer.

Silently congratulating himself on his pseudo-psychological interpretation, Gregory drained his cup. He could see the signs of stress behind Sharon's vivacious facade. She fidgeted while she spoke, and her gaze was more restless than usual, never lighting for long at any one place. Even the skillfully applied make-up couldn't disguise the dark shadows under her eyes. He felt sorry for her, thrust into his predicament, a pawn in somebody else's game. Better for her, perhaps, if she had never met him.

"I'm going to bed," he announced after a while. "I feel pretty drowsy."

She stood up and carried the cups over to the sink. "I'm pretty tired myself," she said. "Besides, I've got the ideal sleeping potion for you."

She walked over, and, facing him, slipped her arms into his robe, rubbing his back and pressing against him. It wasn't something he had considered, but as she nuzzled his neck with her warm mouth he began to change his mind.

He leaned back, untied her dressing gown, allowed his robe to fall open, and pulled her closer.

"Right here in the kitchen? In front of the bananas and oranges?" she said.

"The floor's too cold, the table too uncomfortable. Let's go to bed." He flicked off the light and led her out.

He didn't find their lovemaking satisfying, not even on a purely physical level. There was a desperation to her actions, and at one point she sobbed and dug her nails into his back, not with passion, but driven by some kind of frustration.

Afterward, as he lay in bed smoking, she asked him what he was thinking.

He puffed on his cigarette guiltily. He had been thinking about Brooke again. How it had been with her. How it would be again if he could ever find her. He considered what he had just completed to be a counterfeit love, a charade, compared to the reality of what he had experienced with Brooke.

"Nothing," he told her. "I wasn't thinking about anything in particular."

"Did you enjoy it?" she asked. "Was it good for you?"

"Yes," he lied hollowly. "You were fantastic —as usual."

Her potion was effective in spite of his dissatisfaction. This time, sleep came quickly, and Gregory soon found out why he had tried to avoid it.

It seemed that no sooner had he closed his eyes than *she* appeared.

He remembered Olga's advice and told himself that the figure standing beside the bed while he was defenseless and asleep was Brooke's mother, Eleanor Harvey; that he shouldn't be afraid, and that he knew who she was and what she was trying to do. But somehow it didn't help much. He was still powerless, still unable to open his eyes, still able only to lie there like a sack of flour and listen to the hateful voice lash at him. Helpless.

"How does it feel to know you're about to die?" she asked. "I told you once—I never lose."

He strained to wake up. He struggled to move his mouth, open his eyes, wiggle a finger, anything to show he had some control over his body. But it was no use.

She laughed without humor, a horrible low sound, ending in an insane cackle.

"How do you like it?" she whispered menacingly, leaning down closer to the bed. "I warned you but you wouldn't listen. You knew better, didn't you? Nobody can say I didn't give you a chance. You always were a fool. Now you're going to pay for what you did to me and to Brooke."

What did I do? Somebody, please tell me what I did.

Her voice became almost conversational, then, lulling him, rocking him. "Brooke had everything to live for. Everything that we had ever dreamed about. Do you have any idea how hard I worked for that? How many years I went without things so that she could have everything, so that we would never again have to depend on anyone? Men! You're all alike. The first time I saw you, I knew you were just like her father. Selfish, irresponsible. Soft, weak, just like Bob. You would have ruined Brooke. Ruined everything for her. For me.

"And then," she continued, "when you knew you'd lose her, that I'd win, you killed her, killed us. Look at what you did. Look!"

She lifted a hand and threw back the cowl that had hidden her face from him.

Gregory wanted to scream, but even that was impossible.

He looked at the blistered, ravaged flesh, the hairless scarlet pate, the pustular mass covering the head, and again he wanted to scream, to scream in terror, to scream in repulsion.

It was Eleanor Harvey. Beneath the devoured skin, he recognized her. And this was how she must have looked during the fire when the flames were licking at her. Her eye sockets were black holes, her mouth an empty tube, her nostrils covered by melted flesh. Sealed.

Trapped inside his body, tortured by the vision, he would have given his life to scream.

And perhaps I will . . .

The face now seemed to be only inches away
from him. He imagined he could smell the burning flesh, the suffocating smoke, the encroaching
heat.

"Pay! Pay! Oh God, at last you'll pay."

And then, just as abruptly as she had appeared, she left.

But something was wrong. The acrid smoke
smell still lingered. There was still heat. The
crackling sound of flames leaping.

Gregory suddenly had the horrible feeling that
this was real. This was no dream of fire. It was
real.

He willed himself to wake up. Concentrated.
He knew he was sweating although he couldn't
lift his hands to feel his face or body. The heat
was increasing. The crackle had changed into
a roar.

Sharon! What about Sharon?

Move the arm over to touch her, nudge her.
Wake her up. Brain to nerves to muscle. Brain
to . . . short circuit. Burnt fuse. Brain to . . .
gap. Concentrate. It's purely mechanical. You
can do it. Brain to nerves to muscles. Jump the
gap. Jump.

Try!

He tried. Failed.

*Sleep. Sleep is all I need. I'll wake up in the
morning and laugh at my nightmare.*

The heat would be gone. The roar, the smell,
the siren. He'd wake up and laugh at his foolish
nightmare. He slept.

Siren?

The word partially broke through the barrier
of his slumber. It hovered on the edge of con-

sciousness, faint in the distance. But it grew louder as it approached. Louder still. Closer.

His eyes shot open. He sat up in bed. Awake.

The room! Smoke billowed in angry clouds. The wall opposite him was a mass of flame and the heat was unbearable. The smoke burned his throat and he coughed.

Sharon! She wasn't in bed.

Foolishly, he ran to the bathroom to see if she was there. She wasn't. He wet a towel and put it over his mouth. Caught a quick glimpse of his wild-eyed image in the mirror.

The door leading to the hall was blocked. That entire wall was a solid barrier of flame. He heard noise and shouting from the other side of the inferno, but there was no way for him to make it through. The flames had begun to creep around to the windows, but they were lighter there. He'd never be able to open a window though. There wasn't enough time.

He had enough presence of mind to grab a blanket from the bed and wrap it around himself first. Then he began to run. He left the ground about four feet from the nearest window, rolling himself into as small a ball as possible, twisting his body in midair so that he hit the wood and glass side-on.

Wood splintered, glass shattered. And then he was out. Gasping the fresh air, tears running down his face, miraculously alive.

He ran around the house to the front, still clutching the blanket. Men were unraveling hoses from the fire trucks. A tall, helmeted man was shouting orders in a hoarse military voice. Gregory grabbed his arm.

"My girl friend. I think she's still in there."

The battalion chief looked at him fiercely. "You the owner?"

"Yes. My girl?"

"Is that her over there?" The man pointed back at the grass. There was a white bundle lying on it. Sharon. Gregory ran over. It was she. She seemed to be unconscious, her face pale, her breathing heavy.

The chief had followed him over. "Is that her?"

"Yes, thank God."

"Anybody else in there?"

"No, just us. Nobody else."

The chief ran back to the engine, his voice raised in command again. A few seconds later another fireman ran back. He was carrying a green resuscitation box and he put it on the grass beside Sharon.

He examined her briefly. "No hyperventilation," he said to Gregory.

He took an oxygen mask from his box, and, placing it over her nose and mouth, set it for inhalation. After a minute she began to stir and then her eyes flickered open. They focused weakly on Gregory.

The man took the mask off. "She'll be all right," he said to Gregory. "No need for the medics."

Sharon spoke. "Gregory, what happened? What's happening?"

Hysteria threaded her voice. She tried to sit up, but the man grabbed her shoulders and pushed her back down.

"It's okay, miss. Just lie there for a minute. Everything's okay now." He added to Gregory, "Just let her rest a while." Then he packed up his box and went back to the fire.

"How did you get out here?" Gregory asked.

She raised her hand and touched her face, as if she didn't believe it was there. "I . . . I don't know. What am I doing out here? I can't remember. I went to bed with you and then . . . I can't remember. Oh God, what's happening to me? Did you bring me out?" she asked, grabbing Gregory's arm.

"No," he said. "I found you out here."

He sat on the grass beside her and looked at the house. The flames seemed to be centered in the back near the bedroom, but he could see the glow through the windows and front door. Perhaps they would be able to save most of it. He wondered how they had gotten there so quickly.

Sharon whimpered miserably beside him. He took her hand in his.

"You're okay," he said. "Don't worry now."

The swirling orange lights on the fire trucks blinded him. There were two fire engines, a hook-and-ladder truck, and a pumper connected to the hydrant in the street for backup. Above the shouts of the men he could hear the sound of splintering wood. He didn't care. He was alive and that was what counted. And Sharon was alive.

He had cheated that demonic bitch. Not like the last time.

Now he remembered vividly what had happened when he and Brooke had died.

The fatal fire had not been an accident.

Chapter Twenty

BROOKE'S DEPARTURE to New Orleans had left Michael in a vacuum. Without her, his life seemed to lack meaning or significance, although it wasn't anything dramatic, just a kind of robotlike emptiness that found him going through meaningless motions to fill in the time.

They spoke to each other daily over the telephone, but the thin metallic voices, diluted by distance, did little to console either of them. She tried to amuse him with news of the shooting and he told her lame jokes to cheer her up, but no sooner did he replace the receiver than the familiar emptiness assailed him.

His novel had almost come to a standstill. When he wasn't staring blankly at the typewriter keys, he was looking out the window of his study, as if expecting to see Brooke's face there at any moment. But all he saw were the same dull avocado leaves and an occasional curious bird. When he wasn't doing that, he walked a lot, trudging manfully up and down hills, telling himself he was thinking about the direction of the book. But all he could think of was Brooke and how much he missed her.

On the third day, however, he did have something of note to tell her.

"Your mother hasn't given up," he said.

"What happened?" Her concern breached the distance between them.

"I came home last night and found a man going through the house. After a little persuasion, the guy told me who hired him. Seems like your mom has got herself an ally."

"Who?"

"Your boss. Good ole Harry Shankman. I found this guy going through the drawers in the bedroom. Guess what he was looking for."

"What?" Her voice was faint.

"Your clothes!" He laughed. "He was looking for evidence that you were staying with me. If he'd found it, ole Harry would have jumped all over you. You know how he is about morals."

"My God! The nerve of him! What did you do?"

"I called Harry this morning."

"And?"

"He said, 'Of course, vy not? I sent the man. I protect the reputation of my stars.' Then he told me that marriage to an inexperienced girl of your tender years would be a grave mistake with quote, serious consequences, unquote.

"Apparently your mother visited him and said we were intending to get married and that you would probably give up films if that happened. Nothing upsets Harry more than the thought of losing a rising star—unless they leave on a stretcher or he fires them."

"So what did you say?"

"I told him to shove the telephone receiver up his ass."

"Was that wise, Michael? He could make it hard for you to get work."

"That's what he told me. The hell with it. I've got too many friends in this business."

"Yes, but you know what fair-weather friends people can be in Hollywood, Michael."

"Yeah, I know, but I have a few I can count on. Anyway, don't worry. Harry will cool down and the whole thing will blow over. What would you have done, anyway?"

"I would have handled it differently," she chided. "Probably I'd have told him to shove it up his rectum, not his ass."

"Exactly what I thought," he said.

The following morning, Eleanor Harvey called him.

"You have been very foolish, Michael," she said.

"Is that all you called to tell me?" he said rudely.

"Harry Shankman will ruin you," she said, and he could hear the satisfaction in her voice. "He's not the only person I can talk to, either."

"Have you talked to your daughter?"

"She no longer knows her own mind," she said, dismissing the question as irrelevant. "Are you going to persist on this destructive course of action?"

"Brooke and I are going to be married. Nothing you or anyone can do will change that."

"For the last time, I am urging you to reconsider," she said. "Otherwise, I will not be responsible for the consequences."

Michael, never a particularly patient man, had

reached his limit. "You can take that telephone receiver," he said, "and do the same thing I told Harry Shankman to do with it." He waited for the gasp. It came, and he hung up.

He stood there shaking with anger. He'd fight every last one of the sons-of-bitches if he had to. Why couldn't they leave them alone? Nothing on heaven or earth would come between them. He wouldn't allow it.

That night, when Brooke called, he told her about her mother.

"I'm going to call her right now and get her to stop this," she said impulsively.

"Don't do that," he said. "It won't work. She's absolutely obsessed. She's convinced herself that you don't know what you're doing, so nothing you can say will change her mind. She's past the point of rationality, Brooke. I think it would be better if you gave her the silent treatment. Don't accept her calls, don't talk to her. Maybe she'll get the message that you really mean what you say."

She agreed with his strategy.

The next day Brooke called and told him excitedly that she was coming home a day early. The last scenes were to be completed in the morning. Delighted, he arranged to meet her at the airport the next evening.

Michael sat in the waiting lounge chain-smoking, impatiently consulting his watch and eyeing the antics of two small boys who had come to meet their father. As usual, the plane was late.

He went over to the observation window and watched the plane taxi up to the ramp. The people in the lounge moved as if on cue to the door where the passengers would exit and stood around it in a broken half-circle, anticipation coloring their faces. Michael stood well back to one side, tall enough to see over the roof of swaying heads.

Brooke was one of the first to disembark. He stood and watched her eagerly search the faces around her. She was one of the few women he knew who could travel in a white suit and look as fresh and radiant by the end of a journey as she had at its beginning.

She saw him then, and ran through the crowd. They held each other, not speaking, eyes closed, oblivious to the people around them. She sobbed and laughed happily, and he buried his face in her golden hair, experiencing a feeling of fierce protectiveness toward her.

They collected her baggage and decided to go directly to his house where they could be alone. In the car, she unbuttoned his shirt while he drove and rubbed her hand over his chest.

"I can't wait," she said. "I think I'll tear the clothes off your body right now."

He knew that wasn't her style, that she was only trying to express the depth of her passion, and he loved her for it.

"Let's get married," he blurted out. He'd been thinking about it all day. "Let's screw them all and get married."

"That's a helluva reason to get married," she said.

He grinned over at her. "You didn't think I'd marry you because I love you, did you?"

"Big ox!" She pulled at the hair of his chest. "Actually, I've been thinking the same thing. We've been intending to do it, so we may as well do it now. It might put an end to the harassment."

"You're right. People tend to be more careful about coming between a married couple."

"Where do you want to get married?" she said, excited now. "I don't want to go to Vegas, and I don't want to get married in a church."

"We'll figure it out in a day or so. Just so I heard you say yes."

"Yes," she said. "Yes, yes, yes."

She had another thought. "Damn!"

"What?" he asked, looking concerned.

She held up her hand and pointed to the large silver-and-turquoise ring on the second finger of her left hand. "It won't like being beside a gold ring. I don't much care for gold myself."

"You can have the gold set with a turquoise stone," he said.

They were driving down Franklin near his house when she confided her fears to him.

"I was relieved to see you at the airport," she said.

"Relieved?" It struck him as a strange choice of words.

"Yes. I had this feeling all day that something terrible was going to happen. I don't know what it was. Maybe that you weren't going to show up for some reason, that something had happened."

Her face was serious, so he stifled the joke he had been about to make. "Well, nothing happened, so stop worrying, darling. We're together, just as we should be."

She nodded and smiled, but a small, barely noticeable frown hovered on her forehead. He turned into the driveway and pulled up outside the front door.

"Your new home, milady," he said with a cavalier bow when they were out of the car.

He scrambled in his pocket for the key and got the two suitcases from the trunk. She took the key from him and opened the door. It was dark and cool inside, and there was a strange smell.

"Is that gasoline I smell?" Brooke said.

Michael sniffed. There did seem to be a faint smell of gasoline in the air. He thought he heard a sound in the rear of the house and stepped into the living room, flicking on the light. The living room and dining room were connected to the kitchen, forming half of the bottom floor. He had a clear view of all three rooms. He could see nothing out of the ordinary.

"I don't know. I can't smell anything now," he said.

"Well, I'm sure I smelled it," Brooke said. "Why don't you check while I go to the bathroom? I can use a nice long shower. Then you can make me a drink."

"All right. Do you need your suitcases?"

"Not right now. I'll just take the small one up and get out of this suit."

Michael walked into the dining room and peered into the kitchen while she went upstairs. Nothing. He got some ice from the refrigerator and took it into the living room.

The low mahogany bar formed a small alcove on the far side of the room. He took the ice over and mixed them each a martini, checking the taste to see if it was dry enough. He'd almost forgotten something. He reached into his pocket and pulled out a locket. It belonged to Brooke and he had had the catch fixed while she was away. It was a heart-shaped silver locket, set with a round turquoise stone. Inside was a small picture of him. He'd give it to her when she came back downstairs. She'd be surprised. He was sure she had expected him to forget.

There was a noise in the kitchen. It sounded like the back door closing. For a moment he thought that it was Brooke, but then he realized that she couldn't have gotten there without passing him.

"Who's there?" he said, stepping out from the bar and walking toward the kitchen. The locket dangled from his hand on its silver chain.

His first thought when he saw her was incongruous—he wondered why she was wearing a raincoat. And then the full significance of what he was looking at hit him.

It was Brooke's mother. She wore a gray plastic raincoat. In one hand she held a lighted candle. In her other hand was a five-gallon gasoline can. The liquid was dripping to the floor.

Michael was too astounded to speak at first. He just looked at the bizarre apparition. When he recovered himself, he stammered. "Wh . . . what, why . . . what the devil are you doing?"

"I didn't expect you back so soon, Michael." Her voice had a strange lilt to it. Her smile was a deformed grimace. "I was just beginning to prepare things for you when I heard you drive up. It doesn't matter though. Your little interruption doesn't change things."

Her face was taut and her eyes glittered nervously. Her voice, too, had changed: she almost cooed when she spoke, all the time leering at him with that evil smile. My God! he thought, horrified, she's cracked!

"What do you intend to do?" he asked, eyeing the can. It was old and battered and covered with grease. The filth explained the raincoat: she didn't want to dirty her clothes. She held the can at an angle and the gas dripped from the top where it had spilled out. There was no lid on the can. Even as he watched, he knew that the fumes were gathering in dangerous clouds, reaching up for the flickering flames of the candle.

"I don't intend to let you get away with ruining my life," she snapped, her voice cracking. "I said I'd stop you. I warned you. I gave you every chance. Now I'm going to have to deal with you. I'll just change the plan around a little now that you're here."

"What were you planning to do?" he asked cautiously, playing for time. He took a tentative step toward her.

"Don't!" she said, tipping the can and sloshing gas onto the floor. "Don't come any closer."

"All right, all right," he said placatingly. "I'll stand right here."

"Very good," she crooned. "You do that. The plan? Why, Michael, I was going to perfume your house from the back door to the front. When you walked in the front door, I was going to light the trail from the kitchen and give you a big surprise." She laughed. "When Brooke comes back tomorrow, she'll find you all charred and cindered, in no position to trouble her anymore."

"Brooke is here, you damn fool!" he cried. "She's upstairs right now."

"You're lying. She's not arriving until tomorrow." She narrowed her eyes maliciously. "You'll have to do better than that to get out of this." Her voice rose angrily. "You . . . turning a girl against her own mother, her own flesh and blood. Getting her to a state where she won't even talk to me. Won't accept my telephone calls."

She walked closer to him, splashing gas onto the floor as she moved. "Get back," she said. "Move back."

He debated rushing her, diving for the candle, kicking the can away. There was no guarantee he'd reach her before the candle dropped. Neither could he be sure he wouldn't grab the candle and fall in the rush. Either way, the fumes were gathering above the floor. She held the candle almost level with her shoulder. Lower it a foot or two, and—boom!

She walked around him, slopping gas at intervals of a foot or two. She intended to move from the kitchen to the dining room, to the living room, to the front door, trapping him. She reached the entrance to the living room. Now he'd be able to run for the kitchen and make it out the back door. Probably he'd beat the flames if she dropped the candle. Maybe even if she threw it.

But what about Brooke? She was upstairs and if there was a fire, she'd be trapped. He couldn't leave her, it was out of the question.

"Brooke!" he screamed at the top of his lungs. There was no answer. He screamed again and again. Still no answer. She must still be in the bathroom, he thought, taking a shower.

Mrs. Harvey looked at him triumphantly. "So much for your clever lies," she said.

"Listen, can't we talk this over?" Surely Brooke would be finished with her shower if he could just stall for a few more minutes.

"Too late," she said. "Too late for talking. Too late for anything now, Michael. I gave you your chance."

She was crazy, he knew, but that didn't matter. What mattered was that she was going to murder him. And Brooke along with him.

Mrs. Harvey went through the living room door to the passage and splashed more gas there and on the floor beside the front door. Then she moved back into the dining room, not taking her eyes off him.

"Now I have you where I want you," she said, her eyebrows arched in triumph.

"I swear to you, Brooke is here," he said quietly. "She's upstairs changing, and you'll kill her, too."

"You already tried that. It didn't work." She circled him, still pouring gas.

"I swear to you," he said desperately. "Let me go upstairs and get her. No, you go up and get her. You'll see she's there."

"And leave you to escape? You must think I'm crazy."

He did, but it wouldn't do to point it out at the moment. "I could have run out through the kitchen when you went to the front door," he said persuasively. "Why do you think I didn't? It was because Brooke *is* here."

She looked at him, a flicker of uncertainty crossing her face. Then she smiled. "You were too scared to run. You're looking at your own death and you're petrified."

Oh, God, he thought. Now what? He began to feel a rage at his position, at his helplessness before this crazy old woman.

And then Brooke appeared in the doorway behind her.

She wore only a bathrobe. She had showered and her hair was wet, plastered close to her head.

"Mother, what in the world *are* you doing?"

Eleanor swung around, her face a mingling of shock and horror.

Brooke stepped toward Michael. "Stop," he said. "Get back, Brooke!"

She ignored his order and walked to his side, looking disdainfully down at the gasoline as she stepped through it.

"Mother, what in the hell do you think you're doing?" she said.

Eleanor's face was white. She swayed where she stood, her mouth open, trying to speak, but the words were unable to pass the barrier of terror and shame at being discovered by her daughter.

The can dripped gas, the candle dripped wax.

"Get out of here, Brooke!" Michael said urgently. "Please, please, get out."

"Don't be silly . . ." she began.

And then Mrs. Harvey reached out both hands imploringly, anguishingly toward her daughter.

The candle dropped.

To Michael, it seemed like slow motion, the way it fell, turning and just beginning to flip over when it hit the layer of petroleum vapor.

Brooke's mother didn't even have time to scream. The explosion engulfed her in a sheet of bright-orange flames. And then everything happened very fast. Much too fast.

The force of the blast knocked them back, blinded them. He fell on Brooke. She screamed, but he must have been partially deafened by the blast, because the scream seemed to come from a great, great distance. He tried to cover her body with his. And then the flames were on them.

His screams joined hers in a single terrible wail.

He had time only to think, "It *can't* end this way. I won't let it. We'll be together somehow, somewhere . . ."

His hand tightened on the locket.

And then they were silent.

Gregory cried quietly to himself as he sat on the grass. Sharon, still lying slightly behind him, couldn't see.

His grief was mixed with relief that he hadn't been the one to cause Brooke's death, but the sadness was dominant. Wasted, he thought bitterly, wasted. But he couldn't dredge up any anger. That would come later, he realized.

He sniffed and wiped his eyes with the back of his hand. He was still wrapped in the blanket, naked beneath it. The glow in the house seemed to have subsided. Apparently the firemen had it under control.

"Are you okay?" he asked, turning to Sharon.

"Yes," she said dully. "You?"

"Fine."

He scrambled to his feet and walked to the house. The battalion chief approached him. He was carrying a can.

"Arson," he said, swinging the can forward. "We found this gas can in back. Seen it before?"

Gregory looked at it. "Yes, I keep it in the garage. Spare gas. How . . ."

"Somebody spread it all over, then lit a match," the man said. He wiped his face with his forearm. "How did your girl friend get out?"

Gregory thought quickly. He didn't need Sharon involved in an arson investigation. "Well," he could imagine himself explaining, "she probably lighted the fire, but then she's not really responsible, because I think at the time she was possessed by the spirit of a dead woman." They'd love that.

"I carried her out through the kitchen," he said. "Then I went back in to try and get a manuscript I left in the bedroom. I'm a writer, you see. I couldn't reach it, though. Then, when I came back out, she wasn't there. It scared the hell out of me. I thought she'd gone back in, too."

"Well, she must have wandered around to the front before she collapsed," the fireman said. "Is she all right?"

"Yes, she's not too bad. More shocked than anything else," Gregory said, relieved to see that the man had accepted his explanation.

"Good. Well, I've called in an A-unit, an arson unit, and they'll be here shortly. They'll have some questions for you."

"Of course," Gregory said. He'd have to get Sharon to tell a similar story, but that would be easy. She was so confused she'd accept anything he said. "How's the house?"

"You're lucky. The hall and bedroom are badly damaged, but the rest of the place isn't bad."

"Please thank your men for me. I appreciate what they're doing," Gregory said.

The chief looked pleased. He probably didn't hear that too often. "I certainly will," he said.

Gregory walked back to Sharon and sat down heavily beside her.

"Do you remember now what happened?" he asked.

"No," she said. "I remember falling asleep. Then I woke up out here with an oxygen mask on my face. That's all."

"You're sure?"

"Christ, that's what I just said, isn't it?"

"All right, all right," he said quickly. "Don't worry about it now. You're safe, that's the important thing."

"How did the fire start?" she said, calming down.

Gregory turned to face her. "Somebody poured gas all over the house," he said.

Her hand went to her mouth and her eyes widened. "Just like the . . ." She covered her mouth, cutting off the words.

"Just like what?" Gregory said, grabbing her arm. "What do you mean?"

She drew back from him, fear on her face. "I don't know," she said weakly. "It just came out. I don't understand. What's happening to me?" She began to sob.

Gregory removed his hand. "Don't worry," he said. "You'll be okay in a little while. There's nothing to be afraid of. You're just suffering from a little shock right now. There's something we have to do, though."

"What?"

"Arson investigators are going to arrive in a few minutes. That story of your not remembering will make things too complicated. I want you to say that you vaguely remember me dragging you out the back door, and then you can't remember from that point on, okay?"

"All right," she said. She took his hand. "God, Greg, I don't know what's happening. I'm really afraid. Afraid for both of us."

"Don't worry. There's nothing to be afraid of —it's all over now."

He wished with all his heart that it were true.

Chapter Twenty-one

GREGORY WOKE UP wondering where he was. He sat up and rubbed his eyes, remembering what had happened. The questions and most of the flames had died out at about five in the morning and he and Sharon had driven off to get some rest in a motel on Sunset, both exhausted and quiet, limiting their conversation to essentials.

The questioning had gone well, Gregory thought. The two arson investigators were tough, experienced men, but he was sure he hadn't aroused their suspicions. Luckily, Sharon's obvious shock condition had excused her from speaking much. There was no doubt that arson had been committed, but the investigators had drawn a blank as to a suspect.

Gregory looked at his watch. It was about eleven. Sharon looked innocent and relaxed beside him, her mouth open and her breathing even. He got up quietly and slipped into his clothes. He didn't want to use the telephone in the room, so he left, closing the door quietly behind him and pocketing the key.

He found a telephone in the restaurant and dialed Olga's number, praying she was back.

"Hello?" It was she.

"Olga, thank God you're back."

"Gregory? Whatever is the matter? I tried to return your call, but there was no answer."

Her composed voice calmed him. He managed a bit of gallows humor. "Oh, since I saw you last there've been only two attempts on my life, and I've been burned out of house and home."

"You had better explain," she said.

He told her what had happened, starting with Sharon's attempt with the knife and ending with the fire of the preceding night. "It appears that Eleanor Harvey has been using Sharon to get at me, controlling her body either through outright possession or some kind of hypnotic command system. The poor kid doesn't know it, but she's hanging on to her sanity by her nails."

"She claims she knows nothing?"

"Right. Some kind of blackout, I think. Oh, there was one strange thing. When I told her last night how the fire had started, she began to say something, then she stopped. She started to say, 'Just like the . . .' and then stopped. I asked her what she had been about to say, but she didn't know. Now, the interesting thing is that at last I've remembered how Brooke and I died. . . ."

He went on to tell her about the fire that had destroyed them.

When he finished, Olga exclaimed, "My God, the woman was totally insane! I never thought she had gone to such lengths. I need to think about this."

Gregory held the telephone, listening to the silence at the other end.

"I want you to bring Sharon to my home right away," Olga said at last. "It seems to me that the only way to reach Mrs. Harvey is through her. I don't know if we can reach her, but we must try to force Mrs. Harvey to confront what happened that night. I think her attacks upon you are based on the fact that what happened then is too horrible for her to face. She has made herself believe that you started the fire because her guilt at murdering her own daughter is too much for her to bear."

"How do we reach her through Sharon?"

"I'm not sure. I'll try to have the answer to that question by the time you arrive. But it's the only chance I see. We know she had to use Sharon's body, correct? Then it's the only avenue of communication we have."

"All right, I'll be there as soon as possible," Gregory said. "What can I tell Sharon? I know —I'll tell her you've invited us refugees for brunch."

Olga managed to chuckle. "I can take a hint," she said. "See you soon."

Gregory once again found himself traveling up the hill to Olga's house. Sharon sat stiffly beside him, not speaking. She had been withdrawn since awakening and hadn't said more than a dozen words. When Gregory told her a friend had invited them to brunch, she got dressed as obediently as a child, asking no questions. All of her attention was directed inward, and he was growing more and more concerned by her withdrawal.

Olga greeted Sharon with a friendly smile and a searching glance and invited them in. Sharon, far from her normal vivacious self, merely mumbled a greeting.

They went into the breakfast room off the kitchen and sat around a blue-tiled table with a yellow sunburst in its center. Olga poured coffee, served scrambled eggs, bacon, and croissants, then sat down and joined them at brunch.

For a moment, nobody spoke. Then Olga broke the silence. "I'm glad to see you are both all right," she said. "Was the house damaged badly?"

"No, not too bad," Gregory said. "I'm going to have to rebuild the bedroom and a couple of walls, but we'll be back there in a few weeks. Luckily, a neighbor saw the flames and called the fire department. It could have been much worse."

"How fortunate," Olga murmured. She sipped her coffee.

"Sharon was lucky," Gregory said casually. "She got out before it became an inferno. I had to jump through the window."

"Oh? How *did* you get out in time?" she said, directing the question at Sharon. She put the cup down in its saucer.

Sharon looked up, her eyes flicking nervously to Gregory.

"It's all right," he said gently. "You can talk to Olga."

"I don't remember what happened. I just woke up outside," she said, speaking down at the table.

"I see," Olga said. "And you also don't remember attacking Gregory with a knife. Is that correct?"

Gregory was startled at the tack Olga was taking. Sharon pushed her chair back from the table, as if preparing to escape. "Who is she?" she said to Gregory. "What right does she have to ask these questions? What have you told her?"

"She's a friend," he said. "She just wants to help."

"I don't need help. I don't need anyone meddling in my affairs. I want to go." She began to rise from her chair.

Gregory placed a restraining hand on her arm. "Wait a minute, Sharon. Calm down. No need to get upset. She just wants to talk."

"I'm not going to put up with an inquisition," she said, a whine entering her voice. "You can't force me to."

"Sit down!" Olga's voice rang with authority. It filled the room, cowing Sharon into obedience. She abruptly sat down in her chair. Her lower lip trembled and her eyes began to brim with tears.

This was a different Olga from the one Gregory had seen before. She seemed to have magnified in size and presence. Her eyes were remorseless, her face devoid of warmth or pity.

"I'm going to ask you some hard questions," she told Sharon. "And you are going to answer them. If you attempt to leave, Gregory will hold you in that chair if he has to. Do you understand?"

Sharon looked at Gregory in confusion, fear showing in her eyes. Gregory was more surprised than ever at the change in Olga. He thought . . . what had he thought? That Olga would just chat over coffee and get Sharon to talk? He really hadn't thought at all. He'd been afraid to. He'd been willing to leave it all in Olga's hands, and that was how he would have to continue.

"Listen to her," he said to Sharon, as sternly as he could.

Sharon switched her frightened gaze back and forth between Olga and Gregory, cringing in her chair.

"Now, I want you to listen carefully," Olga said firmly. "It is very important and your life may well depend upon it. I believe that you have been used by the spirit of a dead woman to attack Gregory. That is why you have not been able to remember what has been happening. It is imperative that, as a first step, we get you to remember."

As Olga spoke, a change came over Sharon. She now looked defiant and angry. "Possession?" she cried. Sharon's voice rose to a shriek. Olga's words had struck some core of final resistance. Sharon looked from one to the other and laughed coldly. "You're both crazy. Certifiable fruitcakes. First reincarnation—and now possession. I blacked out, that's all that happened. Plenty of people suffer from blackouts. You've both been watching too many horror movies."

Gregory shook his head. "Sharon, there was no physiological reason for a blackout."

"I still think you're both nuts and I want out of here now!"

"You are *not* going anywhere," Olga said firmly. "The only reason you are unable to remember is because you are afraid to. Now, let us take the night you attacked Gregory with the knife. Tell me what happened after you went to bed."

"You take it!" Sharon shouted. "I'm not listening to any more of this. I'm leaving."

She stood up. Olga nodded at Gregory and he

grabbed her arm. "Sit down, Sharon. And stay there!"

She tried to pull her arm away. He stood up, took her by the shoulders, and forced her back into her chair.

"I'll scream," she said, looking at Olga.

"No one will hear you," Olga said calmly. "Now, tell me what happened when you went to bed."

Gregory looked at both of them: Sharon, suddenly defiant; Olga, with the velvet glove removed from the iron hand he never knew she possessed. He didn't like what was happening. It wasn't in his nature to use bullying tactics. And yet, he told himself, he had no other choice than to trust Olga.

"What happened? I don't remember," Sharon protested angrily.

"Yes, you *do* remember," Olga said. "You are just refusing to look at it. Think back."

"I told you, I don't remember," Sharon said sullenly.

"What happened when you went to bed?"

"I went to sleep. That's all I remember."

"Did you dream?"

"I don't remember."

"What was it you started to say to Gregory after the fire? 'Just like the . . .' "

"I don't know what you're talking about."

"Gregory said the fire had been started with gasoline, and you began to say, 'Just like the . . .' What did you mean?"

"I don't know. It just came out. I was upset. In shock."

"What were you thinking when you said that?"

"Nothing."

"What decisions did you make before you went to sleep that night?"

"I don't know!" she screamed. "I don't know! I don't know! Stop asking me these questions. I can't stand it anymore."

Gregory looked at Olga. "Olga, maybe . . ." he started to say.

"No!" Olga said emphatically. "Let me handle this."

Sharon turned to him, sensing an ally. "Gregory," she pleaded. "Make her stop this. Please."

"Sharon, she's just trying to help you." He was speaking as much to himself as to her. He decided that maybe he wasn't as tough as he'd thought.

"Help me?" she raged. "With these accusations? Telling me that I'm lying. What kind of help is that? I can't remember what happened. Maybe nothing happened. All I have is your word that I attacked you with a knife. Maybe *he's* lying," she said eagerly to Olga. "Did you ever think of that? Maybe he started the fire, too?"

"No," Olga said. "He's not lying. Tell me about the fire."

"I don't know anything about it. I woke up on the lawn."

"And you think you blacked out?"

"Yes! Yes! I blacked out." Sharon put her head down into her hands and leaned on the table. Then she looked up as if she'd just thought of something. "Maybe I didn't. Maybe I fainted inside from the smoke and Gregory carried me out. Maybe he's lying about that, too. Trying for some reason to drive me insane."

Gregory shook his head.

"No, that is not what happened," Olga said.

"What *do* you remember about the night of the fire?"

"Nothing, goddamn you! I remember nothing."

"Would you let me hypnotize you?" Olga said. "Try to get you to remember that way?"

"You're nuts," Sharon said, shaking her head wildly. "I wouldn't let you near my mind with a ten-foot pole."

"Then you will just have to remember," Olga said. She stood up, the perfect hostess. "More coffee, anyone?"

"I can't believe this is happening," Sharon said. "Greg, why are you doing this to me?"

Gregory clenched his jaw. It was one question he *could* answer. "Sharon, someone is trying to kill me. I'm trying to find out why."

Olga filled their coffee cups, then sat down again.

"All right," she said. "Now think back to the night with the knife."

"I can't remember anything about that night," Sharon said.

"What *can* you remember about that night?"

"Going to bed. Nothing. I can't remember."

Gregory began to feel a little dizzy. Their voices droned in his ears. Remember, don't remember. Olga's persistence was like a sharp-bladed knife, shaving off layers of something. He lost track of time. He could have been sitting there one hour, three hours, he didn't know. He wondered how Sharon was feeling if it affected him this way just as an observer.

The hammering continued.

At one point Sharon sat silently, refusing to respond in any way, but Olga just kept battering, asking the same questions over and over again, never changing her tone, untiring.

"Stop!" Sharon pleaded. "I can't let you go on."

"You are not even trying to remember," Olga said. "If you try, you will be able to. Then we can stop."

"All right," Sharon said. "I'll try. I'll try."

"Good. Now the night you got the kitchen knife. Can you remember getting it?"

"No."

"What can you remember?"

"Going to sleep. Waking up with a bruise on my chin."

"Look back at that time. Try to remember what happened after you went to sleep."

"There's nothing there. I can't remember. It's blank. I swear to you."

"You are being evasive, Sharon. Look again."

"I can't remember!"

Olga changed her tactics. "Tell me about Eleanor Harvey," she said.

Sharon's face crumpled. "What? Who are you talking about?"

"Eleanor Harvey. Tell me why she hates Gregory."

"I don't know what you're talking about. I don't know anyone by that name."

"Yes, you do. You know her very well. She hates Gregory. She wants to kill him. She doesn't want him to find Brooke again. Tell me what you know about her."

Sharon was pale, her breathing erratic, her voice faint. *"I—don't—know."*

"Why does she hate Gregory?" Olga persisted. "Is it because of the fire?"

Sharon began to sob soundlessly, her mouth opening and closing.

"Is it what happened with the fire that made her hate Gregory?"

Sharon's hand clawed helplessly at the table.

"Tell me why she hates Gregory. Was it the fire that killed Brooke?"

And then something snapped. Sharon screamed. It was a piercing, ear-shattering sound that reverberated through the room.

"Yes! Yes! Yes!" she screamed with her hands over her ears. "He killed Brooke! That's why. He murdered Brooke in cold blood!"

Sharon dropped her hands to the table, her eyes wide, shock and surprise on her face at what she had said.

"You remember?" Olga prodded quietly.

Sharon laughed.

The sound was so incongruous that it shocked Gregory. He looked from her to Olga, then back to Sharon again, bewildered. And then, it struck him, the fact he had never fully taken into account throughout the entire affair—Sharon was a consummate actress. It was her profession, her life. She was good at it, good enough to fool him and almost anybody she wanted to. She had been acting the innocent all along, but now, under Olga's hammering, she had at last broken down.

He looked at her with fresh eyes and a sense of dawning horror.

Sharon's face was undergoing a subtle change. There was no fear in it anymore. It seemed to grow harder before his eyes, a ruthlessness replacing the uncertainty and fear. She drew herself upright in the chair and looked boldly at each of them in turn. When she spoke, her voice seemed a shade deeper to Gregory.

"I remember *everything*," she said scornfully. "I remembered it all last night after the fire. All of it."

To Gregory, the moment was timeless, suspended in space. He sat there, physically paralyzed, his mind buzzing.

Sharon looked almost amused. "You pair of blundering fools with your talk of possession and spirits," she said. "You're so far off the mark, it's laughable. You are the ones in danger, not me." She paused and smiled then—a cruel, icy smile.

"*I* am not in any danger from Eleanor Harvey," she said. "I *am* Eleanor Harvey!"

They sat, stunned. Gregory looked at Sharon, his mouth open, staring disbelievingly at the apparition before him. Olga stared, in equal amazement, her body rigid. Olga has bought more than she bargained for, Gregory thought. Sharon wore a small, mocking smile.

Olga was the first to recover.

"What do you mean?" she said.

"What do you mean? What do you mean?" Sharon mimicked spitefully. She laughed again. "I mean what I said. I remember everything. I *am* Eleanor Harvey. I died, *killed by him!*" She shot a hateful look at Gregory. "But I was born again."

She plucked derisively at the skin on her arm. "This is just a covering," she said. "This silly, flighty young actress, Sharon Forbes, is just an identity I wore for a while. But now I once again know who I am and what I can accomplish."

She looked at Gregory again, her lip curling contemptuously. "I did all those things," she taunted. "The furniture, the note, the letter. I even killed your cat. God, how I hated that cat!

"I didn't really know I was doing it at first. My identity as Sharon was too strong. To protect herself, the part of me that is Sharon blacked out. But last night, after you told me how the fire started, I remembered everything. Now I am wholly *me* again. Now I can do with full knowledge what I always intended to do— *kill you!*"

Even Olga was shaken by the force of her hate. It had a strength they could almost touch.

"Tell her about the fire, Gregory," Olga said, trying to hide her feelings with a calm voice.

"I don't want to hear anything about it from him," Sharon shouted.

"You are going to listen, even if we have to hold you in that chair," Olga said. She began to rise.

"Don't come near me!"

"Do you remember me?" Olga said.

"Olga Nabakov. Brooke's so-called friend."

"I think it would be wise if you listened to Gregory. He has a story to tell you."

Sharon didn't speak; she just sneered at Olga. Suddenly, Sharon seized the edge of the table as she rose from her chair and, with amazing force, shoved it over. It went sliding on its side halfway across the room, dishes and glasses clattering to the floor and shattering into a hundred fragments.

Gregory snapped out of his mesmerized state. He jumped up, moved behind Sharon, and grabbed her arms, pushing her down into her chair. Sharon twisted out of his grasp, clawing at his face viciously with both hands. Exerting all his strength, Gregory again managed to push

Sharon down in the chair and pin her arms behind her.

"Get something to tie her with!" he shouted to Olga.

Olga ran from the room. Sharon struggled and tried to bite his hand. "You bastard! I'm going to get you."

Olga ran back in with some laundry rope and wrapped it around Sharon's waist and the chair. Then she went to work on her arms, tying them behind the wooden frame of the chair.

Gregory stood back panting and looked at Sharon. She was cursing and screaming, her face livid. Gregory touched his face tentatively, then drew his hand away and looked at the blood smeared on it. Rage surged up in him.

"You killed Brooke!"

He screamed it out, leaning forward toward her, the veins in his neck and face distended.

"You killed us all!" he screamed again.

He stepped around the upturned table, heedless of the broken dishes littering the floor, his eyes bloodshot, a primitive force propelling him on, urging him to use his hands to squeeze the life from her neck. For a moment he stood before her as if undecided, then he raised his right hand and slapped Sharon in the face with his open palm, the blow swinging her head around to one side.

"You killed her," he said more quietly now.

Sharon cringed before the attack.

"You came to my house to kill me," he said. "You brought gasoline. You spread it around the house. You thought Brooke was still in New Orleans. I told you she was upstairs but you wouldn't believe me. You had a candle in one hand, the gasoline can in the other. Brooke came into the room. You dropped the candle. You killed us all. *You* did it. Not me."

The short, staccato sentences rang out like a hammer on an anvil. Sharon looked at him with dull eyes, her face slack.

"Brooke saw you and said, 'Mother, what in the hell do you think you're doing?' And then when I told her to get out of the room, she said, 'Don't be silly,' and those were the last words she ever spoke. Because then you dropped the candle. You killed her, you degenerate, insane woman. Your hate was so consuming you killed the only person you ever loved."

Sharon began to utter a high keening sound, rocking her head and shoulders back and forth against the rope that bound her. Tears flowed down her cheeks.

Gregory straightened a chair and sat down heavily in it, his shoulders slumped, his face gray and haggard. Olga sat quietly for a long moment, then spoke calmly.

"Sharon . . . Eleanor," she said, "you had your chance. As Sharon, you had a fresh start, a new opportunity to make things right. When you met Gregory you had the greatest opportunity possible. You could have made him happy, contributed to his life, and made up for the wrongs you committed in your last life. But your hate was too strong. Once again you became its worst victim."

Sharon broke into a shrill, continuous wailing. Her eyes rolled back in her head. Drops of spittle formed at the corners of her mouth and she began to drool.

"Maybe we'd better untie her," Gregory said anxiously.

Olga nodded. "Yes, I think you are right."

Gregory got up and moved behind her chair, his fingers fumbling with the rope. When he unwound it, Sharon slumped forward, her head bowed almost down to her knees.

"Now what?" Gregory said, turning his troubled countenance to Olga.

"Now we will tidy up my breakfast room," she said.

She took a broom from a closet and began to sweep the broken china and glass that littered the floor.

Gregory put his hand on Sharon's shoulder. She sat up.

"Please don't touch me," she said quietly.

He drew his hand back as if he had touched something hot. Her tear-streaked face was calm, cool as ice.

"Give me a cigarette, please," she said.

He handed her a cigarette. She picked up a book of matches from the floor and lighted it herself, taking a deep draw and exhaling slowly.

"I . . . I don't know what to think," she said.

Olga stopped what she was doing and watched her keenly.

"What you've told me," Sharon said. "What I've done . . . I don't know what to think."

Gregory tried to comprehend the shock she was experiencing. Her entire rationale, the reasons and justifications she had given herself for the terrible vendetta against him, the motivation that had, in a sense, given her life and power— it had all just been destroyed. Thank God, he thought. She sounded as if she was approaching rationality.

"Everything will be all right," he said. "Just give it time."

She shook her head slowly, numbly. "The

things I've done, the things . . ." Her voice choked. She twisted the cigarette in her fingers, her eyes downcast.

"What you did was . . . terrible. But if you know that now, there's still the future."

"Yes," she said. "The future."

She stood up and Gregory automatically flexed his muscles, then relaxed. This shaken, remorseful figure wasn't the same person who had almost demolished the breakfast room.

Sharon turned to Olga. "May I use the bathroom, please? I need to fix myself up."

Olga nodded after only a split-second's hesitation. "Straight down the hall," she said. "Second door on the left."

Sharon left the room, her steps slow and thoughtful.

"What do you think?" Gregory said to Olga after a few moments of silence.

"That when a woman decides to fix herself up, it's a good sign."

Olga swept the broken dishes and glasses into a neat heap and motioned to Gregory. "Hold the pan for me, please, so I can sweep it in."

He did as he was asked and poured the refuse into a brown paper bag she had placed on the floor. The simple task seemed to reassure him. He smiled wanly. The tension of the last few hours was beginning to dissipate.

"She's taking a long time," he said to Olga, looking expectantly at the door.

"I think that perhaps you are a chronic worrier," Olga said. "Give her a few minutes."

He lifted the table back on its legs and sat down beside it, taking a cigarette out of his pack. He reached into his pocket for matches and didn't find any.

"Do you have any matches?" he asked Olga.

She leaned the broom against the sink. "Where are the ones that were on the table?" she asked.

"They fell somewhere on the floor and then . . ." He stood up, his voice dropping. "Sharon!" he exclaimed.

"I think we had better see how she's getting on in the bathroom," Olga said quietly, but there was a note of fright in her voice.

They walked out of the breakfast room. "You don't think she'd do anything silly to herself, do you?" Gregory said.

Olga didn't reply. She knocked on the bathroom door. There was no answer. She knocked again. Silence. She tried the door and pushed against it, but it was locked.

Gregory stepped forward and tried it. His stomach muscles were tightening up again.

"Break it," Olga said.

He stepped back and hurled himself against the wooden door. His shoulder hurt but the door didn't give. It was easier in the movies, he thought.

"Again," she said, her voice now urgent.

He hurled himself against the door six more times before it burst open at last with a splintering of wood.

He didn't know what he had expected to see— Sharon drowned in the bathtub, or hanging from the ceiling with a towel around her neck, or what. But he hadn't expected to face an empty bathroom.

The window was open.

He walked over to it and stuck his head out. Nothing.

"Our bird has flown," Olga said.

"Goddammit!" he cursed. "The actress!"

"What?"

"I keep forgetting she's an actress. A damn good one."

"Come," Olga said, walking back into the passage. "We'd better find her."

She led the way through the house to the front door. They stepped outside and Gregory cursed again.

"Dammit!"

"What is it?" she said.

"The tires on my car." He walked around to the other side of the automobile. "All of them. Flat."

"She's probably on her way down the hill," Olga said. "Wait and I'll get my car keys."

She darted back into the house. Gregory kicked his tires uselessly. Olga came back out, swinging her keys from her hand. Gregory opened the garage door for her, lifting it above his head.

"There's a smell of gasoline in here," he said, stepping inside. Olga followed.

"Do you keep a can of gasoline here?" he asked.

"No, I don't. God, it's strong!"

"The floor—it's wet," Gregory said, scuffing it with his toe. "There's gasoline all over it. It seems to be coming from under the car.

They each took a few steps forward to look.

Then there was a resounding crash.

The door swung down behind them.

"Light. Is there a light in here?" Gregory said, feeling the first stirrings of fear.

"No, it doesn't work."

A voice shouted from the other side of the door. It was Sharon's.

"I have you now!"

Gregory took a few quick steps to the door and tried to open it, but it wouldn't budge. He adjusted his eyes to the dark and tried again.

"Does it open from the inside?" he asked Olga, speaking softly and urgently.

"Yes, but not if it's locked from the outside. She must have found the outside lock."

The voice came again, loudly, triumphantly. "I have you trapped! Trapped like rats!"

"Sharon," Gregory shouted. "Please, can't we reason with you? I didn't do it—it was you who killed Brooke."

"Yes, I remember. But you made me do it. You left me no other choice. It was all your fault. You *made* me kill Brooke."

"Is there a door out of here?" Gregory whispered to Olga.

"No."

"I said you'd pay for it," Sharon's voice continued, charged with madness. "And you will!"

Olga had been looking below the car. "The gasoline," she said. "She must have punctured the tank. It's dripping under the car."

"She led us here," Gregory said furiously. "She punctured my tires, knowing we'd come in here for your car."

There was a scuffling noise on the other side of the door, and then Sharon spoke again.

"Ashes to ashes!" she shouted, and laughed wildly.

A tongue of flame crept beneath the door, following the trail of gas from where she had lighted it outside.

"Quick," Gregory said, grabbing Olga roughly by the arm and pulling her to car. "Give me the keys."

She handed them to him and he opened the door of the car. He pushed her in ahead of him and got in behind the wheel before she had time to slide over, shoving her unceremoniously to the side.

They could feel each other's fear in the enclosed space. The fumes were not heavy enough to explode from the tiny creeping flame, Gregory realized, but the moment the flame hit the puddle of gasoline under the car, it would all be over.

"Let's hope there's enough gasoline in the tank to get us out of here," he said, inserting the key and turning it.

The engine kicked over, but it didn't catch.

"The car. Won't it explode?" Olga said, sounding more terrified than he would ever have thought possible.

"Let's just hope to hell not," he said.

He turned the key again.

The engine coughed into motion.

"I'm going to wreck your car," he said, putting it into reverse.

"Just get us out of here," Olga said, but the revving of the engine muffled her words.

Thank God it was a wooden door, Gregory thought. If he could get up enough speed, he might be able to do it.

He shifted in reverse and floored the accelerator.

The car lurched into motion, speeding backward with a screech of tires. There was the bang and crunch of metal against wood as the car smashed into the door. Their heads were jerked back with the impact and Gregory felt a sharp pain in his back and neck.

But the door gave way, swerving crazily to one side.

To Gregory, looking backward as he drove, half-turned in the seat, Sharon's face seemed only inches away.

Her laugh had changed to a scream; her face was distorted into an expression of terror.

It was all too fast for her to move, for him to step on the brake.

There was a sickening thud as the car hit her and sent her body flying violently through the air. It landed yards away, arms and legs stretched out grotesquely.

Chapter Twenty-two

WHY DID HE FEEL so guilty? Gregory asked himself over and over again.

When it was all over and the friends and relatives had come and gone, when the explanations had been made, the effects disposed of, and the body buried, Gregory still had his enormous burden of guilt.

Olga thought he was foolish and told him so one day as they were having lunch at the Old World Restaurant on Sunset. They had a window view of the busy Tower Records intersection. People were zipping by, busily enjoying their lives in the warm California sunshine, but Gregory found none of it uplifting.

"You can't possibly blame yourself," Olga kept assuring him.

"If I hadn't remembered Brooke and started this search for her, Sharon would still be alive," he said glumly. "She wouldn't have remembered anything and she would have had that fresh start she deserved, being Sharon Forbes, the promising young actress."

"You cannot know that," Olga said in annoyance. "Anything could have happened to cause her to remember, particularly because she was involved in something as closely aligned to her past as the film business. It is stupid to blame yourself."

"But that *is* the way it happened," he insisted.

"Yes, and we each have to take the responsibility for our own condition. She *could* have overcome her obsession. She *could* have overcome her hate, but she chose not to. That was *her* responsibility."

"Chose not to—that's a strong statement," Gregory said. "I wonder how much choice she had."

"We all have a choice," Olga said firmly. "One way or another, we all have a choice. There are no true victims in this world, although there are many who posture as such."

The conversation drifted on, resolving nothing. Intellectually, Gregory knew she was right, but his emotions were another matter. It was difficult for him to look at Sharon-Eleanor as two sides of a coin, for the memories of Sharon as he had known her at her best were bright in his mind.

"So, what are you going to do now?" Olga asked.

"I'm going to search for Brooke," he said. "The only thing that will give this experience any value is finding her again."

"What about the book you're writing?"

Gregory shrugged. "I suppose I'll finish it, though my heart really isn't in it now. Still, as far as stories go, it's a good one, and that's my job, I guess."

Olga toyed with the silverware. "You know,

that book—in itself, it could be a worthwhile tribute to Brooke, a monument of lasting value to her memory," she said.

Gregory looked up sharply. "Monuments are for the dead," he said. "Brooke is no longer dead. She's somewhere in the world of the living— and I'm going to find her."

Gregory's resolve to find Brooke did not diminish, but hope that he would succeed, that he wasn't chasing an illusion, varied from day to day.

According to his understanding of things, there was only one encouraging possibility—it was likely that Brooke, whoever she now was, probably was involved in some way with films. It wasn't a certainty, of course, but there did seem to be a good chance; after all, he was a screenwriter again. In the final analysis, though, it wasn't terribly heartening. She *could* be an actress, but she could also be a theatrical agent, a musician, or even a drama teacher in some midwestern hamlet. Still, it was all he had to go on. So he operated on the assumption that she would once again be an actress.

Faith also played a part in his mission. How would he recognize her? Different body, different name, different person. That's where faith came into it. He believed that somehow, if he ever saw her, he could not fail to recognize her. Nothing—social condition, appearance, occupation, age—nothing could change the part of her that he loved, and he would surely know her when he saw her.

When he considered the resources available to him, he realized that they were hardly extensive. The Screen Actor's Guild didn't keep photo-

graphs of its members—just biographical information and resumés filed in a computer by
Social Security number. His first and best re-
source was the Academy Player's Directory.

The Academy of Motion Picture Arts and
Sciences had its offices on Wilshire Boulevard
in Beverly Hills. He went there feeling as if he
were going to a Vegas casino. The directory was
divided into two volumes: one for male actors,
the other for actresses. It came out three times
a year and contained photographs of the players
and the names of the agents who represented
them. The main drawback was that only those
who wished to be in the directory were listed.
It wasn't all-inclusive.

Gregory spent an entire day at the Academy,
starting with the most recent 937-page directory,
and then, after examining that, poring through
the back issues. Although he saw many actresses
he recognized, there was no hint of that special
person he was seeking. There were pretty faces,
plain faces, vapid faces, but he didn't see the
face that would send his nerve ends tingling. He
discovered that a Player's Guide for stage actors
was also available, and spent another day looking through its issues with the same end result
—frustration.

The next part was the hardest—visiting every
agency in town and looking through their files
of actresses. It took a week of frantic activity,
crisscrossing the sunbaked streets of Hollywood,
visiting flashy new offices, dust-ridden old ones
filled with failure and disillusionment, climbing
stairs, waiting for elevators, talking, explaining,
looking.

The photographs all began to look as if they
were of the same small group of women, an

indistinct blur of coy smiles and posed attitudes. He'd never realized how many women were, or wanted to be, actresses. At first he'd looked at the pictures and tried to imagine the stories they portrayed. The delusions, the dreams, the nature of the mythical, magical pot of gold that drew these women from all corners of the world to these frenetic, hastily erected few square miles called Hollywood. But the novelty of it soon wore off, and he found himself looking at the pictures quickly, voicing a silent *no* that soon became a swell, a roar of frustration in his ears.

Nothing rang a bell—either in his heart or his mind. He began to doubt the validity of what he was doing. Photographs were such lifeless, one-dimensional things. Maybe he needed to see Brooke in person to recognize her, particularly that part of her he sought—not a thing, but a quality too ethereal for any photograph to capture.

It was on a Thursday that he finally listened to his own counsel and gave up searching through photographs. He got up, dressed, and ate in the restaurant of the motel in which he was staying. He tried to plan his activities of the day over coffee and realized that as far as photographs were concerned, he'd explored just about every avenue open to him. There was nothing left to do that he could think of.

"Now what?" he said aloud to himself.

He didn't know. And no mysterious messenger appeared at his table with an answer. He didn't know what to do except wait, the most painful of all processes. *Just wait*, he said, relying again on faith, *something will happen*.

Something did happen, and it sent hope flaring up like a fast-rising flame.

Maggie, Richard Willmer's secretary, called him at his motel.

"Gregory! How are you?" She spoke with her usual fervor, overwhelming him with her enthusiasm.

"I read the outline for the book you're doing," she said. "I loved it. It's a beautiful story."

"Thank you, Maggie," he said cautiously.

"Well, the reason I called," she explained, "is because I met this girl. She's a total Brooke Ashley freak. Even looks like her. She's an actress, too. Walks like her. Talks like her. It's quite amazing."

"Oh?" he said, not allowing the flame to flare.

"Well, I thought you might like to meet her. You know, seeing as how you're basing your character on Brooke Ashley and all. And you and Richard plan to do a film based on the book. She might be ideal for the part."

"Who is she?"

"As I said, she's an actress. Her name's Jessica Walton. Do you want her phone number?"

"Yes," Gregory said, finally allowing the excitement to build. "Yes, I do."

Maggie gave him the number. He wrote it down on the cover of a matchbook, thanked her, and hung up.

He picked up the receiver again and dialed the number.

A girl answered. Her voice was light, breathless.

"Miss Walton?"

"Yes, this is she."

"Hi. My name's Gregory Thomas. Maggie . . . Maggie . . ." There was a hysterical moment when he realized he didn't know Maggie's last name. "Richard Willmer's secretary gave me your number."

"Oh, yes. She told me about you."

"Well, I thought that since we're both interested in Brooke Ashley, we might get together."

"Oh, I'd love to. She's wonderful, isn't she?"

"Yes," he said. "May I come over and see you?"

"Oh, of course. I live at the Chateau Marmont on Sunset, Three B. Would you like to come over now?"

"As soon as I can get there."

"Yes, that's fine."

He grabbed a jacket, wallet, car keys, an extra packet of cigarettes, and ran for the door.

God damn! he said to himself. God damn! Could it be? Could this be what he was looking for, just lucking into it like this?

When he slipped into the driver's seat of his car, he stopped himself. He took out a cigarette and lit it. His hand, he saw, was unsteady. He told himself to cool it, not to get his hopes up. It could be just another false lead.

But as he drove down Sunset, he couldn't suppress the hope or stop it from growing almost to a feeling of certainty.

The girl who opened the apartment door made him gasp in spite of his resolve to maintain a calm exterior.

She had long, blond hair swept softly back, just like Brooke's. The features were different, but the eyes were the same shade of blue.

"Hi. Come on in," she invited, standing aside.

He walked into the center of the room and turned to look back at her. She closed the door and walked toward him, using the same smooth motion Brooke once had.

"Please sit down." She indicated the couch. It had a striped blue-and-white cotton spread over it.

He felt her eyes on him while he sat. When he looked up he saw that she was smiling nervously.

"Would you like some coffee, or something else to drink?" she asked.

"Coffee would be fine, thank you. Cream and two sugars, please."

It was a small one-bedroom apartment, comfortable enough for a single person. A large white shag rug covered part of the hardwood floor in the living room. Two halves of a barrel made up the end tables and driftwood adorned one of the shelves. On the wall facing him were prints from the Los Angeles County Musem of Art, and the table beside him was covered with half-a-dozen books and a selection of magazines. The obligatory *Hollywood Reporter* and *Variety* newspapers formed a neat pile on the other table.

She came back and put the coffee down on the table beside him, pushing aside the books and magazines.

"Maggie told me about the project you're working on," she said, sitting at the other end of the couch. "It sounds *very* exciting."

"Thank you."

"I saw your last film. I think you've got the Oscar sewn up," she stated with oracular certainty.

"Well, we'll see," he said uncomfortably.

He noticed that she had a nervous habit of running her tongue over the arch of her top lip when she wasn't speaking. The motion was fluid and practiced and he had the feeling that someone had once told her it was sexy. It irritated him.

"Where are you from, Jessica?" he asked.

"Eugene, Oregon," she said brightly. "The home of the paper mills, and the wettest spot I know. I've been out here about three years now."

"You're an actress?"

"Yes. Did you see *Charlie's Angels* two weeks ago?"

"No. I'm afraid I missed it."

"Well, I had a part in it. Just a small one, but speaking."

"Do you get much work?"

"It's getting better," she said. The perennial Hollywood optimism, Gregory thought. Everybody's favorite survival mechanism. "I'm much more interested in feature films, though, you know. Television is such a drag for anybody with any real talent. I think I'm more than ready to tackle a solid feature part, but, of course, those parts are hard to come by, especially for women. I think the character in your story that you based on Brooke Ashley would be a fantastic part," she concluded.

"You . . . er, know a lot about Brooke Ashley?"

"Oh, everything," she said, clapping her hands together. "I've seen all her films, studied her inside out. She could have been one of the truly great actresses if she'd lived, you know. She was fantastic in *The Flight of an Eagle*. That scene at the ball where she discovers that she doesn't really love Robert. She handled that with such incredible understatement. When she . . ."

Gregory half-listened, his heart sinking into the hardwood floor. This wasn't Brooke. This was a hungry young actress trying to impress him in order to get a part in a film about Brooke. The hairdo, the walk, the enthusiasm—it had all been created to impress him. It was all an act, and not a particularly good one. The hope he had felt earlier died while he sat there.

"Do you want some more coffee?" she offered.

"Uh, yes, just half a cup." He thought he needed it, but he wished it were something stronger.

She took his cup and went into the kitchen. He rubbed his hand wearily through his hair and fiddled with the books on the table beside him. The book on the bottom of the pile, he noticed, was the biography of Brooke he had bought at Larry Edmunds'. He opened it casually and saw the sales slip inside. It was dated a few days earlier.

He smiled and shook his head ruefully. That Hollywood hustle again.

She came back, handed him his coffee, and sat down.

"When did you first become interested in Brooke Ashley?" he asked.

"Oh, years ago," she said. "I've been into her since I was a kid."

"I thought perhaps it was only a few days ago, when Maggie called you," he said, forcing a smile to soften his words.

Her cup halted between the table and her mouth. "What do you mean?" she said, uncertainly.

"Come on," he said, still smiling. "You know what I mean."

She put her cup down and wet her lips nervously. There was an awkward silence and then she said, "Are you angry?"

"Hell, no," he said, getting to his feet. "You have to do what you can to get work in this town."

"Maggie told me about your book," she explained hurriedly. "She also said it was almost certain to be a film. I just thought that I'd get my bid in early and that maybe you'd be able to whisper a word in the casting director's ear." She stood up. "I didn't mean any harm."

"No harm done," he said, touching her shoulder reassuringly. "But you really did waste your time, you know. Maggie should have known better. I have nothing to do with casting. I probably won't even know who the casting director is."

"Well, it was worth a try," she said with a feeble smile.

Gregory's nonchalant pose deserted him in the elevator. Childishly, he slammed his fist against the metal wall. It hurt.

Gregory lay on the bed in his motel room, carelessly flicking the television set's remote control from channel to channel, the pictures not really registering in his mind.

He hadn't yet reached a stage desperate enough to avail himself of the motel's specialty —closed-circuit pornographic movies—but another few days in the place would get him there, he thought. Repairs on his house hadn't yet been completed, although the contractor had promised him faithfully that it would be ready for him to move back in three days. Promises, promises. Contractors and film producers had a lot in common, he thought.

He went to the bathroom and washed his face

in cold water. Always, always, he said to himself, it's the straw that breaks the camel's back, and not the bale of hay.

Jessica Walton had been the straw. After leaving the actress, during the drive back to the motel, the full disappointment had sunk in, leaving him in a morass of futility and hopelessness. There was nothing else he could do to find Brooke. No one to see, no one to talk to, nowhere to go. As captain of his ship, master of his fate, he'd been quite a failure, he decided. All he had to show for his attempts was Sharon's death. That and his own despondency.

He went to the telephone and dialed.

"Maggie? Gregory. Richard, please."

Richard came on the line. "Howya doin', babe?"

"I'm leaving town for a few days. Going for a drive up the coast. Just thought I'd let you know."

"Hey, don't forget the Oscar awards ceremonies next week," Richard reminded him. "And the word is you have a good chance, babe."

"Mmm." He didn't care. There was only one award he wanted and that seemed hopelessly out of reach.

"Hey!" Richard sounded worried. "You *will* be back, won't you? It wouldn't be cool for you to miss them."

"Yeah, well, I'll try and make it," he said apathetically.

"Is there anywhere I'll be able to contact you? Where are you going?"

"I dunno. I'm just going to drive north until I feel like turning around."

"Look, Greg, don't do anything dumb. All right?"

"All right, Richard. I just want to get out of this god-forsaken town, that's all."

"I know, babe. That's cool, but make it back for those Academy Awards. There might be an Oscar with your name on it."

"I'll see you later."

He depressed the button with his finger, juggled the receiver in his hand. He took his finger off and dialed another number.

"Hello," she said.

"Jenny?"

"Gregory?"

"Yes. How are you?"

"I'm fine. Listen, I was sorry to hear about Sharon. I tried calling you at home a few times, but there was never any answer."

"Yeah, well, I've been staying in a motel."

"In a motel? Why?"

"Well, it's a long story and it doesn't matter, anyway."

"Are you okay? You sound down."

"Yeah, I'm okay. Hey, I'm going for a drive up the coast for a few days. Would you like to come with me?"

"When are you leaving?"

"Now."

"You'll be back in time for the awards next week, won't you?"

"If you like."

"Okay, then I'll come."

"I'll be there in forty-five minutes. Can you wait that long for me?"

"That's better. At least you're trying to be amusing. I'll be ready."

He hung up and threw his suitcase on the bed. He tossed in the few items lying around the room. Pretty Jenny. Maybe she'd be able to soothe the fevered brow. It would be pleasant to let her try, anyway.

He closed the suitcase, picked it up, and went to the door. He turned for a last look at the room to make sure he hadn't left anything. All clear. Good-bye forever, he thought with relief.

Chapter Twenty-three

IT WAS A SMALL COVE, just a nick in the coast, that couldn't be seen from the road. It was reachable only by a precipitous rock-laden path that wound aimlessly down the steep cliff. There were only two people on the narrow belt of sandy beach, a man and a woman.

The man was tall and slim and his skin was just beginning to tan and lose its lobster hue. His attractive curling brown hair matched the color of his eyes. His mouth was firm and masculine, but it had a sensitive twist at the corners.

The woman was also tall. She had a sleek, well-proportioned body, with breasts just an inch larger than perfection. That defect did not seem to bother the man. Her skin was browner than the man's. Her mouth was wide, bordered by lines from habitual laughter.

They were both naked on the sand.

She lay on her back on the sand and the man kneeled over her. He poured oil onto his hands and massaged her breasts. The large nipples rose, glistening in the morning sun.

"You're getting a hard-on," he said with a chuckle.

She moaned contentedly and lifted her hips a few inches off the sand. As he knelt above her, he could feel the tip of his hardening penis scrape against the sand.

He poured more oil onto his hands and moved them down to her stomach. The movement of her hips grew more insistent. Her legs opened. He moved his slick hands down and found what she wanted him to find.

Her head began to roll from side to side and her hands sought him.

"Oh, God! Enough massage," she said. "I want *you* in me now. Right *now!*"

Her eager hands pulled and guided. He filled her and her back arched, straining up. They found their rhythm and rode with it.

Afterward, as soon as they were both breathing normally, Gregory pulled Jenny to her feet and ran with her into the surf, where they laughed and cavorted like children. When they came out and lay down on the sand, he lighted a cigarette, rolled onto his back, and looked up at the gulls as they wheeled effortlessly along the currents created by the cliff. Jenny lay silently beside him, touching him only with her elbow.

After he had finished the cigarette, she spoke. "You're ready to go back, aren't you?"

"Yes."

"Well, it was great while it lasted."

He rolled onto his side and looked at her. She was on her back, breasts lolling to each side.

"It was more than great, it was wonderful," he said.

She turned her head slightly to face him. "But

you haven't been able to forget, have you?" Her eyes were squinting in the glare, unreadable.

He sat up and lighted another cigarette.

"Is it Sharon?" she asked.

He shook his head. "No. It was long before that."

She pulled herself up beside him and sat with her arms entwined around her knees. "Well, why don't you go to her?"

"I can't find her." There was a pause, and then he felt the need to explain himself further. "There was a time when I thought you might be she, but I was only fooling myself."

She took his words figuratively, which was not how he had meant them. He meant to say, "We kept on bumping into each other and in the back of my mind was an idea that grew, that you might be Brooke, but now I know that, as lovely as you are, you aren't she, are you?" But he couldn't speak the words. They were forbidden.

She accepted his remark silently and he hastily added, "I didn't mean that the way it sounded. You're an amazing and lovely woman, and in my way, I love you, Jenny. But it's not fair—to either of us, I guess. I can't love you wholeheartedly while she's still out there someplace. I should be able to, I know, but I can't."

"Who is she?"

"It doesn't matter," he said. "Jenny, I've got a lot to thank you for, even though you may not realize it. When I left L.A., I was a bit of a mess. In these last few days, you've helped me get it together again. Whatever happens now, I know I'll be able to cope. I've had a wonderful interlude, but now I have to get on with my life, my work."

"Hey, it's been my pleasure," she said with a grin, and he knew it was all right with her. Everything usually was, and he realized how lucky he was to have encountered Jenny.

They kissed with a tenderness that neither of them had shown before.

"I don't know how you'll take this," he said hesitantly. "I'm not offering it as a consolation prize. But you've turned out to be one of the best friends I've ever had. I hope you always will be."

She gave her cheerful grin again. "It's a lot more than a consolation prize," she said. "It's second prize, and anyone who wins the silver medal with you is doing fine."

The Academy of Motion Picture Arts and Sciences was born in 1927 in the wily mind of MGM's head, Louis B. Mayer. Originally, it was a group of industry leaders banded together to arbitrate labor disputes and to encourage the profession with awards of merit for achievement. Labor unions soon did away with the necessity for this type of arbitration, and the other purpose took precedence.

The first award banquet was held on May 16, 1929. The Best Picture was *Wings*, Best Actor was Emil Jannings, and Best Actress was Janet Gaynor. Since then, things have changed. The advent of sound ruined the careers of a number of prominent actors and actresses. Color made the art of film more lifelike, and other innovations had their effect. The practice of giving the awards at banquets was stopped in 1942.

But some things never change, and one of these is the little golden statuette so coveted in Hollywood today. This small man, with his crusader's sword, standing on a reel of film, has remained unchanged in design since first conceived. The gold-plated, eleven-pound statue costs less than a hundred dollars to produce, but its value in the film industry is inestimable. The golden statuette, as it was first called, became "Oscar" sometime in the early thirties, although the origins of the name are still debated.

There is a mystique to the little fellow. Some schools have claimed that he has jinxed more careers than he has assisted. The legend began in 1937 when Luise Rainer became the first person to win two Oscars in a row, only to have her career take a nose dive. Oscar has been praised, damned, belittled, berated, and worshiped, but through it all, in the history of the Academy, only a very few have refused to accept him.

The Academy Awards ceremony is Hollywood's biggest night, a magical parade with an excitement that nothing can dispel. It is a tribute to the men and women who are part of a medium that is perhaps more glitter than glamour, yet one which has changed man's ways of talking, thinking, and behaving, and has transformed an entire world. And it all revolves around a coveted little thirteen-and-one-half-inch homunculus named Oscar.

Gregory was nervous and excited in spite of his determination to remain cool about the whole thing. He was going to the awards show with his friends Steve and Liz Sherman, and so he arrived at their house at about four in the afternoon. Because of television requirements in the East, the show was scheduled to begin at seven in Los Angeles, a small indication of how television has become the Great Dictator of our society.

Gregory wore a black velvet dinner jacket, feeling very silly to be so attired in broad daylight. He was, however, greatly reassured at hearing the sincere compliments of his host and hostess.

Without doubt, however, the chief attraction was Liz, sexily svelte in a tight, full-length, off-the-shoulder red dress.

Steve began to ply Gregory with drinks as soon as he arrived. Gregory concluded that reverse psychology was at work. Steve seemed much the most nervous of the threesome and was probably projecting his feeling of uneasiness onto Gregory. It was strange, Gregory thought, since Steve had nothing at stake, and Gregory, if one were to accept the gospel of the Great God Oscar, had his whole future at stake.

"You're going to win, man," Steve said, holding up his glass. "I've got a gut feeling about it. And my gut, she is never wrong."

"All you've got *is* a gut, honey," Liz commented.

"Thanks for your vote of confidence, Steve," Gregory said, "but the odds are against me."

"What do you mean, the odds are against you? Your script is better than the others."

Gregory laughed. "That's debatable. But there *are* others, right? Three, or is it four? Whatever. So that makes the odds four to one before we even start."

"Ah, bull," Steve said derisively. "That doesn't compute for crap. That's just pure pessimism. I told you, I've got a gut feeling. Don't hand me that odds manure."

"I wonder what odds Jimmy the Greek has

given you?" Liz said. "You know he does it for the Oscar Awards, just like for a football game. Let's call Vegas and find out."

"Forget it," Gregory said. "Between Steve's gut and the Greek's odds, a guy could go bonkers."

"Well, go bonkers," Steve ordered, filling his glass again. "Because you, my good man, are going to walk out of there tonight with a real little Oscar in your hand."

"Can it, will you, Steve?" Gregory said. "Whatever happens will happen."

Steve refused to be put off. "What kind of attitude is that? I've told you—you're going to—"

Steve broke off, catching a signal from Liz. By now, even he could realize that his attempts to bolster Gregory were only making him more nervous.

"Hey," Liz said, "how about something to eat?" She went into the kitchen and came back with a tray of hors d'oeuvres.

Gregory took a cracker and munched it slowly, thoughtfully.

What if?

Ah, bull, he told himself. It didn't matter. It was just an overrated golden statuette. The public was the final judge. They'd liked the film and that was enough for him. But another devilish little voice in his mind said, Who do you think you're fooling, Mr. Cool? The public liked the film, sure, but what they liked was a composite effort consisting of the story, the stars, the photography, the music, the pace, the editing. But an Oscar was another matter. That was recognition of the excellence of his script. That was a tribute by his peers, people who competed and knew the values, and he had no right to underestimate it.

He tried to stop the insistent voices competing in his head. He'd been doing a lot of that lately, he realized. He'd tried to stop thinking about Brooke in the past few days as well. At least, he'd tried to stop dwelling on the things they'd done together, those little vignettes of their life that played so entrancingly on the screen of his memory. So far, he'd done pretty well. Now, however, the alcohol, together with the strain of the evening, was undoing it all. As he sat there sipping his drink, the images crowded into his mind, obliterating everything else. Goddammit, he had to stop! He bit angrily into his cracker.

"Polly want a cracker?" Brooke held it out playfully. He leaned forward and took a bite. They were on the beach at Malibu, loafing in the sunshine, both playing truant. He picked up the champagne and poured it into their glasses. "Brookey, want a drink?" he said in the same cadence she had used. "To be brutally frank about it, Brooke wants you," she said, rolling over on top of him, sending the glasses spinning into the sand. Her damp swimsuit was cold against his chest, her bare flesh warm. He pretended to struggle, but then he kissed her fiercely, wanting her as much as he always did.

"What?" he said, focusing his eyes back into the room.

"Is Jenny going to the awards?" Liz repeated.

"Oh. Yes. She's going with someone else. We decided to cool it for a while."

"God, you're a dingbat!" Liz exclaimed. "She's a great chick. Just right for you."

"Hey, I like her a lot," he protested. "It's just that . . . at the moment . . ."

"Want to tell me about it?" she said.

"No, Mom. I don't," he said.

Steve looked at his watch impatiently. "Where the hell's the babysitter? It's almost time to go."

"Cool it," Liz said. "You're not up for an Oscar." She went into Cosmo's room to check on him.

The doorbell rang on cue. The babysitter was a young teenage girl, gangling and ill at ease. She had pimples and put her hand over her mouth when she smiled to hide the braces. Gregory felt for her. He remembered the times he'd hated being a teenager, awkward, never knowing whether he was doing the right thing or not.

Liz went over her duties with the girl for a few minutes in the bedroom, then came back snapping her fingers.

"Okay, boys. Let's go, *if* you're together enough."

Gregory stood, draining his glass. He wasn't sure how together he was. Nervous, he was sure about that. He straightened his jacket, feeling suddenly like an imposter who was going to turn into a pumpkin at the magic hour. God, what a crazy time of the day, he thought. I should be working now, not traipsing off to a beauty contest.

The loyal fans were there. They thronged the street outside the Dorothy Chandler Pavilion—four, maybe five thousand of them.

Hastily erected wood and scaffold grandstands

had been set up to accommodate the fans. Others lined up on the street behind cordons of ushers and security men. Gregory peered out of the limousine window as it pulled up. The crowd peered back, staring hungrily, wondering who would emerge from the car.

As they stepped out onto the sidewalk, the crowd drew in a deep breath of suspense. Then there was a deep sigh of disappointment when nobody recognized them.

A Channel Five reporter stuck a mike under Gregory's nose after a short introductory spiel.

"How do you feel about your chances tonight?" he asked.

Scared shitless, he wanted to answer, but instead he said, "There's a lot of competition. They all deserve to win."

"Jesus Christ!" Liz said under her breath as they walked away. "I hope your acceptance speech is better than that."

A young girl managed to reach him and asked for his autograph. She'd seen him interviewed by the television cameras. He had to be someone.

He scrawled his name on the pad she gave him and handed it back. She looked at it uncomprehendingly.

"Who are you?" she said.

"I'm a writer," he replied.

"Oh, a writer," she said disappointedly. He felt as if he'd betrayed her and had to suppress a ridiculous urge to apologize.

An usher showed them to their seats. A couple of people he knew shouted, "Good luck!" as he passed down the aisle. They had good seats, fairly near the front.

The pandemonium outside was matched in the

hall. It was created mainly by the television crews. There were about six television cameras in the room, two right in the center of the audience. Hundreds of spotlights swung from the ceiling, connected to one another by a jungle of wires.

Gregory looked up at the blazing lights, squinting under their glare.

Brooke held his arm nervously as they stepped out of the limousine. Michael looked at the spotlights, six of them, weaving enticing patterns in the night sky above Grauman's Chinese Theater. The crowd of bystanders began to clap when they saw Brooke.

It was their first premiere together. Previously they had managed to stay out of the Hollywood limelight as they had originally intended. She had gone to premieres like this with people the studio had chosen for her. He went alone, if at all. But the day before, she had said to him, "Michael, I want you to take me tomorrow night." He was puzzled. "But what about . . ." She tossed her head at him. "I don't care anymore. You're my man and I want everyone to know it. I don't care about anything else anymore." So they found themselves walking through the crowd, smiling at fans who wondered who the tall, rough-looking man with Brooke Ashley was. Inside the lobby, the small clique of celebrities looked at them speculatively. When they sat down in the dark, Brooke took his hand and pressed it to her lips. He could feel her lips move against his palm but he could not hear her. "What?" he said, leaning toward her. "I love you," she said. "What else is there to say?"

Gregory rubbed his eyes, then he adjusted his black tie. He wondered what he was doing there. He had an urge to walk out and go home and watch the presentations on television. At least the television audience would get a better view of it all. He resisted the impulse to flee, and looked around. He didn't know any of the people in the immediate vicinity, but he recognized most of the famous faces. Gene Hackman, Jerry Lewis, Robert Redford, Faye Dunaway, Paul Newman, James Caan, Dinah Shore. There were others—the great and not so great. Hollywood had turned out in splendor for its night. The women were untouchably glamorous, the men strikingly handsome. This, the cameras seemed to be saying as they panned in on the nominees and other notables, is what Hollywood is all about. The final incestuous touch was provided by the two giant monitors on either side of the stage, showing the audience what the home viewers were seeing.

"There's one of your rivals," Liz said, nudging Gregory in the ribs and pointing to a monitor.

The camera had closed in on James Norton, the screenwriter nominated for the script of *Hurricane*, a highly successful adventure film. Gregory envied him, not for his achievements, but for his calm as he chatted comfortably with the woman beside him. An old pro, Norton had been through it half-a-dozen times before.

The orchestra started events rolling with a fanfare. There were short, obligatory speeches, and then the entertainment got under way with Sammy Davis, Jr., singing one of the nominated songs. Gregory tried to enjoy it, but his chest had a band around it and butterflies were crawling around in his stomach. Busy little bastards.

He put his hand in his jacket pocket. Brooke's locket was there. He carried it with him everywhere these days. He touched his car keys and rubbed them ruminatively with his thumb.

"Have you got the keys?" he asked Brooke. "No. I gave them back to you." He stood beside the car, searching through the pockets of the clothes he was carrying. The sun had dropped, cooling off the beach. "I don't have them," he said. "I gave them to you when I got out of the car, just before we went down to the beach." She shook her head. "I held them for you, then gave them back." He clicked his tongue. "Look in your bag." She looked. "Nope." He put the clothes on the hood of the car. "Are you sure?" "Sure I'm sure." He grimaced. "Well, if you don't have them and I don't have them, they must be in the sand where we were sitting. Come on." They walked back to the beach. "We were sitting here," she said. He pointed with his finger. "No. Here. These are my cigarette butts." They got on their hands and knees and scrambled through the sand. He found a quarter. "This is a nightmare," he said. "Well, you might get rich," she suggested. "This is a nightmare," he repeated. "Well, don't blame me." "I'm not blaming you, Brooke. But look through your bag again, will you?" "It's a waste of time," she said. "Well, do it anyway." He continued running his fingers through the sand. He found a comb. "Popular spot," he said. Fifteen minutes later he told her to look through her bag again. "For God's sake, Michael. I've already looked twice!" "Again," he ordered sternly. A moment later he heard her cough and looked up. The keys were dangling from her hand. "Where?" he

said ominously. Her face was red. "In my bag,"
she said. "I had them in a side pocket." "Jesus
Christ, Brooke! What a way to earn a quarter!"

"What are you laughing at?" Liz said curiously.

"Oh, just thinking . . . just, ah . . . nervous,
I guess."

The monitors were featuring clips from the
nominated films in the Best Cinematography
category. He joined in the applause after each
one, but his heart wasn't really in it. He wished
they'd hurry and get to his category. Get it over
with, please; win, lose, or draw. His throat
was dry. He wanted a drink.

He woke up shouting from a dream in which
he was drowning. Brooke stood above him, a
champagne glass in her hand. The contents of
the glass were being poured over his face.
"Christ, Brooke. You scared the hell out of me.
I thought you weren't coming over tonight." She
fell on her knees beside the bed. "I'm sorry,
darling," she said. "Here, let me help you." She
began to lick the champagne from his face. They
both started giggling.

Bob Hope was at the podium, doing his traditional monologue. If it was funny, Gregory was
in no condition to know it. The crowd laughed
uproariously and applauded heartily.

Liz dug him in the ribs again and pointed with
her head. Somebody was gesturing at him from
three rows ahead. It was his agent, Richard
Willmer. He waved back. Willmer gave him the
thumbs-up signal, changed it to a circle with his

thumb and second finger joined, and ended with a clenched-fist salute.

Liz laughed. "Well, he certainly knows his sign language," she said.

"She won't come between us," Brooke said hopefully. She was talking about her mother. "We won't let her," he said. They were lying in bed. He was leaning on an elbow and looking down at her. They had just made love and her cheeks were flushed the color of pale pink roses. She was always at her prettiest then, he thought. "We won't let anyone come between us, ever," she said. "Lady, you've got yourself a deal," he replied.

The Jonas Foster Dance Troupe had the stage, dancing to another of the nominated songs, an instrumental number. They were very energetic. Gregory began to feel exhausted watching them.

Steve leaned past Liz to speak to him. His expression was encouraging. "Hold on, man. Just a few minutes and you'll be off the hook."

Gregory smiled back feebly.

Another comedian took the podium.

Gregory half-stood. "I've got to go to the john," he said to Liz. He made his way down the row, mumbling apologies to the four people nearest the aisle.

When he got to the washroom, he drank water from the faucet, then splashed it over his face, rubbing as hard as he could. It helped. Then he stood in the lobby and smoked half a cigarette. That helped, too.

He arrived back just in time to hear a soft, French-accented voice say, "Thank you," and see a woman walk off the stage to applause. Even from the only view he had—of her back—he got the impression she was extremely beautiful.

"Who was that?" he asked Liz after he took his seat.

"Monique Rousseau. Best Actress in a Foreign Film."

He had never heard of her. He didn't keep up much with foreign films. Brooke had acted the role of a Frenchwoman in *The Flight of an Eagle*. Although the exteriors were done in New Orleans, the interiors were shot at the studio soundstage.

He was watching from an inconspicuous vantage point behind the cameras. Brooke stood wringing her fingers nervously in front of the cameras, but as soon as the director called, "Action!" she was all calm professionalism. It was the final scene. She would recite the full monologue, though part of it would be cut later in the editing process. "I've loved you since the sun first rose," she said. "I've loved you through God-sent catastrophe and manmade disaster. I've loved you though my heart stopped beating and my eyes ran dry, through time and in spite of it, for our love has its roots in eternity, and cannot fall victim to time or death. My love has no shame, no pride. It is only what it is, always has been, and always will be. It is yours. All yours. Only yours." He stood there, knowing the words were meant for him. She kissed her co-star and he knew the kiss was meant for him. The crew applauded spontaneously at the end of the scene, and she walked quickly off the set toward him. They held each other, emotion clogging any words. The crew continued to applaud.

Steve Martin took the stage and had Gregory laughing in spite of himself. In recent years the Academy had tried some of the younger comedians to forestall criticism that the awards were appealing mainly to the Geritol set. The audience applauded Martin wildly.

"No one, nothing can ever separate us," Brooke said fiercely. He tenderly stroked her hair. Her head was on his chest. "If we're ever separated, for any reason," she said, "let's make a pact to get back together no matter what the obstacles." He kissed the top of her head and said, "I told you long ago that our love has its roots in eternity and cannot fall victim to time or death. Remember?" "I remember," she said.

"And now," someone was saying, "to present the award for the Best Original Screenplay, here is Miss Monique Rousseau."

Gregory sat upright, the butterflies kicking to get out of his stomach. He looked at Monique Rousseau's close-up on the monitor. He turned pale, all thought of his own stake in the ceremony completely vanished from his mind. Then, suddenly, his face became flushed with color. The adrenaline was pumping wildly through his body.

She had fair hair that fell to her shoulders; full, curving lips, mocking blue eyes. She was wearing a white strapless dress that clung to her body as far as her hips, then fell gracefully to the floor. Who is she? *Who is she?* he thought insistently.

She stumbled charmingly over some of the names as she read the cue cards announcing the nominees, eliciting good-natured laughter from the audience.

"And now, the envelope, if you please."

Somebody came out of the wings and handed her an envelope.

Gregory's eyes began to film over with gray dots.

She tore it open and took out the paper slowly.

"The winner is . . ." she read slowly, "Gregory Thomas for *The Hunter*!"

Gregory saw himself on the monitor as it flashed her picture away, his mouth partly open. Steve stamped his feet and yelled a war-cry. Liz kissed him exuberantly and whispered urgently in his ear, "Go! Stand up, dummy! Go!"

He stood up and walked down the aisle as if in a dream, drifting through the warm cocoon of applause.

Our love has its roots in eternity and cannot fall victim to time or death.

He stumbled up the stairs and had to use his hand to save himself. Laughter mixed with the clapping. It was thunderous. It deafened him.

Our love has its roots in eternity . . .

He walked across the stage toward the actress. It seemed to be taking forever. She was smiling radiantly at him with that warmth he knew so well.

. . . and cannot fall victim to time or death.

Her eyes met his and they both felt the shock of it as she handed him the Oscar. He saw past the gold of the Oscar, he even saw past the beauty of her face. He saw in her beauty the spirit that had made Brooke Brooke, and that now made Monique Monique.

He kissed her on the cheek. "I've found you,"

he said clearly. "For always." Puzzlement clouded her eyes, but she continued to smile.

He took the podium, the Oscar in his hand. *I've won the Oscar*, he thought. *But that's nothing! I've won everything.*